SWEET dreams

C.L. EASTON

Dear Hannah,

Words cannot express my gratitude for your unwavering support while writing this book. I truly appreciate you being by my side every step of the way. I am so fortunate to have you in my life. Thank you for everything.

AUTHOR NOTE

WELCOME TO THE TOWN OF HOLDEN. IT SEEMS LIKE NICE QUIET TOWN, BUT A MASKED MAN LURKS AROUND AT NIGHT.

DUB-CON/NON-CON, STALKER, PUBLIC PLAY

PLAYLIST

- GIRL IN RED- WE FELL IN LOVE IN OCTOBER
- TOMMEE PROFITT, FLEURIE, MELLEN GI- IN THE END
- KALEO- I CAN'T GO ON WITHOUT YOU
- NINE INCH NAILS- CLOSER
- SAINT MOTEL- MY TYPE
- HOLLYWOOD UNDEAD- ANOTHER WAY OUT
- BILL WITHERS- AIN'T NO SUNSHINE
- THE INSECTS- NEVER MET A GIRL LIKE YOU BEFORE
- BAD OMENS- THE DEATH OF PEACE OF MIND
- THE ZOMBIES- TIME OF THE SEASON
- GHOST- CALL ME SUNSHINE
- BRING ME THE HORIZON- CAN YOU FEEL MY HEART
- THE KILLERS- ALL THESE THINGS THAT I'VE DONE
- GHOST, PATRICK WILSON- STAY
- WUKI- SUNSHINE (MY GIRL)
- LORD HURON- THE NIGHT WE MET
- LANA DEL REY- SAY YES TO HEAVEN
- NF- PARALYSED

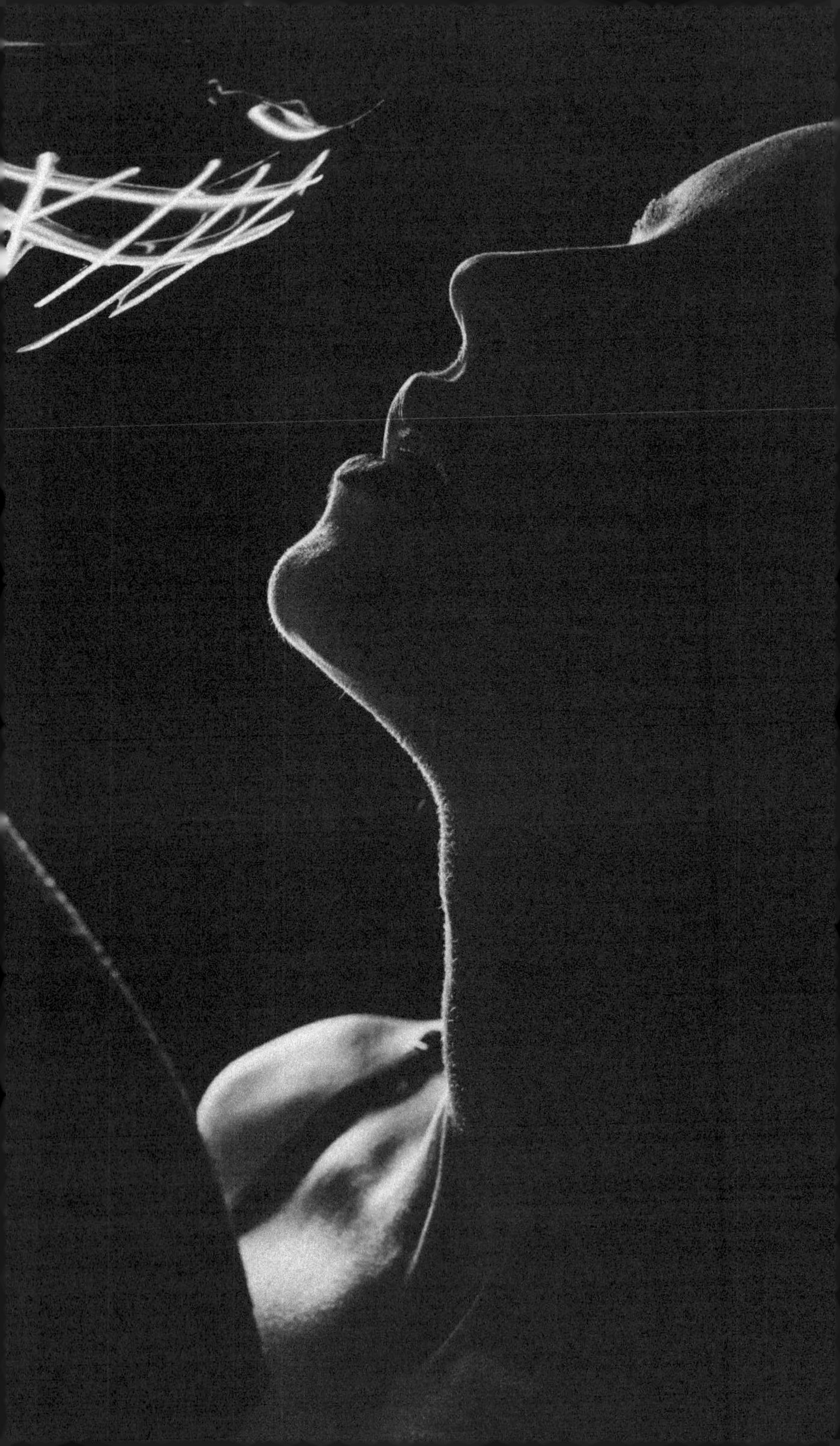

ONE

Her side of the bed is still warm as I slide further under the covers, breathing in her scent. I'll never get tired of this; there's only one thing that will make it better; having her here with me. But I can't rush these things. It has to be perfect. No matter how often those thoughts have been running through my mind, they must be planned perfectly.

She has always been mine.

As I gently slide my hand into my pants, I can feel the arousal building within me. The image of her peacefully sleeping in her silk nightgown from last night plays in my mind.

It moved with her body, like how I imagined my hands would slide against her hips. I pump my hand faster, squeezing the tip wanting nothing more than it being her pussy. One day, I'll have her screaming my name as I fuck her without remorse. She's been teasing me for too long, and if I don't get a taste soon, I'll steal it when she's sleeping.

My stomach muscles clench, and I release myself. I can't come yet. I need the warm embrace of that pussy.

I roll out of her bed and slide out the window into the night like a ghost.

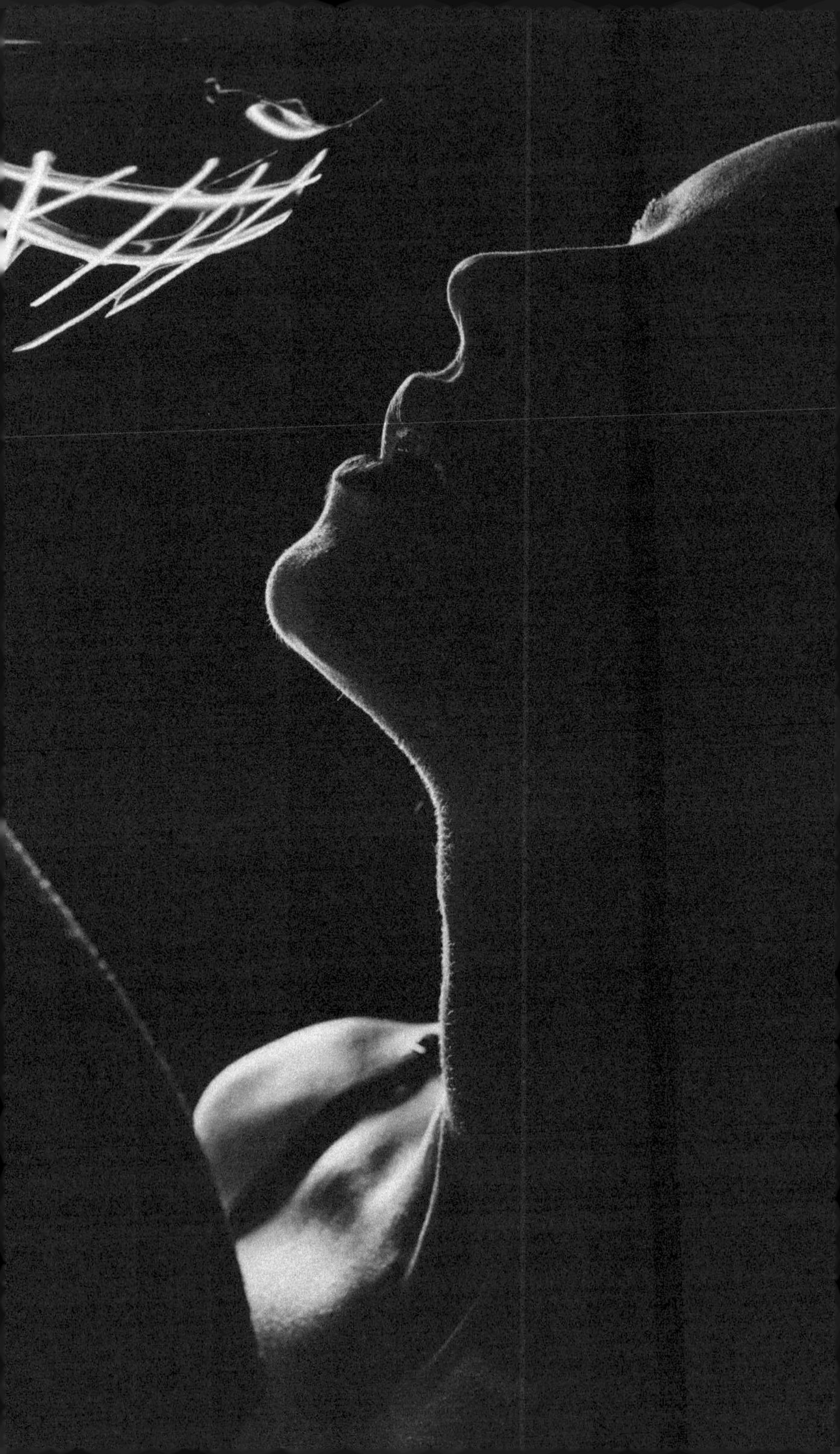

TWO
TEAGAN

My feet barely hit the cement, and the crisp fall air hits my soul. If anyone tells you Fall isn't the perfect season, they are wrong, and you shouldn't be friends with them. There is no place for negativity. The walk to The Dancing Goat Bookshop is only a few blocks from my house. I was lucky enough to have found the perfect location for the shop. Being in a small town also has its benefits; everything is close no matter where you live.

The downfall of living in a small town. The rumour mill is strong. No one can stay out of anyone's business, and unfortunately, that includes my own business. There will be messages on my phone about the latest affair or who moved into the abandoned house before I lock up the shop—every day.

The town gossiper is our leading lady, Elma. I try my hardest not to open up when she visits daily, but she has a way with words and the next thing you know. Your business is being spread around like a fast-growing STD. The words of Elma are hotter than the morning paper.

I adjust my bag; I might have a problem ordering items to the house that are meant for the shop, but when you're up late at night and find something bookish, you can't help but buy it. The house is filled with books waiting to be brought to the shop. There are only a few more blocks to go, and I guarantee Elma will be waiting for me to unlock the shop with her morning gossip.

The Dancing Goat Bookshop is nestled between a closed record shop and a trendy clothing boutique on Main Street. It's a peaceful location, ideal for relaxing and reading before purchasing. I round the last corner and spot Elma already there, waiting patiently. She glances up, and a warm smile lights up her face.

Here we go.

"Teagan honey, how are you? I've been waiting for what seems to be hours. Is everything alright?"

I fish the keys out of my bag, and as I stick them in the lock, I hear Elma inhale deeply. I swing around in a panic. "What's wrong?"

"Him, honey."

I shift my eyes around the street and roll them. "It's Silas, Elma. He wouldn't hurt a fly."

"Something is off with that man."

"Maybe something is off with your spidey senses. And don't start a rumour just because you don't like him." I finish unlocking the door and hold it open for her. The sooner she's inside, the better it is for everyone.

I take one more glance at Silas, his inky black hair tamed by his baseball hat, and his piercing green eyes stare back at me. Even from across the street, I can see his full lips twitch into a smirk. Silas has been a mystery since he moved to Holden a few months ago, hence why Elma has her panties in a wad over him. He'll come into the shop once Elma leaves but never sticks around long enough to start a conversation.

The bell above the door rings, and I can practically hear Elma squirming. Note to self: get a cat to talk to so I don't turn out like her.

"I swear, Teagan. You are too nice for your own good. One day, it'll get you into trouble."

"Elma, being nice doesn't mean anything. Have you ever tried it?" I flick on the lights, lighting up the shop.

Her nose crinkles, and she blinks slowly. "Teagan, if I didn't know your mother, I swear you were being rude."

I shrug, making my way to the back office. The other downfall of a small town is that everyone knows everyone.

"Teagan. I have news. Don't you want to hear about it?"

Her heels click along the tiled floor; it's a little after nine, and she's already drained me. I swear she must've been a vampire in her past life because she is sucking the life out of me.

"Elma, I honestly don't have time for your morning gossip. I have a delivery arriving soon, a Mom and Tot program starting in an hour that I desperately need to set up for. I can't chit-chat." I drop my bag onto the office chair, avoiding the mess on my desk for the tenth time this week.

"It won't take long."

Why can't people listen to me when I talk? I try to be forceful, but they still never listen. "Go ahead, Elma," I tell her, evading her eyes.

"Wonderful." She claps her hands.

An hour later!

Elma took over an hour to talk about shit that I didn't care about, and even when the delivery showed up, she followed me, still talking. No matter how much I told her I had stuff to finish, she still never left. Now, I'm scrambling to set the backroom up for the Mom and Tot program. I'm beginning to think there are a lot of downfalls in this town. Me being one of them.

That stupid bell above the door rings as I throw the last cushion on the floor. It's about to get loud in here. I make my way to the front, and a pile of one- to two-year-olds run rampant through the shop as their moms gossip. I have to remind myself it's worth renting the backroom; it helps pay the rent.

"Morning, everyone. I hope you're having a terrific Tuesday. The room is all ready for you."

Holly, the mom in charge of this chaos, steps forward with her daughter. "Thanks again, Teagan. This means a lot to us. The kids love coming here."

I take another look around, books tossed on the ground. I'm sure they do. I laugh nervously. "Yeah,

I can tell. I'll see you all in an hour. If you need anything, I'll be out here."

The older kids run screaming toward the room while the moms hold steady to the younger ones who haven't yet discovered their working legs. God have mercy on them when they finally do. I look at the mess the little monsters left me, another thing to add to my busy day.

I'm stacking the last of a fantasy series when the bell goes off again. It's been a steady flow of customers, and I can't seem to get anything done. The gust of wind blows in the smell of decomposing leaves, and I inhale as much as possible. The hairs on my neck stand up, and my hand freezes. I glance over my shoulder and come face to face with a crotch. My cheeks flame up, but I can't seem to look away. His dark-wash jeans don't leave much to the imagination. I watch his hand slowly sink into his pocket, and my mind wonders if he can feel his dick.

He clears his throat, "Teagan?"

I blink, jolting backward into the bookshelf. When I take a look, Silas is gazing down at me. Oh, sweet baby Jesus. I was just checking out his fucking dick. I struggle to stand, slipping on books. I reach out for the shelf but grab Silas' hand instead. His touch sent bolts of electricity throughout my body, a feeling I'd never felt before. I quickly snatch my hand back and shove myself upright.

I dust myself off and avoid glancing at him. "I'm sorry, Silas. How can I help you?"

When he speaks, I damn near melt on the spot. "I was eagerly looking forward to getting my hands on the new fantasy book I had requested." his husky voice is hard to resist.

Fantasy book, what fantasy book? Oh my god, my brain is mush right now. I still avoid him as I turn and walk to the counter. I wiggle the mouse, waking the computer after a few clicks, I'm in the ordering system.

"Can you freshen my memory? Which book was it?"

He chuckles. "It was The Cursed Sorcerer. I do believe it's book two, if that helps."

It doesn't help, not when he keeps staring at me. I try to type the words, but my fingers won't cooperate. And I can't lie and say we have it because he'll want me to show it to him. I will my brain to focus.

"You're in luck. It says it arrived this morning, but I've been so busy that I never noticed it come in. I'm not even sure I stocked it yet, to be completely honest. It's been a nut house here. I'm sure you can hear it." I glance to the backroom and cringe. I'm not looking forward to cleaning it.

Silas pears over his shoulder, and his body shivers. "How many kids are in there?"

"Ten kids plus their moms. If you want to avoid it, every Tuesday is Mom and Tot at 10."

"Noted. Kids give me the creeps," he grumbled.

A snort escapes before I can stop it. I slam my hand over my mouth and blink at Silas; that only encourages him to laugh.

"Shut it. I'll go find your book while you enjoy the sound of the children." I step around the counter for the storage room.

"That isn't funny, Teagan," he calls out.

That's the most I've ever talked to Silas. Something is different with him today; usually, he finds a book, pays, and then leaves. A few words are exchanged, but nothing like this. I've never been able to joke around with him, nor have I embarrassed myself so much.

The stock room is a mess and if Elma had left me alone this morning, all these books would've been put away by now. I might have to break down and hire an extra set of hands. Christmas season will be a nut house around here, and I know I won't be able to keep up.

"Sorry, Silas. It's ridiculous back there. Here is your book. How many more are there in the series?" I ask, stepping out of the storage room, but Silas isn't where I left him. "Silas?"

I scan the shop, but he is nowhere to be seen. I didn't hear the bell ring, so he has to be here somewhere. It's a tiny ass shop, and he sticks out. I make my way to the backroom, peeking in on the group. They have twenty more minutes before the little monsters destroy the shelves again.

"Silas?" I call out near the bathroom.

I've never hunted down a grown-ass man in my shop before, but I must say it's exciting. My heart races when I check every aisle, but I'm stumped when I come up empty-handed. A person doesn't disappear, can they?

Holly opens the backroom door, and chaos explodes. All the moms look tired, and the kids look like they could go on for hours. I try to avert my eyes as books go flying, and the moms apologize, but I keep reminding myself. It helps with the rent.

I drop the book that Silas wanted on the counter and get back to work. If he had wanted it that badly, he would've stuck around.

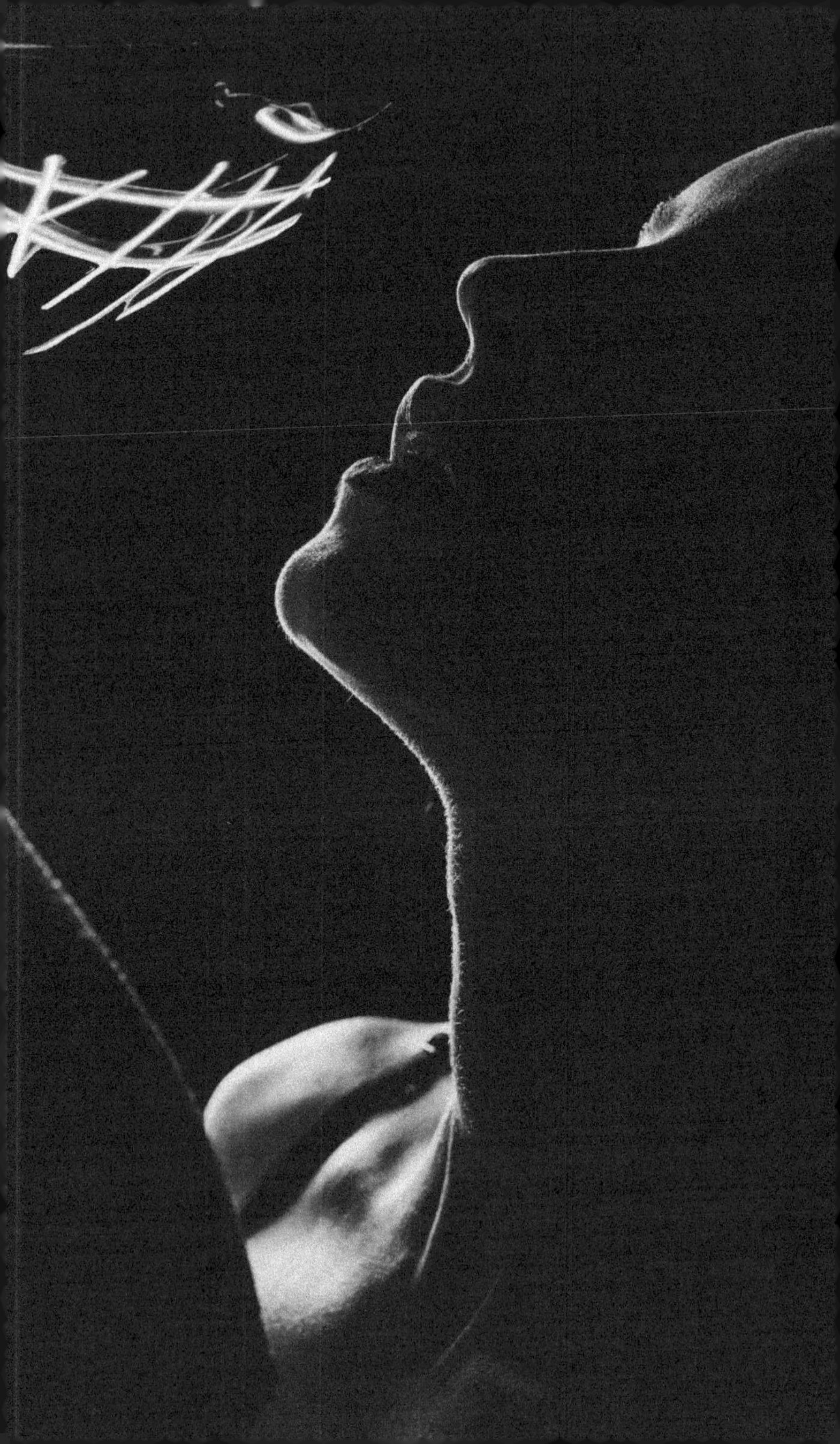

THREE

TEAGAN

This would be the perfect morning if I weren't running down the block, shoving a piece of toast in my mouth, hoping I don't choke all because my alarm didn't go off. I don't understand why it didn't go off. I never turn the stupid thing off; it's my phone, for Christ's sake. It's supposed to be reliable.

I turn the corner, prepared for Elma, but I'm blown away when it's Silas standing there. His black hat pulled low, making his eyes concealed. He must've scared Elma away, and if I'm being honest, I'm glad. I don't have time for her this morning.

"Morning, Teagan," he says, slowly turning his head toward me. His eyes send shivers down my spine. They are emptier today.

I move closer to the door, moving my bag in front of my stomach. "Silas, how's your morning so far?" What I want to ask is if everything is okay, but I don't know him that well, and I know personal boundaries.

"It's going. I'm here for that book. Sorry about yesterday."

"No worries, I'm sure wherever you went must've been important."

He gives me a grim smile but doesn't explain further. We're all entitled to our secrets; he would've told me if he wanted to share.

I unlock the door and hold it open for him. When he doesn't move, I head in. I'm in the middle of the shop when I stop. Something is off.

"Did you hear the bell ring when I opened the door?" I stare at the door, puzzled. I can't remember if it went off yesterday, either. I know in the morning, but after that, nothing. Silas turns to the door, adjusting his hat.

"I don't think it did."

I walk back to the door, pushing it open. Nothing. No ding. I look up at the bell, but it's gone.

"The bell is gone." I stare at nothing in shock.

"Who would steal a bell?"

I turn to him and shrug. "That's what I want to know. Is there some creep out there getting their rocks off with bells?"

"Should we be alarmed by the bell thieves?"

I point my finger and laugh. "Funny. But seriously, where did it go?"

"Sure it didn't fall off and roll away?"

Who knows at this point? "Let me turn some lights on, and I'll get that book for you. You disappeared so fast yesterday I thought I was losing my mind."

He removes his hat, scratches his head, and then replaces it. "I'm sorry about that."

When he says nothing else, I move along, readjusting books as I go. I flick all the switches when I reach the office, and the shop comes alive. This is my favourite time of the day; it's when the magic starts. Heading back to the front, I swipe Silas' book from behind the counter and pray he's still here.

I swing around and bump into his chest. I pull in a breath of his woodsy scent through my nose, and my body turns to jelly.

"The book?" his voice snaps me out of my stupor.

I back away and slam the book into his chest. "Here. Enjoy." My God, how many times have I embarrassed myself in front of him already? He probably thinks I'm a nutcase. The warmth of his hand wraps around my wrist, and I glance at him.

He taps the book with his other hand. "I still need to pay for it."

I shake my head; it must be because I'm still running behind. "I swear I'd lose my head if it weren't screwed on. My alarm didn't go off, sending my entire morning into a whirlwind." I turn the computer on, and wait for another wave of embarrassment to pass by. At this point, I hope Silas never comes back.

"How long have you owned this bookstore?"

I am delighted by how far this shop has come since opening. So much blood, sweat and buckets of tears have gone into it. Every time I switch the sign from closed to open, it reminds me it was all worth it.

"I opened it around two years ago. One town council member wasn't overly excited about it, and they fought me, but in the end, I won." I roll my eyes at the memory of Nancy picking a fight with me.

A frown creased his forehead. "Why wouldn't they want a bookstore in town?"

"Nancy Montgomery. She kept denying my building permit. She's had a hate on, for my family for decades. Realistically, I should've known better."

"Nancy sounds like a cunt. But I'm glad it worked out in the end. This place is amazing."

"Thanks. I'll give you a piece of advice. Stay away from the Montgomery family; they will make your life a living hell."

He pulls his wallet out and tosses two twenty-dollar bills down. "I'm not afraid, Teagan. Take care."

He should be. That family has more pull in this town than anyone; poor Elma doesn't even gossip about them. If they found out she was spreading rumours, her ass would be blacklisted from every business in this town. The only way I was able to get my building permit was to give up the café that I wanted to include. After I talked things over with my parents, we both determined it wasn't necessary and would only add more stress. If Nancy thinks she won over that, let her.

I watch Silas walk out before moving to the back room. I honestly need to hire more help. Now that the bell is broken, I have no way of telling when people walk in. I'm only grateful it's not Mom and Tot day. I would be losing my mind. As much as I hate to admit it, Elma has yet to grace me with her presence and daily dose of gossip. I must be coming down with something if that's what I'm looking forward to now.

I load a box of books onto my cart and haul it out front; the worst part of unpacking is entering books into the system—another reason to hire someone.

But it comes along with owning the joint. I wouldn't be here if I didn't enjoy it. The storage room will be ready for next week's order, with the last box unpacked. And now I'm prepared for the cycle to repeat itself once more.

The slam of the door brings my attention to the front of the shop; that bell is sadly missed—in a way. It's quieter.

"Teagan, hun. Where are you?"

Elma. I thought too soon.

"I'm back here. Give me a second." I park the cart out of the way of the back door and hang the clipboard before walking out and finding Elma searching the romance section. It's not the section I would ever think of finding her in. Considering she constantly bashes the books for having sex in them. When she sees me watching her, her cheeks flame a bright crimson.

"Teagan. I was only passing by. I have news to tell." She turned away from the books and walked toward me.

That gleam in her eye shines bright, which only means the gossip is extra juicy. I lean against the counter, waiting.

"It's about your friend Jace and his girlfriend Ivory."

I raise my hands, making her stop. "Nope. Not listening. If Jace has shit to tell me, he would call me. You are not spreading jack shit about him around this town. I draw the line there, Elma. Not to be rude, but you don't know anything about Jace or Ivory to be spreading shit around. The only one who gets to talk smack about him is me, the best friend. The one that knows him. You don't get to. And whoever you got your sources from should be ashamed of themselves." I'm beyond pissed; my hands are shaking, and I have to shove them into the jeans of my pockets.

Elma stands there shocked, hand pressed to her chest as if I killed her cat. I'm not sure what she expected. I'll tolerate anything, but you don't know my friends; do not gossip about them.

"My apologies. I didn't mean to upset you. But perhaps you should give Jace a call. I'll leave you alone."

I give her a tight-lipped smile and nod. It would be wise for her to leave. As soon as that door closes, I reach for my phone. Hitting Jace's name, I wait for him to pick it up. Usually, if he has shit to tell me, he doesn't wait, so if Elma knows something, it can't be good.

"Tee, what's up?"

"I don't know, J. You tell me." I tell him, giving him a snarky tone.

He's quiet on the other end, too quiet. The sort of quietness where your mind wonders to the deep dark corner of who the fuck did he murder or did Ivory get pregnant by some other man. Kind of dark corner.

"Jace, fucking tell me because Elma is spreading a rumour about you two, and I already bitched her out, so my fisty train is in the station."

He releases a slow, long breath. "Tee, it's nothing that you're thinking. Elma is like a dog who gets a scent and goes with it. She honestly needs to retire at this point before she talks about the wrong person. I swear. And it's not even about Ivory."

"I hear, ya, but seriously, what's the news? Don't make me beat it out of you."

"I was promoted to chief, and of course, a certain member was pissed and said that I didn't deserve it because I'm not a local to Holden, even though I've been here since I was ten."

"Let me guess, Nancy's son Blaine."

"Ding, ding. You are the winner. What a joke. I've done more for this fire department than that asshole ever has. He's only here because Nancy is a bitch, and everyone knows it."

"You didn't take the chief's position, did you?"

"No."

I can hear the heartbreak in his voice. Jace has talked about being chief ever since joining the fire department. It was his big goal, and to be presented with that honour is monumental. But of course, Blaine bitched to his mommy. God, he is such a bitch boy. You can't do anything in this town with the Montgomery's being up your ass for it.

"It is what it is. I have to let you go, Tee. I'll talk to you later. Thanks for the call, and I promise next time, you'll be the first to know anything new."

"Yeah, okay. Bring Ivory over for supper one night. We need to catch up. I love you."

"I love you, too."

I wish there were something I could do for him. He's been there for me more than I can count, and I'm useless. Blaine Montgomery needs to fuck off, same with his mother. They aren't the rulers of this town, and it's about time someone reminded them of it. It takes everything in me to finish the rest of the day. Trying to smile at customers when you are pissed is more complicated than it seems. All I know is closing time will be a sweet relief.

I'm halfway home when something suddenly feels off. I stop walking and glance over my shoulder. Of course, nobody is there. I've officially lost it.

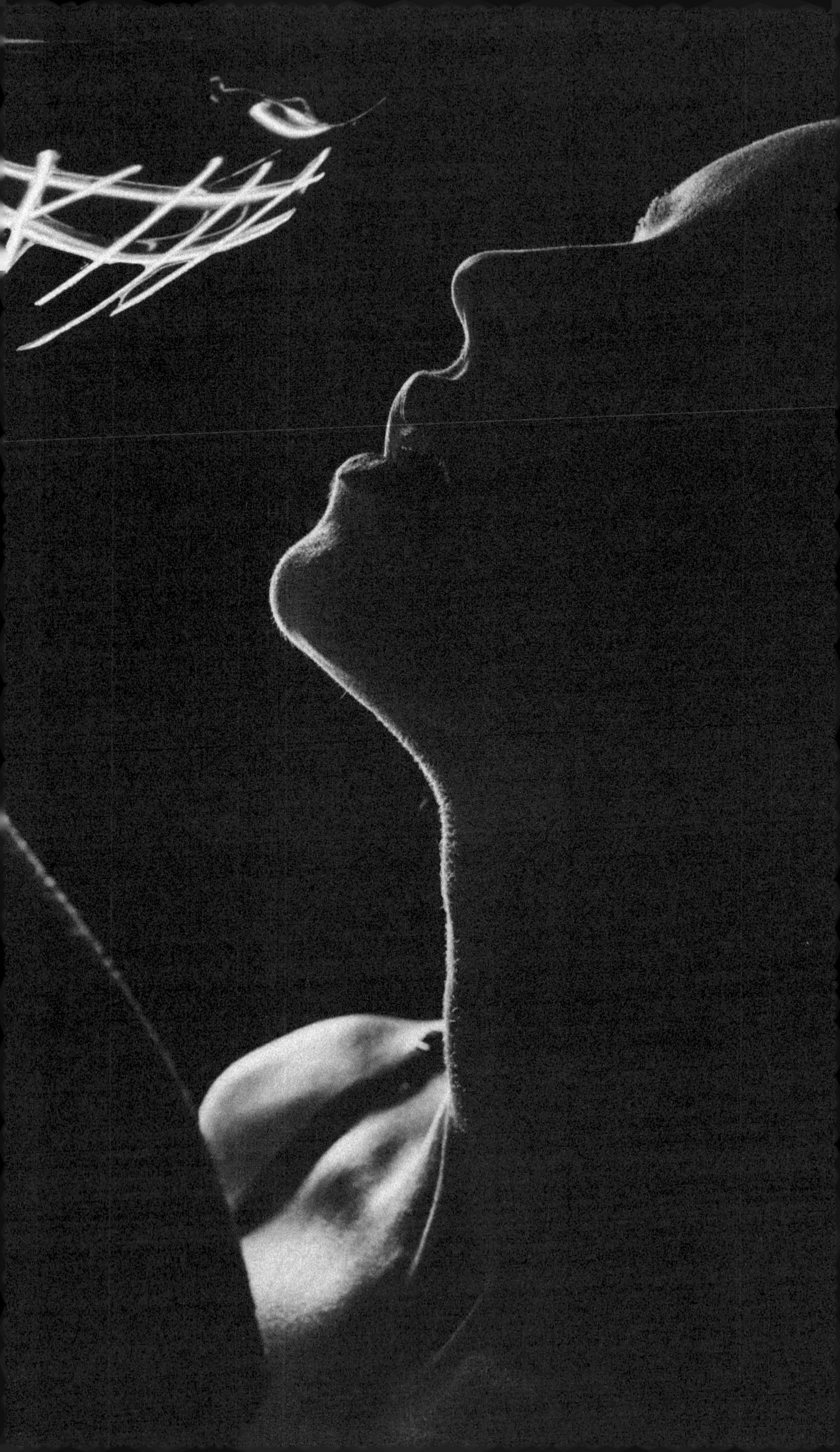

FOUR

SILAS

There's something about this town that I can't place my finger on. Holden has a way of sucking you in. I wasn't meant to be here; I should be in the city, living my life to the fullest. Instead, I'm here doing dick shit, chasing zero dreams. I'm dreamless.

Fuck I hate this town. Every person is annoying, sticking their nose in your business. And the one that is the worst is that cunt, Elma. I certainly don't help matters by constantly popping up wherever she happens to be. I love seeing the old hag lose her shit when I show up. It's how I keep myself entertained.

What else am I supposed to do here?

Most days, I catch myself loitering at the bookstore more than I care to admit. And that's saying a lot coming from someone who's not exactly bookworm material. But then there's Teagan. There's something about her that gets me hooked. From the moment she noticed me, she didn't do the typical small-town move of running in the opposite direction. No, she actually welcomed me with a smile so sweet it could melt ice. And those dimples of hers? Let's just say they had me weak in the knees. She's the real deal. Genuine in a world full of fakes.

But deep down, I know she'll never go for a guy with a shady past like me. It's just not in the cards. It's never going to happen. If any of the guys show up, I'm screwed, it's another reason why I had to move, the past can't follow me. If it does, I won't think twice about packing and leaving. I'll be nothing in this town. That's why I need to stay a mystery. The less people who know about me and my past, the better it'll be for me.

My burner phone rings for the umpteenth time, and I have no desire to answer it. What I should do is throw it away. But every time I try, something holds me back. I can't let the past go. The survivalist in me needs a fallback, and if shit ever hit the fan, I know the old life would be there with its arms wide open, waiting for me. I'm determined to banish it from my thoughts and live free from its grip. Yet, no matter how hard I try to shove it out, it always manages to sneak back in through the tiniest openings. It's like a relentless game of hide and seek with my sanity.

I can't handle being cooped up in the house any longer; I've reached my limit. Cabin fever is creeping in fast, and it's only been a few days. I'm about to lose my marbles. Then again, if I leave the house, it's not like I'll find anything exciting to do. As much as I love pissing Elma off, I can't always keep doing it. I'm surprised she hasn't sent the cops after my ass yet.

I watch from the living room window the wind whip the loose leaves around the street and con-tempt about leaving. But if I don't leave, I'm about to lose my marbles, and I'll be talking to the fuckin' walls soon. I grab my hoodie from the back of the sofa and dread my decision. I can't be a hermit for the rest of my life, even if that's what I want most.

There's something about Main Street Holden that sets it apart. It's like living in a real-life Hallmark movie. Every shop is decked out with cheesy autumn décor, like every shop owner got a memo say-ing, *"Fall has arrived, so throw up some decorations!"* I wouldn't want to own a business here. My decorations would be lacklustre if I even bothered trying. It seems like a lot of work. God, I am not looking forward to seeing what happens at Christmas. For all I know, it's gonna look like Santa bent over and took a shit, and Santa Ville fell out.

Before anything registers, I find myself outside of The Dancing Goat Bookshop. A particular blonde owner always manages to draw me back in. I must be crazy to keep returning; maybe I should've just picked up my phone.

I can't always be running to Teagan when I'm bored. I need to find a hobby or something, and reading isn't one of them. No matter how hard I try, I can't resist Teagan's irresistible charm. I'm like a dog in heat, unable to stay away.

Stepping inside the bookshop, I take a deep in-hale. Something about the way books smell calms me. Even though I'm not an avid reader, it's calming in this shop. Or maybe it's the owner that calms the inner demons.

I watch a few customers mill around the shop, picking up books, kids running around wanting something, and their parents telling them no. A few catch me watching and pull their kids closer to their side like I'm a predator. I've never had a parent pull their kid into their side before; this town is unbelievable.

I move down another aisle, trying to avoid any other mishap, when I bump into an asshole taking up the entire space.

"Watch it, you no good for nothing asshole," a stocky, muscular bald guy says to me.

"Excuse me? I'm minding my business. Maybe you should try it." I stand to my full 5'9" height, shoving one hand into my pocket, showing him I'm not giving a fuck.

He looks around like he wants a crowd to watch him, but no one can be bothered. "I was trying it until you ran into me." He raises his voice, now drawing the attention of a few people from the next aisle.

"If your wanna-be muscles weren't in the way, this wouldn't be a problem. Find a gym, bro."

He clenches a fist, all while I still haven't moved a muscle. If he thinks that will intimidate me, he has another thing coming. I've been hit with worse than a fist.

"You're lucky we're in a store and not on the streets, or I would've kicked your ass."

I smile and nod. "Okay, bud. Whatever you need to tell yourself to get through the day. But if you wanna take this outside, I'm game."

"Problem, gentlemen?" Teagan interrupts our manly fight.

"No, ma'am. I was just leaving." He leaves giving me a dirty look.

I salute the prick as he walks away.

"Seriously, Silas. Did you need to stroke your ego?

I turn to her, smiling. "What ego, Dimples. I was a perfect gentleman."

She laughs, making those dimples pop. "Right, and I'm Mary Poppins. Did you need anything? It's busy today, and I can't be here babysitting your ass."

I take off my baseball cap, run my fingers through my hair, then put my cap back on. "It would be hot if you were Mary Poppins." She rolls her eyes laughing. "Did you want my help? I'm not good with book stuff, but I can try."

"You want a job?"

I shrug. "I mean. I got nothing else to do besides sit at home stroking my ego."

"Yes, the ego. You should give it a break. The little thing must be tired."

"Nothing little about it." I smirk, adjusting my jeans. She quickly looks down before rolling her eyes.

"Whatever helps you sleep at night, Silas. Come, I'll show you how to work the till or if you want to avoid people, I can show you the stock room. Choose."

"stock room. Fuck people."

I follow her to the back, where a mountain of boxes awaits me. That is not what I expected to be doing when I walked in here today. But the lack of oxygen to the brain makes you do stupid things, and let's be honest this is better than sitting at home, listening to a phone ring nonstop.

"Unpack and stock. That's it. It's easier than it seems. If you need help, I'll be out front. You've saved me so much time, I owe you."

"No, Dimples. I owe you."

I've been working for years, but never legit that it seems foreign. The thought of not being busted or being shot at is refreshing. Then again, it's not nearly exciting. I thought leaving was what I wanted, but maybe it wasn't. I'm so confused about what I want. Now I'm sounding like a bitch boy.

Teagan should've informed me that I would still be interacting with people. Stocking books is great, but when someone asks where to find a book, that's above my pay grade. I don't even know where half of these fuckers go. It's a guessing game at this point. Hopefully, my new boss doesn't mind my fuck ups.

When I glance at the till, I see Teagan laughing and chatting with a customer. Her carefree attitude spreads to those around her. It's hard not to be when all she does is smile. She catches a glimpse of me, grins, lifts her arm, taps her wrist and holds up five fingers. I pull my phone out and check the time, only now realizing how late it is. It's quittin' time.

"Are you finished?"

I look up, and she's standing over the bookshelf, watching me. "Um, yeah. Are you?"

"I only need to cash out, and I'm done. You've saved me a lot of time today. I'm not sure how to thank you."

"Can I take you out for supper in celebration of me not fucking up too much?" I spit out before my brain can think to stop it.

"You want to take me for supper?" Her brows raise. You swear I asked her to marry me.

"It's only supper. You have dined with the other team before, right?"

She rolls her eyes. "Yes, dummy. I wasn't expecting you, of all people, to ask me out, that's all."

I'll be the one to shoulder the responsibility. While I may not be the master of small talk, and my people skills may need a little boost, but my charm makes up for it. Or at least, I hope it does. My style is usually wham bam, thank you, ma'am. Taking a woman out for supper is out of the norm for me; I swear this town is changing me.

"Pick a place. You know Holden better than I do."

She licks her lips and starts listing off places. "You have the café, The Lucky Dragon, or the hotspot everyone goes to."

I raise a brow. Clearly, I have never ventured much into this town.

"The Holden restaurant. And yes, that's what it's called," she says with a slight laugh.

A laugh broke free. "Get the fuck out of here. Who named it that?"

She shrugs. "No idea, it's always been named that, no matter who owned it, they never changed it. This town is strange, Silas."

I watch as she finishes around the shop, and I try not to let self-doubt seep in. Building a new life is the whole point of the move, but if she did find out about my past life, then what? It would be hard for me to move on; Teagan is slowly sinking into the depths of my soul. I should've stayed away. I'm only asking for trouble.

"Ready? It's only down the street, so we can walk." She swings her purse on her shoulder and gestures to the door.

"That's the only way I get around. I don't own a car." I gently put my hand on her back to lead her toward the front door.

"Really? What if you wanted to hit the open road for a spontaneous trip?"

"I sold it when I moved here, didn't have much need for it. I don't leave the house much." I kept some of the truth from her.

"I hear ya there. You don't need a car in Holden; it's tiny. I hardly touch mine, although it does come in handy in the winter. It gets colder than a snowman's balls here."

"Snowman balls, eh."

"What's colder than that?"

"Antarctica, to start."

She scoffs. "Use that imagination, Sunshine."

I glance down at her; I don't think I've ever had a nickname before, let alone a nice one. Let's be honest; asshole and prick don't count unless the circumstances call for it.

We keep strolling, and I pretend I don't notice everyone staring at me as we pass. I keep telling myself it's small-town life, and I'm the fresh meat. My heart lurches when her fingers curl around mine, giving them a slight tug.

"Don't pay them any attention. You're doing great. Elma will be your worst nightmare, but you already know that. She only wants to crack you open like an egg and examine you, you're a mystery, and it's pissing her off."

I squeeze her hand in return. "Thanks, Teagan. I feel like I should be on display in a museum. Maybe I'll just slap a mask on and give them something to gossip about."

She laughs, nudging my shoulder. "And do what, stalk all the old ladies?"

I wouldn't say old.

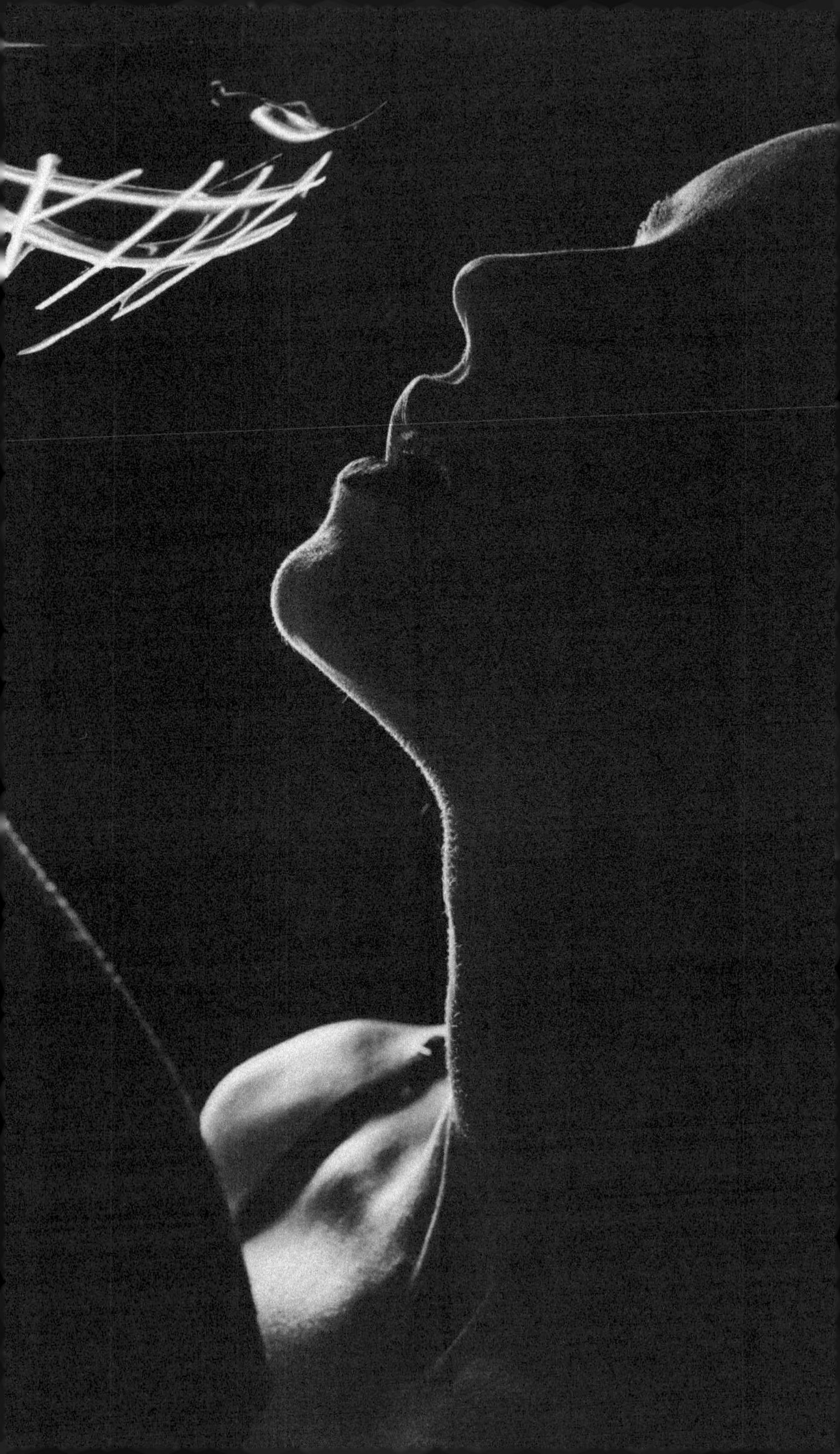

FIVE
TEAGAN

The Holden Restaurant isn't something you would scream from the rooftop about. It's low-key boring inside. From red leather booths to the scuffed-up hardwood floors. It has seen its prime, but the food is fantastic, and I would know; I've been coming here since I started eating solids. The bell above the door jingles when Silas opens it for me and groans as damn near half the restaurant looks up.

"Don't pay them attention, remember." I take his hand and lead him to the back booth, trying to find privacy for him. Maybe The Lucky Dragan would've been better.

"Dimples, it's fine. I'm not gonna let them ruin a good time. Stop worrying so much," he whispers next to my ear; goosebumps pepper my skin from his breath.

I slowly sit, trying to act normal, sliding the menu toward me, ignoring Silas. My dumbass is coming off way too strong, he only just started talking to me, and I had the nerve to grab his hand when all the dicks in this town started staring at him. But I could feel his discomfort; I didn't know what else to do. He didn't pull away from me, so maybe he didn't mind. I'm so far out of my element I need my books.

"Tell me what's good. I have a feeling you're the expert here." He interrupts my dooming thoughts.

"Oh, um. That depends on your mood. They serve breakfast all day, but I usually get the cheeseburger with a poutine on the side."

"Breakfast sounds good. Can never go wrong there." He grins.

I don't know why I'm struggling to strike up a conversation with him now. He spent the entire day working dang near alongside me. You would think small talk would come naturally. I watch Silas play with his cutlery while I find the courage to ask the burning question that has been running through my mind this entire time. I go to open my mouth when Mindy shows up.

"Evening, Teagan." She looks over at Silas and pauses. "And friend. What can I get you today?" Her lip curls in disgust.

I look up at Silas, but he nods for me to go first. "I'll take the cheeseburger and poutine for a side. I'll also get an iced tea. Thanks, Mindy."

"Sure thing, and for you?" She watches Silas like he's some kind of criminal.

He smiles at her as if reading her thoughts. "Mindy, I'll take a stack of pancakes with bacon on the side."

"And what to drink," she cut in.

Silas' head snapped more in her direction, eyes narrowing. "A Pepsi," he spits out,

"Coke fine?"

"Is monopoly money fine?"

Mindy blinked, speechless, leaving me struggling to stifle my laughter.

"Coke is fine, thank you, Mindy." Silas finally puts her out of her misery. I burst into laughter once she walked away.

"You are so mean."

"I couldn't help it; it was the perfect line. You can't say you've never wanted to say it."

"I mean, yeah. But I own a business in this town, so I have to be nice and proper, and I grew up with half of these people, which sucks both ways to Sunday."

He shrugs, leaning back. "Pays off being the fresh meat, Dimples. I can be a cunt, and no one will run off telling my mommy."

This is my chance to ask him. I don't want him to think I'm digging into his past; I'm just curious, and he already knows I grew up here, so he's already one-up on me. Not that it's a competition. My God, now it sounds worse when I think about it.

"Spit it out, Teagan. I can see the smoke coming from your ears."

I chew my lip, and technically, he said to ask it. "Where did you move from, and why, Holden?" The words fly from my mouth before I can rethink them.

He looked away, kneading his neck. He looks back at me, then turns away. Maybe I shouldn't have asked; it's none of my business. We're all allowed to keep things private; Mindy returns with our drinks without saying a word. I guess she isn't a fan of our new resident, either. Silas reaches for his pop and takes a long drink. If this answer is complicated, maybe I won't ask about his family life.

"Short answer." He spoke lowly, staring at his glass. I nod, not wanting to interrupt his thoughts. "Holden wasn't my original destination. Trust me, I wouldn't have picked this shit hole. No offence."

"None taken."

"I planned on the city, needing someplace bigger. But now that I'm here, maybe it was the smartest thing that happened to me." He raised his eyes and smiled at me, making my cheeks flush with warmth.

I clear my throat and try to regain my head from the clouds. Him and that fucking charm. "Where did you originally move from?"

He presses his lips thin, okay then. "If you get a chance, you should visit the pumpkin patch. The corn maze is a lot of fun."

"I'll keep that in mind," He says, giving me a wink. "I know you have another question. Ask it."

He didn't answer the last question. I doubt he'll answer what his previous job was. He doesn't seem to be very open about his past. I'm not good at thinking of questions on the spot; I only wanted to ask those questions.

"That's all I got. If you want to open up, you will when you want to. How's the food?"

"It's perfect. Great recommendation. Any plans for the night?"

"Probably not. Maybe catch up on some shows, or maybe read. I don't have a fascinating life. You?"

"Oh, Dimples. I don't have a life at all."

I shove a fry in my mouth. "That's not true. You read, that's a hobby."

He scoffs. "Please. I barely own any, so I wouldn't classify it as a hobby. It's more trying to kill time when I'm bored out of my fucking mind."

"Well, anytime you want to work at the shop, you're more than welcome to. I'll never turn you away."

He cuts his pancake, avoiding me. "Thanks, Teagan. That means a lot to me."

Supper with Silas was—different. But different in a good way. Surprisingly, I enjoyed his company, and our conversations weren't forced. It was refreshing. I've never laughed so much before, and now my body is running on a pure Silas high. The mystery of who he is has a chokehold on me. Throughout supper, he kept avoiding my questions. No wonder why Elma wants to chase him around town. I would, too, if I didn't know what boundaries were.

He insisted on walking me home, even though I told him nothing would happen. Holden is the safest town I know, but he wouldn't listen. Is it wrong that I wanted more to happen and that things would've gone further? Who am I kidding, I'm not his type.

I'm a bookworm in her late thirties. I'm surprised I don't have a million cats by now. I can't even recall the last time I went on a date, let alone had sex. I'm wondering if I remember how to make a guy come at this point.

Sliding into bed, my mind wanders back to his irresistible smile, and I can tell he's well aware of it. It makes my heart race with excitement. The feel of his hand isn't enough; I crave more. I slowly move my hand under my nightgown and under my panties. Spreading my legs apart, I move my fingers over my clit. The craving for his touch to cover every inch of my body is just the beginning. I wish we could both lie in my bed, a withering mess and be vulnerable. With all our troubles left outside. But those are simply dreams; for now, I'll dream of him this way. With each circle I make on my clit I picture Silas as if he was using his fingers on me, and it's his hand moving along my stomach circling my breast, pinching my nipple.

A quiet moan falls from my lips as I dip a finger into my dripping pussy and press onto my g-spot. My toes dig into the mattress as I picture Silas running his hand through his dark hair; his piercing green eyes look at me with such intensity that I can't help but wonder what's on his mind. Moving my fingers back to my clit, I rub fast, feeling my stomach clench, holding onto the feeling of Silas in my mind. I bit my lip as I explode.

I lay starfish, breathing heavily, not moving.

"Jesus Christ." I made myself come to the image of Silas. How am I supposed to face him after this? It's official, but I've got to ignore him until I lose interest. I'm only fascinated with him because he's new to town, that's all. Give it a few days, and I won't even bat an eye at him.

I try to sleep, but it doesn't come easy; something in the back of my mind tells me something is going to happen. The question is, what? Things have been running smoothly for once, and that can't be a good thing. Chaos is going to erupt, and I don't think I'm ready. I only hope it doesn't happen on Mom and Tot day. That's all I need. Are all these little kids running around the shop when shit hits the fan. But then again, it could happen to the house, or God forbid, to my parents. Why do morbid things come to my mind when I'm trying to sleep?

I swear if Nancy does anything else to ruin me, I won't stand for it. She'll get a taste of the bitchy Teagan. That side of me lays dormant like a volcano and only erupts when needed, and Nancy tests that side almost every time I see her.

After hours of tossing and turning, I finally moved out of bed. The thought of Nancy has pissed me off, and I'll never find the sweet dreams I desire.

I grab a container of ice cream from the freezer and a spoon from the drawer. What else do you do when you can't sleep? You eat. Rocky Road Ice Cream will help this time, or at least it has in the past. Falling on the couch, I grab the remote, find a true crime show and begin my night of research.

Taking my first bite of ice cream, I raise it with a cheers. "Fuck you, Nancy."

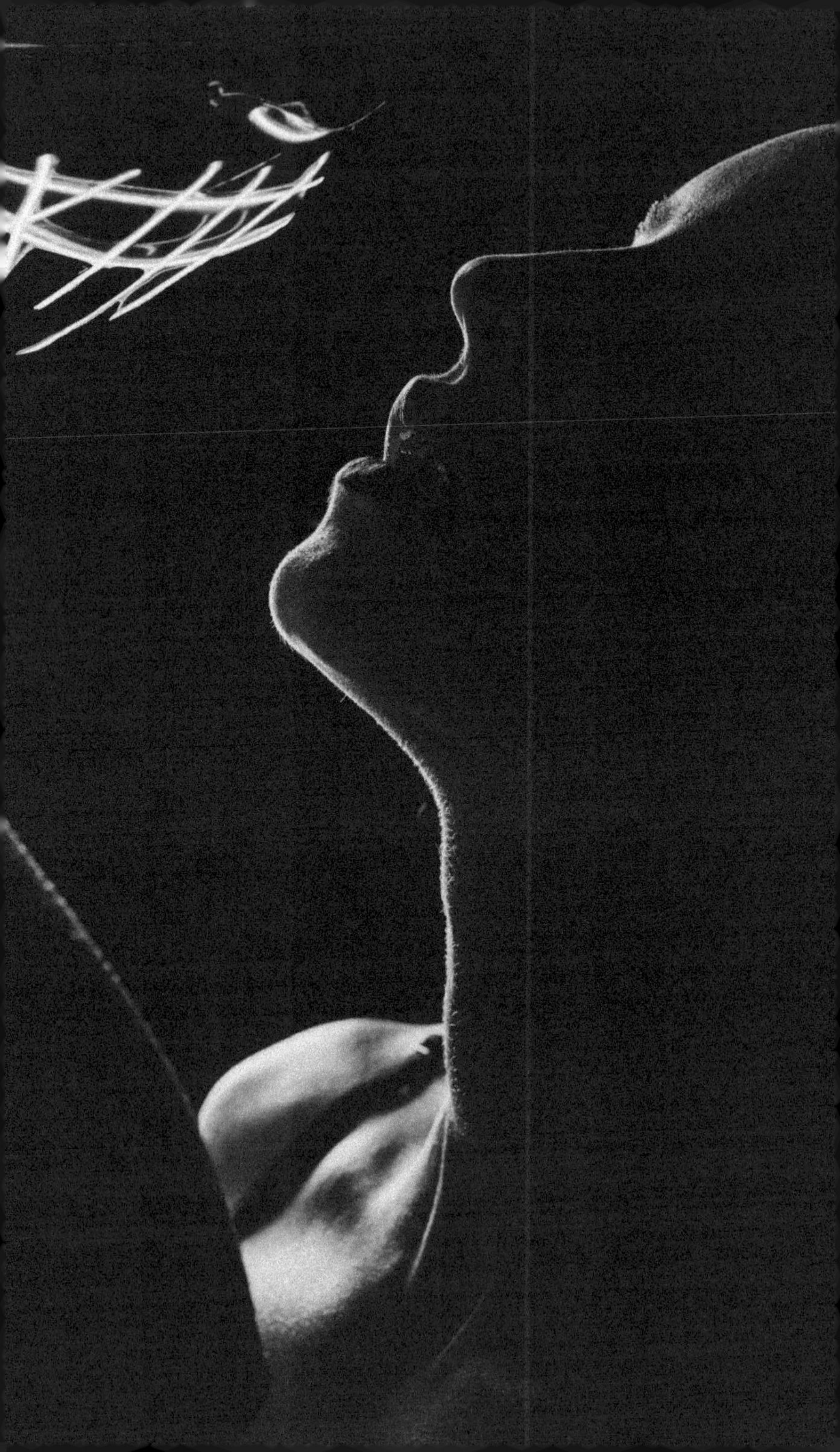

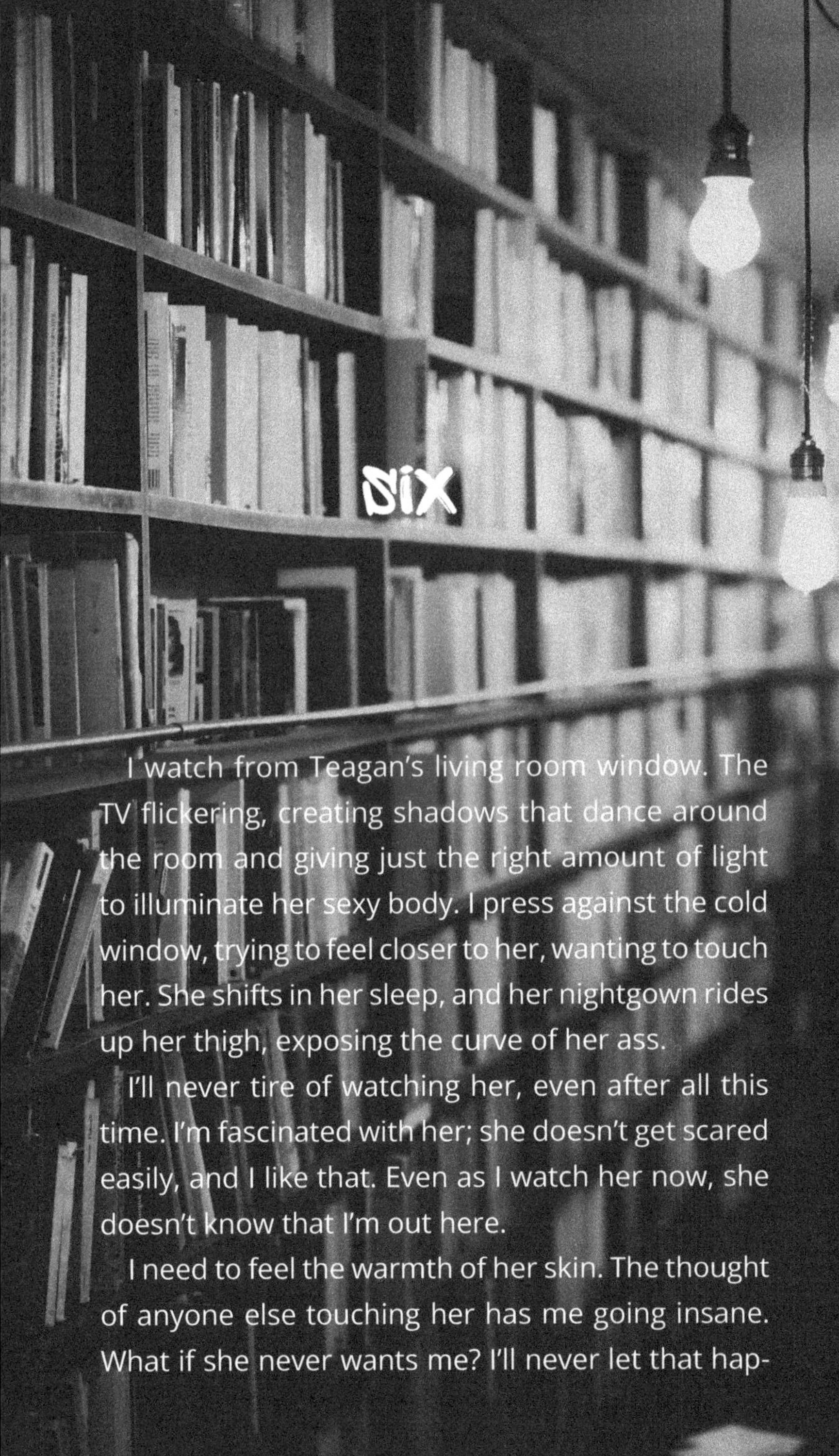

SIX

I watch from Teagan's living room window. The TV flickering, creating shadows that dance around the room and giving just the right amount of light to illuminate her sexy body. I press against the cold window, trying to feel closer to her, wanting to touch her. She shifts in her sleep, and her nightgown rides up her thigh, exposing the curve of her ass.

I'll never tire of watching her, even after all this time. I'm fascinated with her; she doesn't get scared easily, and I like that. Even as I watch her now, she doesn't know that I'm out here.

I need to feel the warmth of her skin. The thought of anyone else touching her has me going insane. What if she never wants me? I'll never let that happen; I'll follow her to the ends of the earth and never let her go.

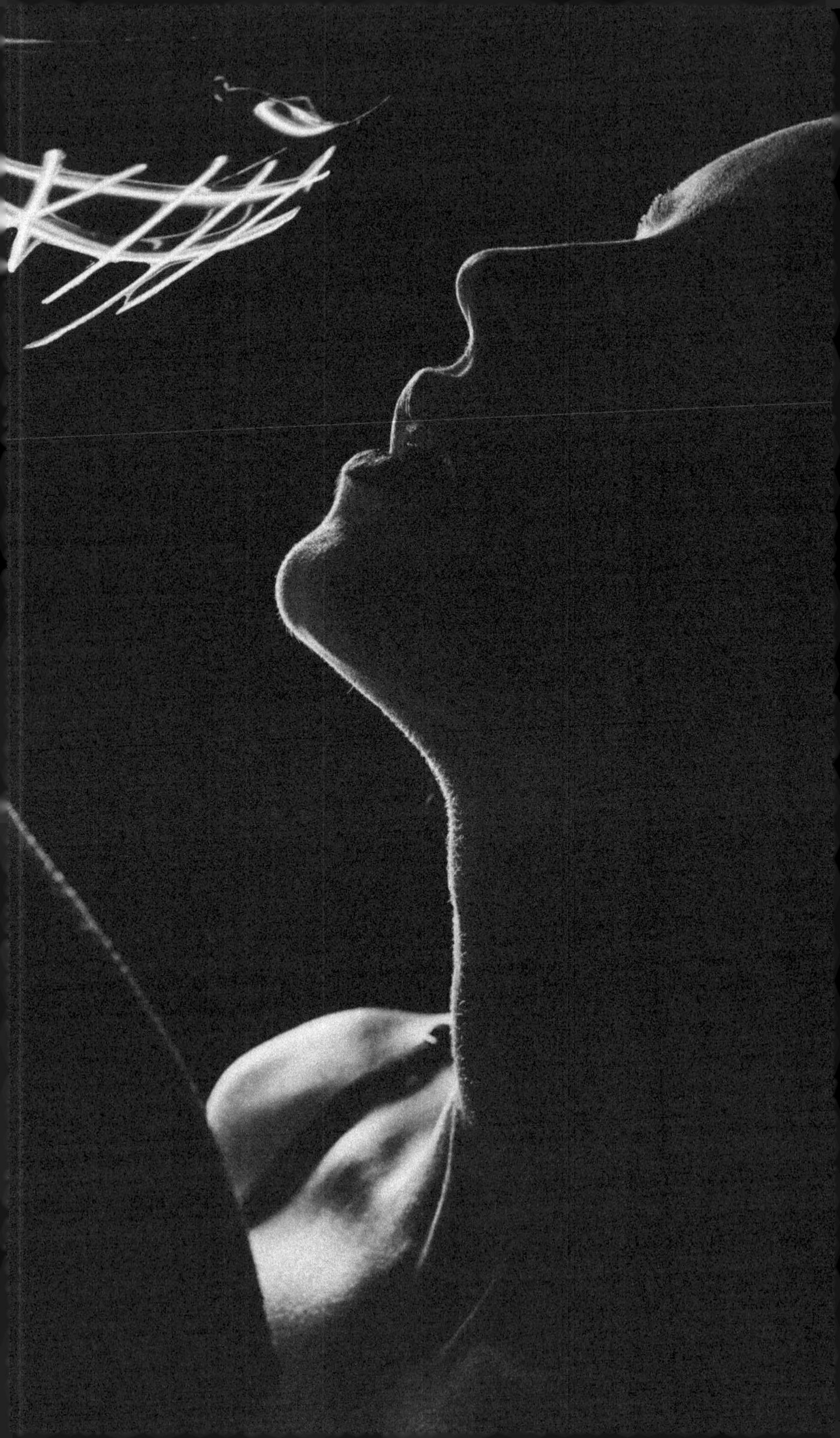

SEVEN

TEAGAN

I startle awake and glance around, trying to figure out where the fuck I am. The only thing illuminating the dark house is the TV flickering. I must've dozed off lying on the couch with my ice cream earlier. I feel along the floor for my phone, turning the screen on to see the time. 3 am. The witching hour.

I close my eyes, trying to go back to sleep, when a tapping sound comes from the front window. My muscles clench, and my eyes shoot open. It's just a branch hitting the window, I repeat to myself. It's nothing more. Until it taps again in a different pattern. I stare at the ceiling, trying not to move. Did I close the curtains?

Oh shit.

I shift my eyes to the window and suck in an air full. A mysterious figure lurks outside, sporting a glowing mask fit for Halloween. The eerie neon light illuminates the crossed-out eyes and stitched smile. He doesn't move; he simply watches me. My body still won't move; all I can do is watch him and wait for him to act. I'm not sure how long it's been, but our showdown continues, with neither of us moving. Finally, when a dog barks, he looks away and disappears into the night.

I lay there trying to compose myself and ensure he doesn't return. I can't seem to calm my racing heart. It's strange to think that after all these years, I've never felt unsafe in my home until tonight. I slowly straighten up, watching the window. Darkness awaits me as I approach it; I don't think, I swipe the curtains closed, sealing the house in.

I check the front door, ensuring it's locked, and then all the windows and the back door. My mind races with disturbing thoughts. What if he broke in? Would he rape and kill me? Why the hell would he choose my house? All those disturbing feelings of being watched, was it him? But why? I'm nothing special. I need to trust my instincts more often; instead, I push them aside and pretend everything is fine. Now look where I'm at. In the worst situation one can imagine. I'm so stupid.

I slip into bed, pulling the cover to my chin and checking my window to ensure the curtains are closed. It's impossible for me to fall back to sleep now. I'll likely be awake for the remainder of the morning with the haunting memory of that mask. It has to be a prank. That's what I tell myself until I fall asleep.

I'm dragging ass leaving the house, and I'm pretty sure my shirt is on backward. It appears that today is not my day. I think Murphy has it out for me. Because guess who is waiting for me at the bookshop when I arrive. Nancy Montgomery herself.

I'm about to unlock the door when Silas walks around the corner. Perfect. He's here to witness the peachiness of Nancy herself.

"Nancy, what brings you down the peasant part of town?" I stop with the key in the door, crossing my arms and giving her the best glare, I can muster.

She smirks at me, holding up a pink piece of hell. "I came by to deliver this, Teagan. I'm sure you know what it is."

"I don't. Refresh my memory, would you?"

She huffs. "It's your business license."

Silas moves next to me, and I try not to remember what I did last night when I caught a whiff of his cologne.

"Teagan, what's going on?" he whispers.

"Why do you have my license? It's not expired yet." I want to ram it down her throat.

She tilts her head and gives me a condescending smile. Yeah, maybe she can have something else rammed down her throat.

"I was reading over some records for all the businesses on Main Street, and yours happens to be the pick of the litter for an inspection. Unlock the door, Teagan."

Fuck, fuck, fuck. I didn't *exactly* get a permit to rent out the extra room. I didn't want to add the additional insurance. I knew it would come around to bite me in the ass. I'm trying not to panic, but Nancy is going to make my life a living hell now.

"What's wrong, Dimples?"

I turn around, facing the door. "Nothing, but you better fucking pray you have a job today." I unlock the door, take a deep breath and bite my tongue as Nancy pushes me aside.

"What a cunt," Silas says, loud enough that Nancy double steps.

"Welcome to my nightmare, Sunshine. Come on, we can be tortured together unless you want to leave. I wouldn't blame you."

He places his hand on my back, and I try not to react, but my stupid heart skips a beat. "I'm in it with you. And if she says anything, I won't hold back."

"I won't either."

We both step into the shop to find Nancy walking toward the back. I hold my breath the closer she gets to the room in question, but she heads for the bathroom first.

"I take it this bathroom is up to code?"

I roll my eyes and move to her. Dumb shit she is, you can't open unless you get a health inspection. "Yes, Nancy. You do know how shit works, correct or do you just sit in your office flicking your useless clit?"

Silas chokes on a laugh behind me, and Nancy snaps her head in my direction with no expression.

"What's this room for?" She points to the rental room.

"Storage," I spit out quickly.

She pokes her head in and notices cushions on the floor. I'm hoping nothing else was left out from one of the kids.

"I think you've seen enough, as you can see. Teagan is within her agreement. Next time you want to be a bully, pick a different business. Leave." Silas moves in her line of sight, standing at his full height. Even with Nancy wearing a slight heel, she still has to look up to him.

"I don't know who you think you are. But you have no right talking to me this way."

"I don't give a shit who you are. Do you know who I am?"

She shakes her head, and now I'm even wondering who Silas is. He's such a mystery that I find myself constantly doubting him.

He grins, stepping close to Nancy. "I'm your worst nightmare. Now move along."

His words seep out with a cold intensity, and I can feel a shiver run down my spine. I can't help but wonder about Silas. As I observe how he moves, a sense of uncertainty creeps in, making me ponder the past he hides. Silas has a unique way of looking over his shoulder as if expecting to discover someone there.

Nancy's face pales, and I watch as she slowly backs away. "I would watch yourself. You may be a nightmare, but I can run you out of this town. And Teagan, I can shut you down before I reach my office."

And that right there is my worst nightmare. I can't let anyone interfere with my business. And if Silas keeps this up, Nancy will shut me down. I watch Nancy leave the shop before turning to Silas.

"You can't say shit like that. Just because you don't care about the repercussions, I do. This is my liveli- hood you are fucking with. Nancy will close this shop down without batting her eyes; she doesn't give a fuck about anyone in this town but herself and her family. Trust me, I know."

"Teagan, I didn't mean any harm."

I walk away, needing a cool-off before I say some- thing I can't take back. I step into the stockroom, leaving the light off. I close my eyes, inhaling deeply through my nose, feeling my lungs expand.

I exhale through my teeth. "Fucking Nancy." I stand there, contemplating how to deal with her when that feeling of being watched returns. I peer over my shoulder, and Silas stands in the doorway.

"Not now, please."

"I need to apologize. I didn't mean anything by my actions. I was only trying to help. Please forgive me."

He steps in closer, resting his chest against my back. He gently moves my hair away from my neck and brushes his lips against my skin with a soft kiss.

"When I apologize, I mean it, Dimples." His fingers wrap around my neck, grazing the bottom of my chin, forcing me to look at him. "Know that I don't want any harm to come your way."

"It's hard for me to trust people, Silas. And I barely know you."

I can't get attached. But Silas makes it hard when he's this close. I'm supposed to keep a distance, yet he pulls me in like a vortex. I have no way of escaping; his presence is consuming.

"Listen to me, Teagan." He stares deep into my eyes, never letting go of my chin. "I can't give you all my trust, but know I wouldn't lie to you."

"What does that mean? Either I get it all or none. I'm sorry, Silas, but I can't risk getting hurt because you can't open up."

He nods, letting me go. "I understand. I won't push anything if that's what you want."

My heart sinks. Will Silas never talk to me again if I tell him that's what I want? I still want to be friends, but to take things further can't happen unless he can open up. I have to protect myself. I'm so lost at what to do.

"I'll still be your friend if you're worried about that. I just won't push for extra." He cups my cheek, rubbing his thumb against my skin and smiles.

The tension in my shoulders melts away. "Thank you. I enjoy your friendship, Sunshine—more than you know."

"Alright then. Tell me what my job entails today, boss." He steps outside of the storage room and waits for me.

While he's in the shop, I'll treat him like an employee and strictly that. I'll have to shelve whatever feelings I have for now.

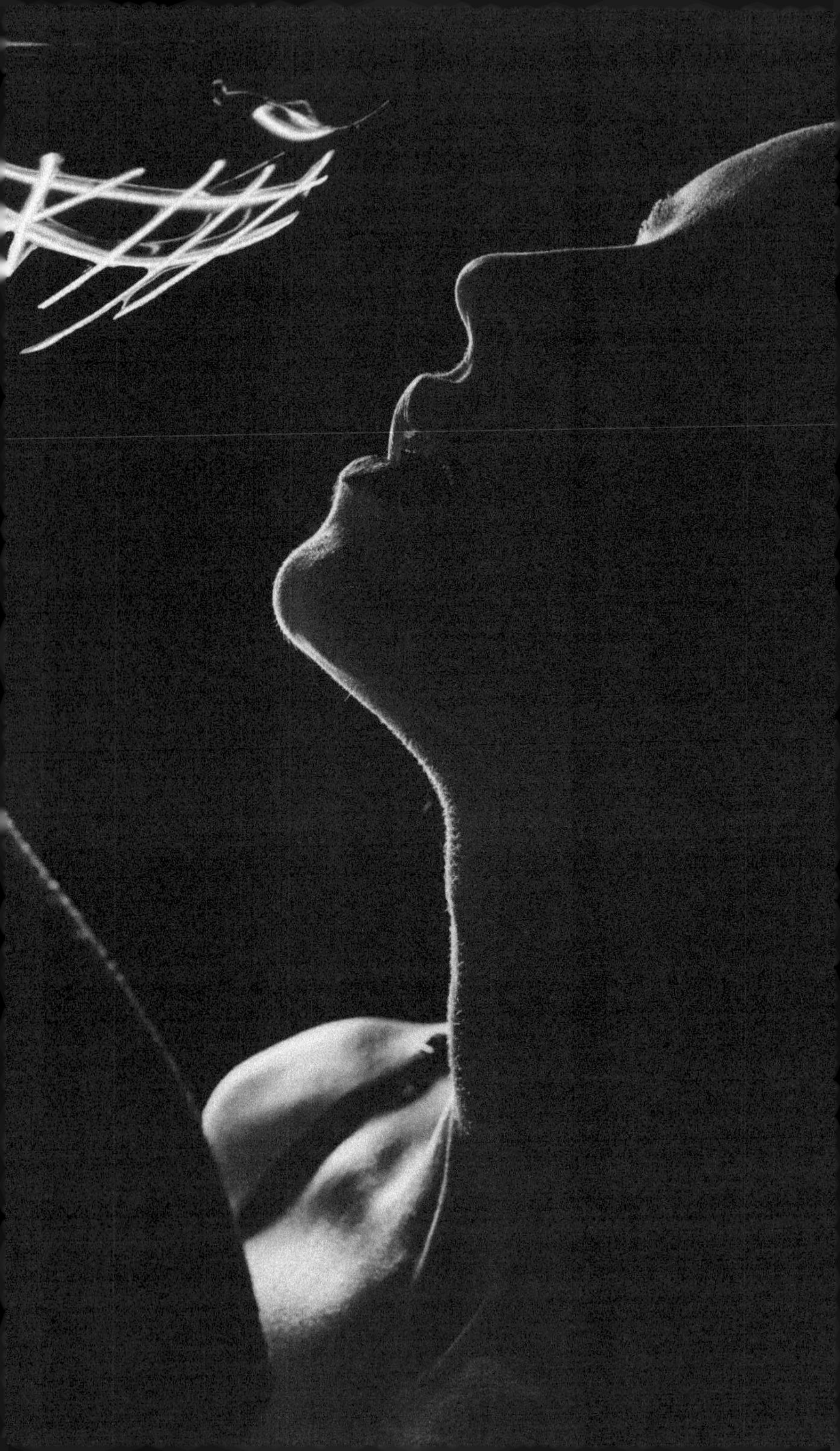

EIGHT
SILAS

I feel like an asshole. I could've been honest and told Teagan about my past, but it's for her safety that I keep things bottled up. I don't want my shit to land on her shoulders. A half-truth is better than no truth, in my opinion. And if anything happened to Teagan because of me. I wouldn't be able to forgive myself.

I watch Teagan work, knowing I almost caused her to lose this entire shop today. I can't control what comes out of my mouth sometimes. But Teagan was right; Nancy is a cunt. I needed to scare her, and she can't keep getting away with this shit.

Whoever this Montgomery family is, they can't have that much of a hold on this town. There's no way. The mayor has to be doing his job, or what's the point of having one? She has to be blowing the mayor to be getting away with all this shit, or she wouldn't be in office still. And what the fuck does her husband do?

"Silas?" her voice comes out alarmed.

I turn and come face to face with Elma. The old bat stares at me, judging me. I know it; she knows it. I don't belong here but jokes on her. I'm not leaving.

"How can I help you today, Elma?" I smile down at her.

"What are you doing here?"

Oh, I love playing these games. "I work here. Didn't you know that?"

"No."

I drop my bottom lip in a pout before smiling in victory. "Wow. Something the rumour queen doesn't know. I'm shocked, to be honest. You must be slacking, Elma."

"You should watch what you say, Silas. I could ruin your life."

"I doubt that. I ruin my own life just by breathing. If you think I'm afraid of an old lady that spreads shit around town worse than a farmer spreading manure, you're wrong. Now find a book or leave."

Her jaw hits the floor, and her eyes nearly pop out of her head. I'm gonna go out on a limb and assume no one talks like that to her. Good thing I don't hold back. Sugar-coating shit isn't in my vocabulary. The way she's still staring at me makes me feel victorious. Gossip is the worst kind.

Elma narrows her eyes at me, moving closer to me. "You'd best be watching yourself. I have ways of discovering things you don't want others to know." She glances at Teagan.

"Don't drag anyone into things you have no business in."

"I'll give you one warning, don't hurt her."

A warning coming from a seventy-year-old is hilarious; what's the worst she's gonna do to me, beat me with a cane? I'm not worried one little bit. I turn my back and get back to stocking books. The more I ignore her, the better. She'll figure it out eventually that threats don't work on me, and I don't scare easily.

The burner phone I keep on me vibrates in my back pocket—another reminder of my past. No matter how much I want to answer it, I can't. I promised myself not to return to that life and am determined to keep it that way, even though some days are more challenging to say no.

Life in Holden isn't exciting, but I'm trying to make it work. It's safe, and right now, I need that. I can't get shot on the streets here, and that's a win in my books. I'm afraid what would happen if I did go back to the city; my ass would be grass.

I definitely didn't see myself getting a job in a bookstore. This came out of left field, but I'm glad I took it. Even if she doesn't want things to move beyond friendship, at least I'll have her like this. Being this close to Teagan is perfect. But it isn't everything; that's why something else comes out at night.

If she ever discovered my secret, she would never trust me, considering that trust is already walking a thin line. What friendship we have would be gone, and I wouldn't be able to handle it. I need Teagan in my life no matter how I get it, even if I steal it little by little.

"Silas? Did you scare away Elma?"

I grin before turning around to find Teagan peeking around the bookshelf. "I might have. She was being nosey like always. Doesn't she get tired of doing that all day long?"

"She gets bored. This is her form of entertainment. Just give her a lie and let her chase it for a little while. It'll make her happy."

"I'm not starting a rumour about myself just to make her happy. That's only asking for trouble,

Dimples." I move closer, tipping her chin to look into her green eyes. "If someone is going to talk about me, it'll only be facts. Now. What else do you have for me, boss?"

She backs away until my hand drops. "I don't have anything else for you. You can head home for the day. And I won't need you for the weekend."

"Oh, why not?"

"It's usually quiet around here, and I'm closed on Sundays. Take the much needed rest. I'll see you Monday." She turns and walks away.

"Um, yeah. See ya."

I'm not sure what went down. She was fine one second ago, and now she's giving me the cold shoulder. Does she want to be friends or not? Is this strictly a work-related situation and nothing more? I need her to tell me what's what. I'm not going to stick around, and guess what our relationship is from now on.

I wrap up what I'm working on before I leave. I tried to say goodbye to Teagan, but she was too busy with a customer. I kind of feel like a dog licking its wound because I didn't get the attention I needed from my owner. I know this is exactly what I wanted. So why am I suddenly acting like it isn't? Having some distance is ideal because it prevents anyone from getting too attached.

Moving outside, I take in the crisp air. It's hard to believe it's already halfway through September, but in a way, I wish it was summer again. Just for the heat, Fall is perfect because the bugs have fucked all the way off.

Now I'm unsure what to do with my time; maybe I should've picked up a different hobby instead of reading and ignoring my phone, which keeps ringing. I almost wish I hadn't sold my car; a trip into the city would have been handy right about now—something to take my mind off her.

It's like the universe is trying to tell me something because the burner phone rings again. And I question myself why I carry the stupid phone around.

"What do you want?" I drew a breath through my teeth, trying to remain calm. I move down a back alley so no nosey Elma can eavesdrop.

"Blackwell, don't be like that. You left us, not the other way around. I still don't understand why. You were on fire here, and now what? You're fucking nothing."

"Leroy, what do you want?" I duck down an alley to stay out of sight. "I got out for a reason."

"Yeah, then why did you answer the phone? There must be a part of you that wants to go back in; that town must be boring. Bring them some action, Silas.

Give the old prunes something to gossip about over tea."

It would be nice to have some action again, the thrill of the chase. I can't believe I'm thinking about going back. Am I so bored sitting around that I would reconsider working with Leroy again? Fuck me.

"Give me the details, and I'll be there tomorrow."

"Attaboy. I knew I could count on you."

I hang up before he can say anything else. What I wanna do is bang my head off the brick wall and watch my brain drip down. I can't believe I did that. Now Leroy owns me again; I'll never get out. A text comes through with the time and place, and the asshole even adds a smiley face emoji.

Now I need to find a goddamn car and fast. If Leroy thinks I'm spending all this time in the city working for him, he's wrong, and I need to be back by Monday. Teagan can't know what I'm doing. All these secrets are too much for me. I'm waiting for the guilt to start eating at me; it hasn't hit me so far, so it must be a good sign.

It isn't till later that night when regret sinks in. Taking this job may not be the most brilliant move I've made in my life—although I've done worse. I just need to remind myself the past and present Silas can't mingle. It would be explosive, and Teagan would never forgive me.

I was lucky enough to find an old beater to use, and if need be, I can always sell it so I can't do this shit for Leroy ever again. I can't do it, it can't happen again. Leroy can't bring his shit to this town, and neither can I.

There's one thing I need to do before I leave. I grab and pull on my hoodie and retrieve the most important thing before heading back to her shop. I make sure to act naturally and not draw attention. I wait in the café until I see Teagan walk across the street; when she's a reasonable distance away, I leave the café and follow her. I sneak into the bush across the street after a couple of blocks and quietly observe her as she goes inside The Lucky Dragon. All I can do now is wait for her; I slip my mask on and cover my identity. She has to know by now that someone has been watching her. I made it obvious the other night by mistake when I kept hitting the branch by her window. Fifteen minutes later, she struts out with a bag of goodies. I casually stock her as I shadow her all the way back to her place. I hug the bushes tight, trying to keep out of sight. When she pauses, I sneak between the bush and a house. With a flick of my mask, I reveal myself. It's even more thrilling now that she knows of my watchful eyes.

This makes the game even more pleasurable—well, for me, at least. Teagan will come around eventually. I step further down the sidewalk when she doesn't move, but she still never moves. Either she's being brave, or this is something she's into.

The game is just beginning.

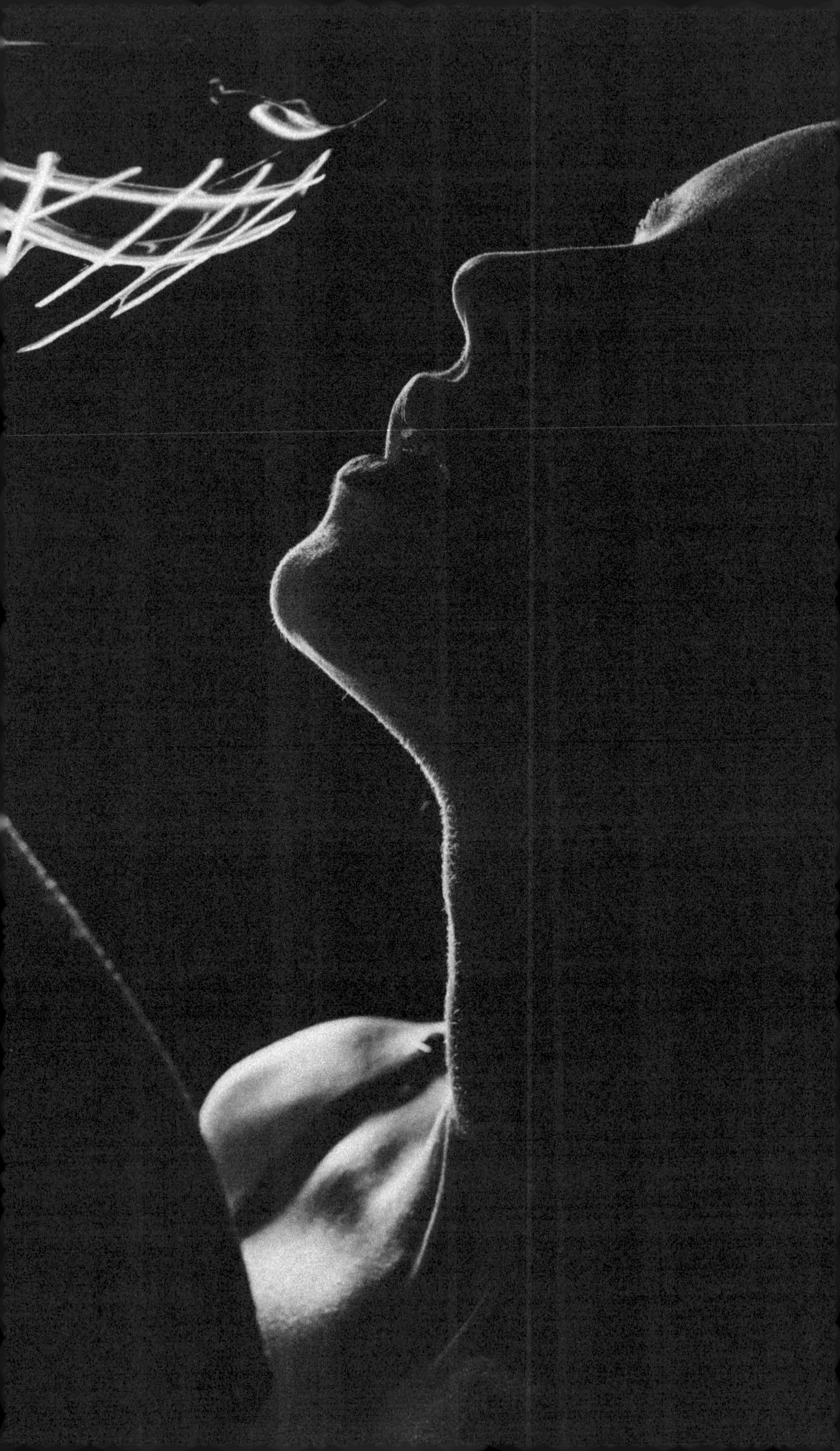

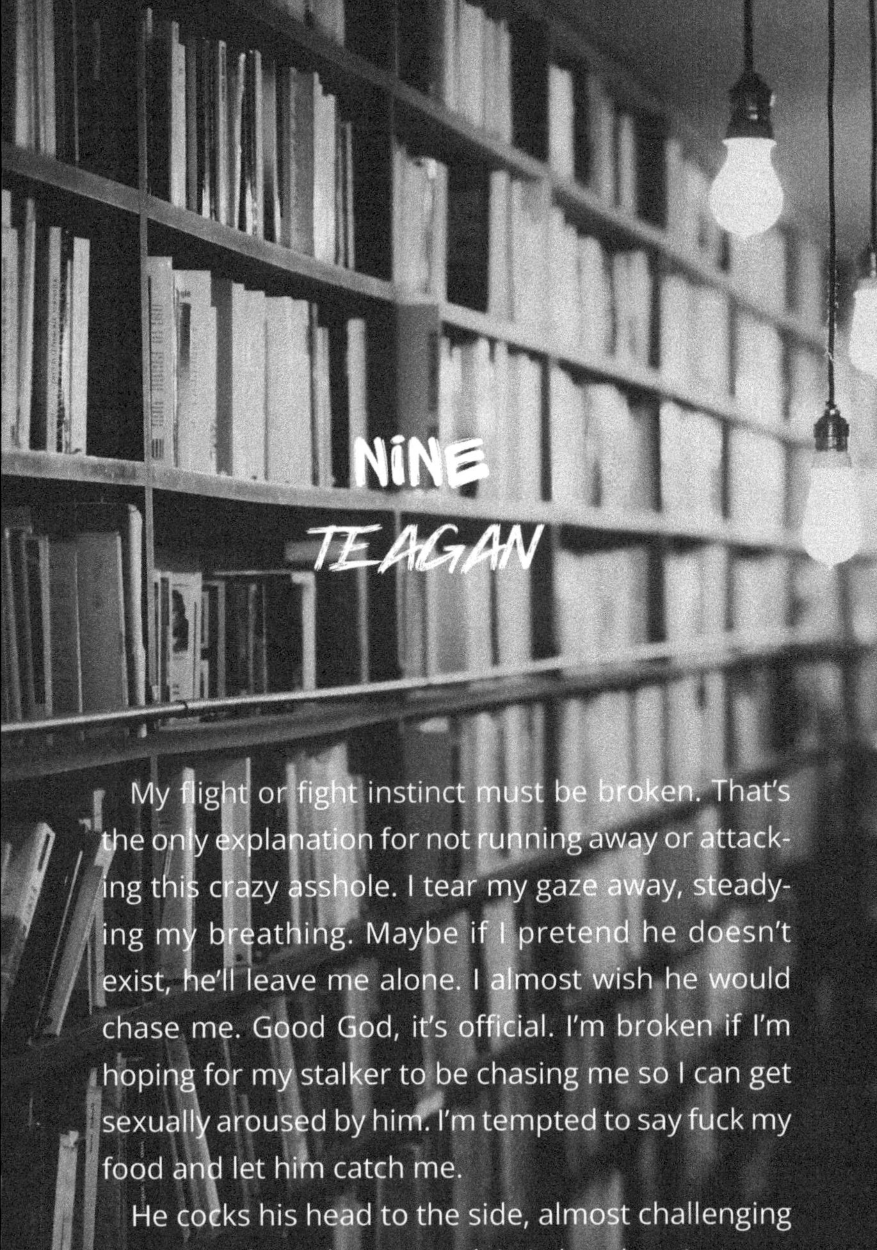

NINE

TEAGAN

My flight or fight instinct must be broken. That's the only explanation for not running away or attacking this crazy asshole. I tear my gaze away, steadying my breathing. Maybe if I pretend he doesn't exist, he'll leave me alone. I almost wish he would chase me. Good God, it's official. I'm broken if I'm hoping for my stalker to be chasing me so I can get sexually aroused by him. I'm tempted to say fuck my food and let him catch me.

He cocks his head to the side, almost challenging me. I don't know how to explain it, but there's something about this person that I find oddly captivating. I want to accept his challenge, but what does that say about me as a person? I'm willing to do anything a stranger in a mask wants me to do. Let alone a stranger who has been stalking me for who knows how long? And what if I don't do what he wants? He knows where I live. I can't hide from him.

I'm fucked either way.

I shake my head, psych myself up, and move my feet. A quick peek over my shoulder reveals he's tailing behind me. My body tingles with anticipation as he pursues me; I try not to think of what he could do to me if he does catch me.

I come to a halt. The school park is to the left, or I can turn right and run home. I swear I hear a muffled laugh coming from behind his mask. Yeah, well, fuck this guy.

Before he can think, I take off down the block, cutting across Mr. Campbell's backyard and then down the back alley until I can see the hole in my fence. Which I probably should get fixed, but that's a problem for a different day. I stick close to the fence line and cut across the yard, climbing the stairs to the back deck. Digging into my bag, I find the keys, but my hands won't stay steady enough to stick them in the lock.

"Jesus Christ, Teagan, calm the fuck down." And I have officially lost it. I'm talking to myself. I slam the key in and unlock the door; I've never felt such relief before. I readjust the bag of food, open the door leading to the mudroom, and silence greets me. Like always. I kick off my shoes and walk past the bathroom and laundry room. I drop the bag of food on the island before heading to the front window. Pulling the curtain back enough to get a small glimpse of the street, I watch and wait for any sign of my new masked friend.

I drop onto the couch, sinking my head into my hands. I'm still trying to wrap my head around what just happened. If I had headed to the school, what would he have done? I'm gonna drive myself crazy thinking of what could've been now. There is no point wallowing in it. I had my chance, and I blew it.

I stare at where I left my food, still amazed that I ran all that way without dropping it. After staring at it, I move off the couch and head into the kitchen. I slide the bag closer and pull out the chow mein and wonton soup, and the smell suddenly sends a wave of nausea through my stomach. Maybe I'm not in the mood to eat, so I place the food in the fridge and check that all the doors are locked before heading into my bedroom.

I slip into my silk nightgown and reach for my Kindle from the nightstand. I might as well finish this book before considering bringing it into the shop. Something about step brothers and a stalker.

I bury myself deeper into my blanket when a breeze glides over my skin. A warm hand wraps around my breasts, and my back is met with a chest. I sink deeper into his warmth. It's been a long time since I've been in someone else's arms. His other hand works up my thigh, causing my clit to throb with need. I must admit it's been a while since I've had this type of dream.

Gripping my thigh, he moves it over his hip, moving his finger beneath my underwear. He traces my clit with such control it drives me insane; my hips move on their own, trying to get him to touch me more in the ways I want him to. He pinches my nipple, and my hand reaches behind me, grabbing onto the material of a shirt instead of his hair. When I try to turn around, he pinches my clit.

"Fuck," I call out.

He grunts in return, driving his fingers deep inside, and I lose my breath as I cling to him. I grab the bedding with my other hand, willfully pushing my body into his. I want this to last forever. He moves his fingers so fast that my body loses all control. I press my heels into the bed and against his thigh as I squirm to get away from his assault, but then he casually moves his hand from my breast to my waist to keep me in place.

"Come," he growls.

I bite my lip as the orgasm hits me like a freight train, leaving me boneless. I turn to look at my mystery man, but he's leaving the room when he looks back at me. It's the stalker from earlier.

When I wake up, I'm covered in sweat. I can't be serious; now I'm dreaming of *him*. Lord, help me. I lie awake thinking about that dream, the way his fingers glided along my skin, moving around my clit, driving deep inside of me. Fuck me, it was only a dream; it's not like any of it was real.

I fling the blankets off and demand myself to get my shit together. But shit, dream me knows how to fucking come like there's nothing. Why can't that happen in real life? It's probably cause there isn't anyone in my life to do said things—no offence to my vibrator.

I throw on another pair of leggings and the hoodie I wore yesterday. Like Dad always says, wear it again if it ain't dirty. It's not like I'll be doing anything productive today, maybe visit Mom and Dad. I throw my hair into a messy bun and redo my wing eyeliner.

Now, I'm ready to take on the world, or at least Holden.

If only that thought had lasted; something felt off when I entered the kitchen. I can't quite place my finger on it, but the feeling of someone being in my house creeps up my spine. I knew this would happen. My paranoia is creeping in all because of this stalker. No one was in my home; I locked everything up.

And tell myself to stop thinking like this as I step outside.

It's hard to concentrate. Even when Dad talks about his latest project around the house, my mind wanders back to my dream. It felt so real, I swear his fingers were inside my pussy. Is it wrong that I want that in real life? There's still this weird feeling that someone was in my house. A vibe I can't shake, like someone was in my kitchen, but I can't pinpoint it. Something felt off, and it's been bugging me all morning.

"Teagan, are you listening to a word I'm saying?" Dad snaps his fingers, grabbing my attention.

"Um, yeah. You want to build a new deck since this one is rotting." I step on the rotting plank in question.

He raises a questionable eyebrow but continues with his story. And I go back to thinking about my masked man.

I shouldn't be.

I should be scared out of my mind like when he peeked in my window. But being followed by him, who knew that would be something I liked. I almost wished he had chased me. It's official. I'm broken if I'm hoping for my stalker to be chasing me so I can get sexually aroused by him.

The mystery of who he is, is what fascinates me. He could be anyone; then again, maybe he isn't a he. For all I know, they could be a woman. That's all I need, is that rumour spreading around town. Elma will have a field day with that.

"I swear, Teagan, you aren't listening. What's on your mind?"

Something that I'll never share with my dad in this lifetime. I'll be taking it to my grave. I wave him off. "Don't worry about me, Dad. When are you going to fix this deck?"

"With my luck, your mother will put me to work soon. Are you sure you have nothing for me to do around the shop? I don't want to start a project in the Fall."

"Sorry. I hired someone to help me around the shop. It's been nice not to be running around like a chicken with my head cut off."

He watches me, and I'm waiting for a lecture to come.

"You hired a stranger before family? Have I taught you nothing? What if this rando stole from you, then what?"

"He wouldn't do that."

"A he. You hired a male." His eyes widen larger than dinner plates.

I can't help but laugh. "Yes, Dad. A male, as in a boy. What's wrong with that?"

"Nothing, I suppose. Just shocked, that's all. Did you tell your mother? She'll be excited to stop by the shop now. Take in the new eye candy, if you know what I mean." He nudges me.

I roll my eyes. "Yes, I got it. You two are so weird. Oh, Nancy stopped by and did a surprise inspection of the shop."

"Oh, fuck her. She is such a nuisance. What did dear old Nancy find?"

"She almost found out that I've been bootlegging my room to rent out. It was a close call, but Silas put her in her place for me. But I'm afraid of what might happen now because of it."

"Mmm, Silas is your new employee, I take it. It's good that he was there, but sometimes, sticking your nose in other people's business does have repercussions. Nancy isn't one to mess with. I wouldn't worry too much, Small fry. If she hasn't done anything yet, she won't."

"I'm not sure, Dad. Her son made a big stink about Jace being chief so he declined it. And we all know how much Jace wanted that."

Dad wraps me in a hug, placing a kiss on the top of my head. "We'll cross that bridge when we need to. Now, let's see if Mom has lunch ready. My stomach is about to rumble, and you know what that means."

We need to eat before he turns hangry, is what it means.

Nancy is coming for me. I can feel it; it's only a matter of when. I'm unsure if I'll be ready for that fight, even if Dad says otherwise.

Ten

TEAGAN

I'm standing in a puddle of water, watching all my dreams drown. Maybe I'm in denial, and it's not that bad. If I ignore all the firefighters storming in and out the front door, splashing water all over the children's books as they try to control the leak.

"Teagan?"

I turn to Jace, forever grateful that he's the one talking to me first. I'm not sure what I would do otherwise.

"Yeah."

"Sugar-coat it or not?"

"Better not. I already have a feeling it's not good, bud." I glance back at the fire hydrant that became my worst enemy.

Jace clears his throat, glancing at the chief before breaking my heart. "It's terrible, Tee. The water damage alone will break the bank, and I can't imagine what it'll cost to replace all the books. The boutique suffered water damage, but nothing like this. First thing tomorrow, call your insurance company, but I'm afraid you are closed for a while."

I don't like hearing those words—damage. From the looks of things, there is a lot of damage. I should've stayed in bed. I'm glad Silas isn't here to see all this, but now that I think about it, I realize he was supposed to show up for work today.

"How did the hydrant blow its load?"

He shrugs. "That I don't know. That's a question for the chief."

From the looks of it, the chief is not up to a chat from a bookshop owner. With the way his arms are flying around, he's pissed. I'm going to assume whatever happened with the hydrant wasn't on purpose; this is going to have Elma's head spinning.

"Thanks, Jace. I guess it's out of my hands now."

He gives me a small smile. "Sorry about all this. If you need a hand cleaning, let me know. I'll get some of the guys to help."

If I don't think about the damage, it's not so bad. It's funny how things turn out, one second, the day was going as planned, and then some asshole named Murphy comes in and says, nope, *let's turn your day upside down.* What a douche. Shove your law up your asshole.

"I'll let you know, but I'll probably take you up on that offer. What a shitty day."

Jace pulls me in for a hug, and when he's in his gear, it's like hugging a bear. My arms barely reach the middle of his back. "Take care, Tee. If this is the worst, it's not that bad."

"I suppose so," I mumble into his chest. I push back and get out of his way.

"Call if you need anything."

I watch all the crew pack and leave, and I'm stuck in the middle of a mess, wondering what to do now. I should call Dad, but even thinking about talking will make me cry.

It's been hours since the great flood, so I decided not to wait and called the insurance company. They advised me not to touch anything until they could send an adjuster to check the damage. I had to beg and plead with them to do it tomorrow; this was an emergency.

The shop will need all new shelving units for the first half, the flooring will need to be redone, and

I'm not looking forward to sorting the books. It's amazing what a few inches of water will do. I walk through the lake and lock the front door.

Before I head home, I stop at my favourite restaurant, The Lucky Dragon.

"Ah, Miss Teagan. How are you?" Mr. Li greets me as soon as I walk in.

I walk to the counter, grabbing a menu even though we both know what I'm getting. "Mr. Li, not good. Not good at all."

He grabs my hand as his callused fingers rub along my knuckles. "Tell me the news, and I get your order in." He turns around, yelling an order of chicken chow mein noodles and wonton soup to his wife. Min pops her head around the corner and grins.

"I knew that was you, Teagan. I get your order done pronto."

Mr. Li chuckles. That's how you know you might be eating out a little too much. Mr. Li pats my hand and gives me a gentle smile.

"We'll make day better."

"I hope so. I had to close shop for a while," I muttered miserably.

Mr. Li's eyes widen with shock. "What happened?"

I glance at the ceiling, trying not to cry. "It flooded." His hand squeezes around mine. "Can you believe that? A bookstore flooding. I would've expected a fire or something, but nope. A stupid hydrant went rapid, and now." I can't even finish the sentence. I'm so upset. All my hard work is gone.

Mr. Li tsk's. "Don't think like that. Persist and keep at it; don't let a little pebble ruin the lake. Think of this as a restart."

"A restart for what? It was hard enough to get a building permit the first time around. I don't think it'll happen so easily this time." I drew my hand away and buried both into my hair. "Nancy is horrible to deal with."

Min comes from the kitchen with a brown paper bag, shaking her head. "Nancy is mean—horrible lady to deal with. I wish you nothing but the best, Teagan."

Short and to the point, that one is. "Thank you, Min. I'll need more than wishes, I'm afraid."

I pay and grab my food. So many thoughts are running through my head about what I have to do now that the shop is on vacation mode. The Mom and Tot program will have to be the first phone call tomorrow, and now they'll be scrambling to find a place to rent. This whole thing has thrown everyone off schedule.

I take things slow this morning; it's not like I have a shop to open. The insurance company said they won't be by until the afternoon. And if I don't distract my mind, I'll think about how nothing is getting done and how the entire place probably smells like mildew. Does mildew set in within hours? I should look that up. I also need to cancel book orders and call the mom group. Who am I kidding? Elma has probably already spread the news like wildfire. This town will know by lunch, and the one who will be the most excited will be Nancy.

As I step outside, the wind blows leaves from the neighbour's large maple across the walkway, another sign that Fall will soon come to an end. The season that I despise the most will be here. I tighten my sweater closer when another gust of wind whips around me; maybe I should've driven.

The further I walk down the street, the busier it becomes. The most popular little joint would be The Coffee Cove. The first thing you see when you walk in is the mint subway tiles behind the baristas. Besides the baked goods, it's the best thing about this place. That's what keeps me coming back, more so the cinnamon buns. They taste like heaven.

I'm mentally going through the list of things to ask the insurance broker when a hand grasps my shoulder. I whip around, and Elma smiles.

"Sorry, honey. Didn't mean to startle you." Her fingers dig deeper.

I reach out, removing her hand. "Trust me. You didn't. I was thinking, that's all."

"About your shop?" she whispers, with pity in her eyes.

And there it is, the gossip of the fucking century coming out of the rumour mill's mouth. The only thing I'm grateful for is that she whispered it but guaranteed she had already told ten people before she walked in here.

I bit back a grin and nod. "Yeah, it's a shame. Bright side. I'll get that vacation after all." I shrug because if I told her what I wanted to say, she would have a field day with it.

"It'll be all right. You'll be open in no time. I have no doubt about it." She pulls me in for a half hug.

"Thanks. I should get going. I have a busy day ahead of me."

I leave the café without ordering. Elma has a way with her words; I'm not in the mood for it. I need to talk to my parents, they'll know what to do.

The family home hasn't changed one bit since I moved out over fifteen years ago. I swear my parents don't know what renovations are. The house still looks like it should be in the 80s. Don't worry; the worst is yet to come.

Floor-to-ceiling floral wallpaper greets me as I enter the front door, and it's something I still haven't gotten used to. I've tried talking Mom into tearing it down, painting it a lovely off-white colour, and adding accent tones. But she shot that down quicker than a sniper can shoot his target.

"Teagan? What are you doing here?" Mom rounds the corner of the kitchen, looking shocked to see me.

I enter the kitchen and find Mom making a tea. "Where's Dad? I need to talk to the both of you." Mom is still looking at me, waiting for answers, but frankly, I only want to retell this story once.

"He's in the garage, I'll grab him." She heads out, but looks at me once more with worry.

I should've known. He's probably tinkering on something that doesn't need to be tinkered with. That man shouldn't have retired. Dad needs a hobby, like fishing, but he doesn't want to leave Mom alone. I'll never understand a romantic relationship, but a few hours by yourself shouldn't be a problem. I think Mom would enjoy some alone time.

I'm halfway through making an apple cider when Dad comes storming into the kitchen like someone just murdered his kitten.

"What's wrong, Small fry?"

I set my cup on the table and look between him and Mom. "Sit." I pull a chair out and sit.

"Fuck, she's pregnant, and the asshole walked out on her." Dad pulls a chair out and slams his fist on the table.

"Whoa, slow your roll, Dad. I'm not sixteen; I'm thirty-five. I'm sure if I did end up pregnant one day, I'd be okay being a single mom. Anyway. The shop flooded, and I had to close it."

Why does he jump to the most extreme? I would've thought something along the lines of something that happened to the house, such as the car breaking. But no, it's my uterus that has finally been used. Mom sits next to me, giving me a small hug.

"It'll be okay. What do you need us to do?"

I spin around my cup of cider, wondering about all the shit that needs to be done. "To be honest. The insurance company is sending someone over today."

"I'll be there with you. Those rat bastards will try anything to scam the smallest thing out of you," Dad interrupts.

"That's a good idea, dear. Dad will not let them take advantage of you. God knows what they'll try to pull," Mom adds, patting my hand.

I lean back in my chair, taking a sip of my cider. Only my parents would try to still treat me like a child. I'm pretty sure I know how to stand my ground regarding my business. I keep my mouth shut; some things are best unsaid, especially around Dad.

Dad parks in front of the shop minutes before the appointment with the insurance broker, and my mind is about to explode. Every what-if scenario is running through. What if the flooring needs to be replaced, the insurance company won't cover repairs, Nancy might not allow me to get a new permit, or God forbid the fire hydrant blows its top again?

"Teagan, it'll be all right. No matter what happens, you have Mom and I standing behind you through the entire thing."

I glance over and see that he's staring at the shop. "Thanks, Dad. We should get in there and take a look around, get my tears out before a stranger sees them."

He chuckles. "You won't cry. You're too tough to cry."

At this point, I could probably cry The Nile. My stress level is through the roof, and today will be my breaking point. I knew owning a business wouldn't be easy, but it's a bookstore, the most relaxing hobby in the world. Yet the owner is stressing.

A blue four-door Sedan pulls up next to us, with EDM blaring from the speakers. I snap my head to the side window, and a twenty-something punk is sitting in the car. If this is the broker, Dad is going to lose his shit.

"It's a punk kid? Jesus Christ, Teagan."

"It's fine, Dad. Don't be a jerk to him. I still need him to do his job." I open the truck door, taking a deep breath. Dad and his old-ass ego can take a hike for a few hours. As I walk towards the shop door, I suddenly feel like someone is watching me. I resist the temptation to turn around and check.

I just want this day to be over and done with.

The only thing that has been keeping me going is the thought of Teagan running away from me the other night. Deep down, I hoped she wanted to try something risky by moving to the school park. I would've bent her over the swing and fucked her in the open without a care.

Instead, I'm sitting in a stolen car, waiting for Leroy to show up. But classic Leroy, he's late as always, even though this is his job, not mine. I should've known this would happen. He pulls this shit all the time while my asshole puckers every time a vehicle passes, and I'm waiting for it to be a cop and bust my ass.

I'm the one to be blamed; I answered the phone and agreed to this. But all I want to do is get back to Holden. Small-town life wasn't in my books, but this seals the deal for me, I can't keep stealing cars and trying to make a living. It's not worth it. I don't think Leroy knows what is involved anymore; he's so far out of touch that it's unreal. All he sees at the end of the day is the dollar signs.

The knock on the driver's window has my skin jumping off my body; when I look over, it's Leroy with a shit-eating grin. I flip him the finger and roll the window down.

"You're an asshole. Get the fuck in before a cop comes by."

He punches me in the arm. "Loosen up, man. I swear you've grown into a stiff since you left. Live a little."

I roll the window up in his face; I'll loosen up when I'm back in Holden and see Teagan. I'm sounding like a pussy, for sure. So much for not wanting to get involved with her.

"Drive, Blackwell. I'll tell you where to turn, you need to get out of that head of yours, or we're fucked for sure."

"I'm not in my head, fuck off." I rev the engine and pull out onto the street. That's the thing about Leroy; he gets in my head more than anyone. He's one regret that I'll never forget, that one reminder of the many fuck ups that I can never take back.

"So, tell me about this town that you ditched me for. It's gotta be something spectacular because I thought you wouldn't leave me for anything."

"Well, if you weren't such an asshole last time, maybe I wouldn't have left."

He flicks his hand and points left. "Turn up here. And I wasn't an asshole. You didn't do your job. It wasn't my fault you pouted like a baby when I bitched you out."

I slam the brakes on, jolting us both forward. I turn to Leroy. "I didn't do my job because you fucked up in the first place. Don't act like it was my fault. Take the blame once in a while. Jesus Christ, Leroy, you could've had me killed, and you probably wouldn't care."

"Drive, Blackwell. We're late."

Deflecting. His fucking specialty.

The spot Leroy directed me to is literally a hole in a wall. The run-down garage is large enough to hide the 71' Bronco that I decided to borrow—without returning. Knowing Leroy, the Bronco won't be sporting its baby blue coat. I dig this colour more than whatever shade they will pick, guaranteed.

"Yo, Leroy. What the fuck is this?" Stan shakes his head when I step out.

"Don't start with me. You wanted a vehicle, so I brought you one. Now pay up." Leroy slaps Stan on the back. "And don't act like this won't sell like hotcakes."

Stan exhales, running his hand through his long greasy hair. "That's not what I'm worried about. These." He knocks on the hood. "Aren't popular. That means it's gonna be hot, and the cops will be watching for it. It's gonna take me forever to make this thing look unrecognizable."

Leave it to Leroy to fuck up again and blame others. This is what I mean by deflecting. God forbid he takes any blame. Give a few, and he'll turn on me since I jacked the stupid thing even though he told me to get something that no one drives.

"I don't care, Stan. Pay so I can get the fuck out of here."

Stan is just standing there, his overalls all gunked up with grease and snug around his belly as he takes each deep breath. "I'm only doing it, so you leave." He walks to his toolbox and pulls out a wad of twenties. "I suggest you don't spend it all in one place."

Once I get my cut, he won't have much to spend. You can't make a living doing this all the time. It's risky, but Leroy doesn't care. It's all about him. I can't do this again. All I know is that come tomorrow, I'll be on my way back to Holden, and I'll be stepping into The Dancing Goat and ready to work.

I unlock the door to my motel room when my burner phone rings. I instantly know it won't be good news if I answer it. It also means I won't be getting back to Holden in time.

"Leroy, this better be great news because I'm about to hit the hay." I step inside, closing the door with my foot. The motel has a hint of mildew and looks like it's straight out of the 60s.

"Don't be like that. It's a quick job, I promise. In and out."

I plop on the bed as gracefully as a sack of potatoes dropped from a roof. "Nothing with you is quick. Now tell me the details."

Tuesday. Fucking rolling back into Holden a day late, and I'm the asshole that never called Teagan to tell her that I wouldn't be showing up for work. I can only hope she forgives me when I walk into the shop.

Except this isn't the bookshop, I remember from last week. A construction crew is working within the small shop. I weave past a few of the workers stepping inside.

The floor is torn up, bookshelves empty, and a distraught Teagan standing in the back holding a clipboard, looking at the scene unfolding in front of her. When a douche walks up to her and says something, she frowns. The second he pulls her in for a hug, I see red. Why the fuck is someone touching her? I don't take my eyes off them as I stalk forward. When bitch boy sees me, he straightens up and whispers something to Teagan. She turns around, narrowing her eyes. She quickly blinks, and her green eyes widen with shock.

"Silas? Where have you been?" She moves away from fucktard and comes toward me.

I slowly relax my clenched fists, jerking my chin to the door. "Somethings came up, and I couldn't get out of them." That's not a complete lie. "What the fuck happened?" I eye nut tard when he steps closer to Teagan.

She shakes her head. "Silas, it's been a shitshow. Let me tell you. I need a goddamn vacation is what I need."

"I told you to take one," fucktard says.

My eye twitches with the way he talks. Who does he think he is? "Anyway. Continue." He glares at me, but he'll learn quickly that I'm not afraid.

"The hydrant exploded, and my shop was on its hit list. I'm thanking my lucky stars. The insurance company pulled their weight and covered it. I'm still footing the bill for the loss of books, but it's whatever."

"Fuck, girl. Is there anything I can do?" I don't wanna come off as needy, but I'm almost at bitch boys level here. I can feel it.

"Yeah, if you see Nancy coming, distract her. I don't have a building permit. The bitch never gave it to me again." She rolls her eyes.

Of course, she didn't. That doesn't surprise me, considering the last visit Nancy sprang on Teagan. Now that I'm here, I dare her to show her face around here.

"I told you before. I'm not afraid of Nancy."

Fucktard laughs. "You should be."

"Well, I'm not. And no one asked for your input, you abnormal shit goblin," I spit the words out; my jaw tightens when he smirks.

"Silas, don't start. Jace, that's enough. Don't you have work to get to?" She turns to Jace, crossing her arms.

Now it's my turn to smirk. That's what you get for being a dick. Except it's me who gets a smack in the face when he pulls her in for a hug. That should be me with her in my arms. But I came off too strong last time, and she wasn't ready for that.

I watch douchebag take off; a little too cocky if you ask me. Asshole.

"Silas, he's a friend. Check the ego at the door next time."

I turn in a circle. "Can't find this ego you are speaking of. Where is it?"

She shoves me, laughing. "Shut it, Sunshine. I'm glad you're back. It's been miserable without you."

I pull her in a hug, inhaling her citrus scent. "I'm here now. Whatever you need, lay it on me. You don't have to do anything alone."

"Thanks, Silas. But as you can tell, I'm not in need of your working skills today. You can head home unless you wanna fill me in on where you were?" She allows the final word to transform into a question casually.

That isn't something I want to share, not yet, anyway or at all. Teagan doesn't need to know I jack cars for a living. I give her one more hug, wrapping my arms around her as she rests her chin on my chest, her pleading green eyes looking up at me. I kiss her forehead before stepping back.

"I'll tell you one day. But if you want me to head out, I will. But call if Nancy shows up; I'll be here in a blink of an eye."

"Thank you." She gives me a small smile. "Maybe we can grab dinner later?"

She's tugging my heartstrings and throwing me for so many loops I'm unsure what direction to head. Do friends have dinner? I'm not sure how this works. Hump and dump, that's how I work, but Teagan is different, and I have to remind myself this constantly.

"Call when you wanna do it."

She shoots up an eyebrow.

"Dinner, you perv."

"I was thinking that. You are the perv, Sunshine." She points at me.

"Whatever helps you sleep at night, Dimples. Be safe here." I walk closer to the door, weaving amongst the mess. "See, ya."

I exit the shop and bump into a body.

"Sorry."

"You should be."

Elma. I'm surprised she talked back to me. She usually runs away with her tail between her legs. I stare down at her, watching her. Her grey eyes narrow at me, and her white eyebrow raises.

"Say what's on your mind, Elma."

"You don't belong here, Silas. How many times do I have to say it? And stop hanging around Teagan."

I move closer until I see every wrinkle on her forehead. "Didn't know this was your town, Elma. I have something for you if you want some gossip to spread." I watch her eyes sparkle, and if she were a dude, her dick would've grown. "There is no Teagan and I. I ditched her like a used condom. I dare you to spread that news."

Elma pulls away, eyes wide and her nose crinkled with disgust. "How dare you speak like that—you filthy animal," she stutters.

I shrug it off. She isn't wrong. I am an animal, alright; it's just not the way she's thinking. The further I push her away, the more she'll leave me alone. Why in the world anyone would want to be up someone's ass about their business is beyond me.

I give Elma a two-finger salute and take off down the street. Elma doesn't need to know the truth that Teagan and I are friends and may never be more. If you are only looking for rumours, I'll give you one to spread true or not. It's not my fault you believe everything you hear. I'll deal with the blonde bookkeeper's fury when she catches wind of this juicy rumour later on.

I'm not afraid of Teagan.

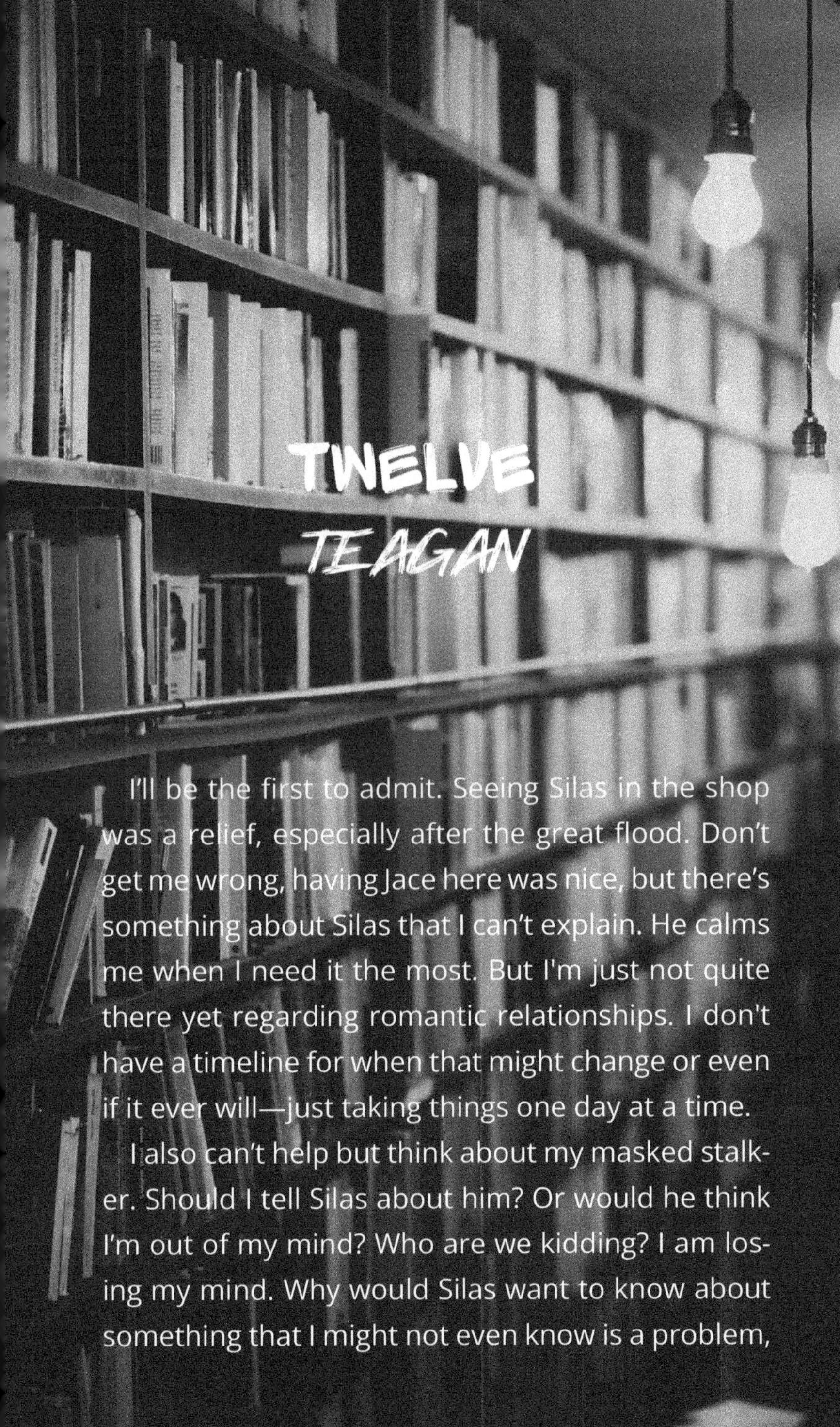

TWELVE
TEAGAN

I'll be the first to admit. Seeing Silas in the shop was a relief, especially after the great flood. Don't get me wrong, having Jace here was nice, but there's something about Silas that I can't explain. He calms me when I need it the most. But I'm just not quite there yet regarding romantic relationships. I don't have a timeline for when that might change or even if it ever will—just taking things one day at a time.

I also can't help but think about my masked stalker. Should I tell Silas about him? Or would he think I'm out of my mind? Who are we kidding? I am losing my mind. Why would Silas want to know about something that I might not even know is a problem,

I haven't seen my stalker in a few days, so maybe they gave up on me.

But my first issue at hand is getting this shop fixed. When I look around, it turns my stomach, and there's no way in hell the crew can get this fixed on time. I need them to work fast before Nancy shows up, or else we are screwed.

"Teagan, can I have a word before you leave?" The head contractor, John walks over, holding his clipboard like he means business.

I groan when he stops in front of me. "John, it better be good news because I don't think I can handle bad news."

He rubs his greying mustache. "Yeah, you might want to call me the bad news train."

"Fuck balls. Lay it on me." I move closer when he lowers his clipboard.

"We're gonna have to replace all the flooring; we can't find the exact colour."

"Okay, that's not so bad."

He chuckles. "The water damage reached further than we assumed. The only thing that saved you is that the walls and subfloor are concrete. We do have to tear down all the drywall on this wall." He points to the wall to the right, the one I share with the boutique and the one closest to the outside door. "It has the most damage, and your shelves need to be replaced. So, if you wanted to change the shop's layout, this would be the perfect chance."

"Would I need a new permit for that?"

"You would need one, yes."

"And if we don't get said permit?"

He grins and shakes his head. "Nancy will ruin everything."

"I was afraid of that. Let's move ahead anyway, and I'll worry about Nancy. Because let's be real, she probably won't give us the permit to move a few walls even if I wanted to."

"What would you change?"

"I wouldn't mind removing the rental room and opening it up for more space. I know it would suck for the Mom and Tots, but I have to think long term and having screaming children in a bookshop isn't where it's at anymore."

"Build your small café that you wanted the first time around."

John was my original contractor, and he was here when Nancy turned into the devil when she tore through here the first time. And shut down the café idea. But now John is right. I could add a small one if I want to. But do I? That's a lot of work, and then I'll have to hire someone to run it and buy all the equipment, which is not in my budget anymore. But I want to build it in spite of Nancy.

"Don't worry, Teagan. I'll tear the walls down and continue with what we are doing. Head home for the day, and don't worry about a thing."

"Yeah, okay. Thanks, John."

I step outside expecting to feel some sort of relief, but nothing comes; my body is maxed out on stress. I'm not sure what my next step is. Do what John says or have a bigger space. I could ask Mom for her opinion, but she'll say don't aggravate Nancy. Dad will ask what does my finances look like. Because he's a responsible adult. And then Jace will say fuck that bitch.

I stop outside the café and pull my phone out. I only have one option left.

Me: Still up for dinner?

Sunshine: That didn't take you long. Miss me already?

Me: No. But I need to ask you something. Yay or nay?

Sunshine: Wow. Humble me much. It's always yes, Dimples. Did you wanna eat out or eat at my place?

Me: Can you cook?

Sunshine: Sure, not well but I haven't died yet

Me: Hopefully tonight isn't that night. OK, if you need me to bring anything let me know.

Sunshine: Just your sassy self

Charmer, that's what he is. Jace always says that a man's charm is his most effective weapon, and I believe it. Silas has a way of making me forget about my troubles. It's refreshing until I stop talking to him, and the world floods back to reality. And that is not a good thing.

I feel terrible showing up empty handed. I should've grabbed a six-pack but what if Silas doesn't drink? Maybe I don't know him as well as I think I do. I'm standing outside his door, debating whether this is right. Perhaps I should've just asked Dad instead.

As I knock, the door swings open, and Silas stands in front of me in his dark-washed jeans, a black Henley long-sleeved shirt, and his dark hair looking tousled without his hat on.

"Dimples. I was getting worried you were gonna walk that little fanny of yours back to your place with all that thinking you were doing."

I roll my eyes and smile. "Shut it. I was wondering how I was going to kick your ass if you tried anything."

He nods. "Sure you were. Come on in before we freeze to death." He moves away from the door and guides me in.

"It's not even cold out here. Don't be such a priss."

"I am a delicate fucking flower, if you haven't noticed."

I step inside his house, and I'm shocked. It's clean for a bachelor living alone. He rests his hands on my shoulder, guiding me to his kitchen.

"I've noticed. Are you hiding a maid in this place?"

He pulls a chair out for me and pushes me down. "No. I know how to clean, and the place doesn't get dirty with only one person living here. Drink?" He gazes down at me with an intensity that's hard to resist. It's tempting to close my eyes as I inhale his earthy scent, but I must stay strong. His playful smirk gives away that he's fully aware of the effect he has on me.

I push back in my seat, trying to clear my head. "Whatever you're having." I watch him move about his kitchen, grabbing two glasses from the cupboard. He peeks over his shoulder and then gets back to work. I have no idea what I asked for, but hopefully, it doesn't kill me.

He places a glass of clear liquid in front of me and laughs. "You asked for what I'm drinking."

"What the fuck is it?"

"Vodka."

"Um, can I have some pop or something to mix with mine?" He winks at me and opens the fridge. "My stomach would retaliate, and we would have a problem if I drank that straight."

"Don't apologize, Dimples. I'll never force you to drink something you can't handle." He pours orange juice into my glass. "I might force you in other areas, though."

Nope, the brain cannot go there. Dinner and talk about the shop. That was the whole point of coming here.

"What's for dinner? I would like to know what my last meal is."

"Don't be dramatic. You aren't gonna die. I made the easiest thing ever. Tacos."

I'd say the most uncomplicated meal. At least I know it's safe. It's the thought that counts; he could've told me no, and I desperately need his input. He's the only outsider I know; he hasn't been jaded by Nancy yet.

"Alright, spill. You asked for this night, so what's on your mind?" Silas asks before shoving half his taco into his mouth.

I wrinkled my nose in disapproval, and just thinking about Nancy turns my stomach. "Nancy and my shop. I need your advice on something, and you are the only one that doesn't have beef with her."

"Okay, shoot."

"The back room is going be coming down. John says to turn it into the café I wanted when I first thought of the shop, and I say leave it for retail or more book space. If we did the café, it would be more money and a permit. To get said permit would be coming from Nancy. I'm not sure what to do."

He sits there, staring past my shoulder for a minute. "Okay. With getting this café, would that bring in more customers to the book side or just to grab food and leave? Would the other café in town get pissed off with you? More work means more employees. Can you handle that?"

"That's what I'm worried about, or would it be easier to have a self-serve coffee bar?"

"That's not a bad idea. Create a reward system where they get a discount on a book or something. This way, it gets Nancy off your back. You don't need a large renovation, the permit shouldn't be needed, and you still have some sort of uniqueness to the shop."

I let out a small exhale. Relief that something has been worked out. "Thank you, Silas. I've been stressing over that all day."

"There wasn't much to it. I only asked a few questions, and you came up with the solution on your own. What's gonna happen to the Mom and Tot program, though?"

I slump forward and hang my head. "I don't know. I love having it." I glance up at him. "But it's loud, and I'm afraid it's driving away business. You saw it firsthand. It's crazy."

"I'm sure they will understand, especially with the flood and whatnot. They can't expect things to stay the same. You have to think of what's right for your business."

"I guess. I feel bad."

"Don't. Where are they having it now?"

"Down at the community hall."

He shrugs, giving me my answer. It's probably better down there anyway; the kids have more room to run around and won't mess with my books or annoy customers.

"Now finish eating."

"God, you are so bossy."

He chuckles. "You have no idea."

In a way, I want to find out, but something is holding me back. Or is it someone?

THIRTEEN

TEAGAN

As I step out of Silas' house, the wind picks up, kicking leaves across the sidewalk. A reminder that October is a few weeks away. And the best time of the year will be here. Halloween. I can't wait to see all the kids in their costumes and hand out candy. It is the only time of the year when you aren't judged for dressing how you truly want.

"Are you sure I can't walk you home?"

"Yes, Silas. I'm fine. I need to clear my head before I go to sleep anyway. I had a great time. Thank you again for supper."

"And hey, you didn't die. That's a success." He reaches his hand out for a high five.

I smack his hand. "Yeah, I'll cook next time, and we'll see if I pass the test."

"I'm sure you will." He pulls me in for a hug, holding me tight. "Be safe walking home. Weirdos are out this late."

"I'll be okay. I can take care of myself. But thank you for caring." He releases me, rolling his eyes.

"Stubborn like an ox, aren't you."

"Yes. The sooner you figure it out, the easier it is for you. Goodnight, Silas."

"Sweet dreams, Teagan."

I leave his place, feeling a sense of relief. I'm glad we came to a solution about the room, and now I need to break it to the moms that they need to re-home their group. I should consider what's best for the business, and potentially expanding into retail with a coffee bar could be the right move.

I was so deep in thought that I completely missed the person sneaking up behind me. I cross the street, giving us space. I don't have to look back to figure out who it is; my instincts are already on high alert. My masked stalker has come to play.

I quicken my stride, trying to add space between us. I head toward the school, which is probably not the brightest idea. The streetlights are too distant to reach this side of the school. I keep going, not letting anything stop me until I finally make it to the slide connected to the tower and bridge.

"You can't run away from me all the time. Let me have my fun." I hear his muffled voice behind me; his mask distorting his words.

"What kind of fun? You sicko." The words are barely out of my mouth when his hand wraps around my hair and yanks me backwards into his chest. Before I can scream, his gloved hand covers my mouth.

"Shh."

My heart is pounding so loudly that I can't even hear what's happening around me. I sense his hand shifting from my hair to my waist, stirring up a sense of familiarity, yet uncertainty clouds my thoughts. His gentle yet firm touch traces delicate patterns on my skin beneath my shirt, summoning a rush of tingling sensations down my stomach, creating a trail of goosebumps in its wake.

I slam my hand over his when he reaches the waistband of my jeans. Clarity is starting to make its way through me. I can't help but wonder, what am I doing here? Is this truly what I desire? Honestly, who am I trying to fool? Embarking on this adventure with a stranger, whom I'll probably never cross paths with again, feels like the most daring thing I've ever done. But they know who I am; they could know everything about me. They could ruin my entire life if they wanted to. They hold all the cards in their hands.

"Trust me."

There's that trust word again. I don't even know this person; how can I trust them? He pushes his fingers inside my mouth until I gag on them. I move my hand away from the one on the waistband to take his fingers out of my mouth. When I feel his palm slide into my jeans, I freeze.

My stalker now knows I go commando. And it's a free pass to the fucking clit. I dig my nails into his wrist, trying to remove his fingers from my mouth, but it's no luck. He pumps his fingers in and out until drool falls from my mouth. When he withdraws them, his fingers in my jeans start moving.

"Fuck." I groan when his finger slides inside.

His hand delves into my hair, yanking my head back and causing me to arch my back. His finger buries deeper as his palm rubs against my clit. I brace myself against a pole by the slide when my legs shake. With each stroke of his finger, my hips meet the stroke of his palm, trying to chase the orgasm that my clit desperately needs. He must notice because he slides his finger out and presses them on my clit.

"Fuck my fingers," he demands.

I don't think twice; my hips move, grinding on his hand, sending shockwaves throughout my body. He releases my hair, wrapping his hand around my waist and lets out a small groan when my ass rubs against his hard-on. His fingers press harder into my clit, the more I push into him. I also want him to come, and I won't stop until he does.

He drops his head on my shoulder, and the glow from his mask reminds me that I'll never know who this is. But it only drives me wild at this moment. He pulls me closer to his body the more I grind into his hand, and I hear his breath hitch and a quiet 'fuck' falls from his mouth. His nails bite into my skin as he chases his orgasm. Just hearing that sends my world tumbling.

As I let out a loud moan, he quickly covers my mouth with his hand to muffle the sound. My legs feel like they're about to give out, but he steadies me by pulling his hand away and wrapping his arm around me for support. That has been the most intense orgasm I've ever had by far. He removes his hand from my jeans, and the cloud slowly clears; I realize what I have done.

I slowly move away, watching him stay where he is. He cocks his head to the side as if he's watching his prey get away.

"This can't happen again. I had a lapse of judgement. Whatever your fascination is with me, you can forget about it. You got what you wanted. Now, leave me alone. I have a boyfriend."

He tilts his head back and bursts into a hearty laugh.

"Whatever helps you sleep at night, Sweets. But we both know you don't."

His nickname sends my stomach into a frenzy and gives me electrifying shivers from head to toe. I can't stand here and be in his presence anymore. It's too dangerous, and who knows what he's capable of. Anything by the looks of it. Jesus, he stuck his fingers in me in public, for Christ's sake.

I step back as his mask switches off, plunging us into darkness. I stand there scared, not knowing what to think. As I reach into my back pocket, my fingers fumble around for my phone. With a quick press of a button, the flashlight bursts to life, illuminating the darkness around me. It's then that I realize I am completely and utterly alone.

"Are you kidding me, you asshole." What am I even saying? Why am I getting angry at him? It's good he left, he's stalking me. Oh, my God. I'm losing my mind.

I swiftly leave the park before anyone notices me. The last thing I need is for Elma to catch wind of this. I wasn't thinking, the pussy was leading the way on this one. I cut across Mr. Campbell's yard like I usually do if I come this way. I'm sure he knows, but he hasn't said anything. Until he does, it shall be my shortcut, mainly to get away from a masked man.

As I turn the key in the backdoor and step inside, a feeling of safety envelops me. As I let out the breath, it fills the room with a sense of relief. I gently push the door closed and lean back, feeling the weight of the night start to lift off my shoulders.

What the hell am I going to do now? He's taken things to the next level, and I'm going to go out on a limb and say he knows my daily routine. Who's to say he hasn't already been in my house? I had a sense of dread one morning. Was it because he was in here? I have so many unanswered questions I'm not even sure I'll get my answers.

I ensure the deadbolt is securely locked before checking the front door. Maybe I'm being paranoid, but I can't help it. I refuse to relax until either he's out of my life for good or I unmask him and reveal his true identity. I swear I will unmask him one way or another. He won't be able to hide forever.

I had the worst night's sleep. The nightmare that woke me kept me up for hours. That's how I know I'm under too much stress when outside shit is plaguing my dreams. The horror of dreaming of Nancy was enough to wake me from a dead sleep. Especially when that dream involved her showing up at the shop and shutting down the construction, that's all I need. I can't afford any hiccups. I hope this isn't a sign of what's to come.

When I turn the corner, I see it. The black Land Rover is parked outside my shop, and only one person in this town drives it. I don't have time to call Dad and tell him to hurry and get his ass down here because World War III is about to start. Nancy's hands are flying around while arguing with John.

Here we go.

"Nancy, what brings you down to the peasant part of town?" I casually walk up next to John, arms crossed, and shoot her my most intense glare.

She smirks at me, holding up another pink piece of hell. "I came back to deliver this, Teagan. I'm sure you know what it is."

"I don't. Refresh my memory, would you?"

She huffs. "I'm declining your renovations."

"Why? It's not renovations, Nancy. I'm fixing the damage the city caused. I'm not altering the structure of the building, so your permit is pointless.

You're doing it out of spite." She doesn't need to know about removing the room. That's here nor there at the moment.

She shoves the paper into my chest, but I refuse to take it. "You will follow the rules, or I'll threaten you." She releases the paper, and it floats to the ground. She swivels on her heels and starts walking back to her blacked-out Land Rover when I call out.

"Have the day you deserve, Nancy. Don't get hit by a fucking bus."

She slams her door shut, reversing from the parking spot and speeding away.

"That lady is a..." John trails off.

"A cunt, John. You can say it. I'm a big girl, and she deserves any word you throw at her." I'm rubbing my temples, starting to feel a headache creeping in. I could use either an energy drink or a strong drink right about now.

"I'll get the crew back to work. We'll work double time to finish this quickly before she can return."

"Thanks, John. That would be wonderful. Did you need anything from the store?" I rub my temples more as the pressure slowly builds.

"No. I'm good." He walks into the shop, leaving me alone.

I can't shake off this morning; I'm stuck in a pit of despair. I'm counting on John and his team to come through so I can start getting back on track. Without my usual routine, I feel like I'm losing my mind.

The walk to the corner store is boring, to the point where I wish Elma would find me and gossip with me. It's been a while since she filled me in on what's happening in this town. It would be nice to know if Nancy is telling lies about me. I'm sure she's already telling everyone that I want her dead, which wouldn't be a rumour; it would be a fact. But Elma is nowhere to be found on my walk, and with my headache worsening, I'm not sure I would be able to handle the gossip. Every step I take feels like miniature jackhammers drilling into my skull. If I don't grab some caffeine, I might not make it back to the shop. Is caffeine the answer? Probably not. But I'm going to say it is.

The bell above the door hits me like a sledgehammer when I enter the store. Another sign that I will not be replacing my bell.

"Morning, Teagan. How are you?" Tom calls out.

I wave him off. Heading for the cooler and grab the beautiful can that'll make me feel better. I don't even wait; I crack it open and slam half of it back, feeling the carbonation bite my throat. Let the magic work.

"Tom, it's been a morning, and it's not even ten yet," I tell him when I reach the till. He chuckles as he scans my can.

"I can tell. I'm sorry about the shop. Elma told me."

"Of course she did. I have a crew working double time to get it back into shape before the end of the week. I can't handle any more delays."

He gives me the look. The one that screams he knows who I'm talking about. "Nancy," he says with a lip curl.

"Yeah. Don't get me started. But I should get back and make sure she doesn't reappear. Thanks, Tom."

"My pleasure, Teagan. Good luck."

I spin around absentmindedly and accidentally collide with a solid chest. My can slips from my hand as I see stars. I quickly shut my eyes and grab my head, hoping the pounding will ease. Arms envelop me in a warm embrace, drawing me in closer, and I catch a whiff of the comforting woodsy cologne.

"Dimples, you okay?"

I groan in response. The thought of talking has flown out the window. I bury my face further into Silas' chest, trying to block my surroundings out. Maybe I should've just gone home. He goes to move me, and I cling to his hoodie.

"We have to move. We can't stay here forever."

"I need to get back to the shop." I groan, slowly pulling away.

Silas lifts his left eyebrow. "You're going to the shop while you have a migraine?"

"It's a headache, and it'll go away once I drink." I raise my empty hand. "Never mind. Sorry, Tom, about the mess."

"It's a little liquid, Teagan. No worries. Get home and feel better."

Silas steers me toward the door, never letting me go. But instead of hanging a left toward my shop, he turns right.

"Where are we going? The shop is the other way."

"I'm taking you home."

"This isn't the way to my house, Silas."

He tucks my head closer to his chest. "My house is closer, and you need the sleep. If you want, I can check on the shop."

"Nancy stopped by; that's why I have a headache. I swear the karma bus will take that witch out one day, and I'll be watching from the sidelines, eating my popcorn and enjoying the show."

"Come on, my little psycho pants, let's get you some meds and into bed before you plan the murder for everyone in this town."

"Not everyone, one particular person, Silas. You have no idea what shit I went through so far this morning. God, I hate that woman."

"It's alright, Dimples. Don't drown in anger. It'll only ruin you." He brushes my hair to the side, and I notice a grim look on his face. When he spots me watching, he smiles.

"Don't worry about me, Teagan. That's a life I left behind. Stop talking, or you'll make your headache worse; a few more blocks and we're at my place. How you feeling?"

I give him a thumbs up, but in reality, my head wants to explode, and I want to tear it off my shoulders and kick it across the road.

He chuckles. "Come on, I've got a bed with your name on it."

At this point, I don't care whose bed it is. I need to lie down. Even though I can't afford to be away from the shop, what if Nancy returns and rains down on everything. John will be left to the wolf, and then what? This isn't how I pictured my day going. All this stress has finally caught up to me when I can't afford it.

Walking back into Silas's place feels natural. His house is minimalist—white walls without pictures, no décor in sight. For one person, a couch and loveseat in the living room seems to be a lot. He guides me up the stairs to where his bedroom is. A bed and a dresser, nothing more.

"Is this thing made out of clouds?" I lay starfish on his bed, making a snow angel in his sheets before finding a comfortable spot.

"Ah, memory foam. Here, take these." He hands me two white pills and a glass of water. I stare at them for a second. "Don't worry, they are only Tylenol, I swear. Want me to get the bottle to show you?"

"No, I trust you. Thanks again, Sunshine." I swallow the pills and close my eyes. The warmth of the blanket wraps around me.

"Rest, Dimples. I'll be here when you wake up." His lips brush across my forehead.

I roll onto my side and breathe Silas's woodsy scent before falling into a deep sleep.

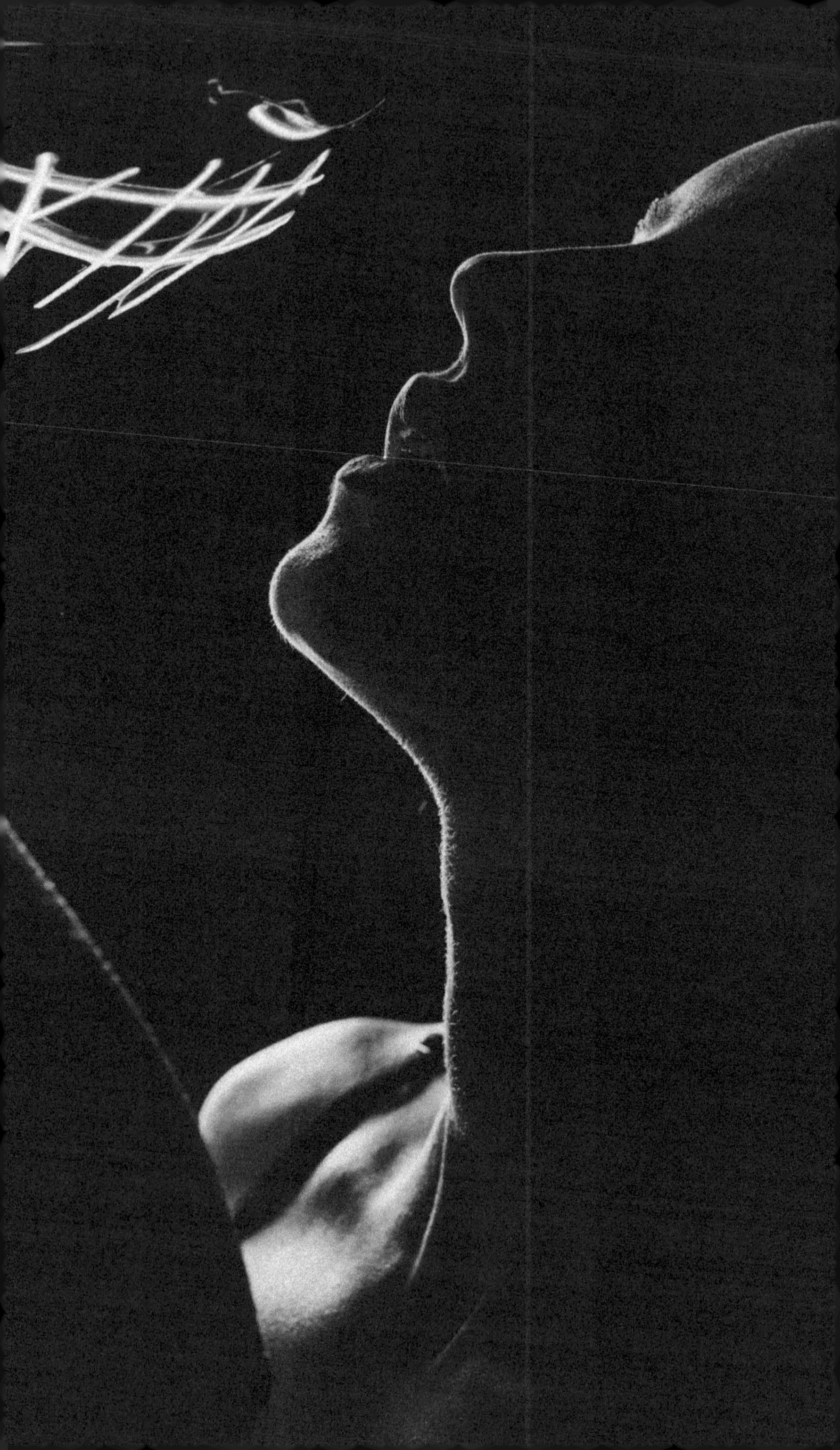

FOURTEEN

SILAS

Last night was fucking hot. I can't believe Teagan would let a stranger do something like that to her, let alone touch her in public. I can't get the thought of her moans out of my head. The way her ass moved across my cock, fuck. It's no wonder I came in my boxers like a teenager. I can't believe I did that. There's no coming back from that. How am I supposed to tell her the truth after all that? I had to fight the urge to pull both our pants down and fuck the living hell out of her.

But I don't want some masked man to be the first to fuck her; I want it to be me. I can only hope she doesn't kick me out of her life when the truth comes out. I should've stopped before my heart fell for her because the last thing I expected was for her to be sleeping in my bed.

I should've seen that coming with Nancy. She needs to be brought down a peg or two. She's like a dog with a bone. Nancy won't rest until everything is buried. I'm nearly tempted to dial up Leroy and have him scare the shit out of her. But call me spontaneous because I'm feeling a tad impulsive right now.

I check on Teagan again, ensuring she's asleep before heading to the kitchen. I'll probably regret this phone call later but right now. I'm pissed off. I've never used this burner phone so much in one month as I have right now.

"Blackwell. Missed me already? I am hard to forget."

"Shut it. I need your help." Those words taste like shit falling from my mouth.

"Hold up. Can you say those last words one more time? It sounded like you needed some assistance. The same person who never listens or asks for anything suddenly needs help?"

I tap my forehead with the phone. "Are you going to listen or not?"

"Shoot."

"There's this lady." I begin.

I tell Leroy about Nancy or as much as I know. Which is she's a cunt, in a nutshell. Leroy had more colourful words to use, which I agreed, but cunt wraps it up nicely. Together, we came up with a plan, but unfortunately, I'm working on Leroy's schedule, and who knows when we'll be able to execute that plan. I only hope it works out before Nancy causes Teagan any more problems. Or Teagan finds out that I'm meddling in her business.

That's all I need is, another reason for her to hate me. I'm digging myself a lovely grave with every minute.

"Silas?" Teagan coughs my name.

I leave the kitchen and find her leaning against the hallway wall, covering her eyes. Even with all the curtains closed, the house is still too bright.

"Teagan, if you aren't feeling better, stay in bed. It's alright."

"No. I have to check on the shop. John probably had another visit from Nancy, and I have to oversee the remodel and order new stock. I can't afford time away."

I move toward her and pull her into my chest; this is gonna make it worse when she finds out I'm a big fat fucking liar. "Hey, it's fine. I'm sure John can handle it; he would've called if Nancy had shown up.

The stock can wait one more day. Do you still have a headache? Want something to eat or drink?"

She groans. "Too many questions, Sunshine."

I shake my head. "It was two. Come. I'll make you something and then get you home."

I get Teagan seated at my small kitchen table. I grab a glass from the rack and turn the tap on until the water runs cold. I watch the water run from the tap, wondering if I should just disappear from her life for good instead of keeping up with all this bullshit.

"Silas, you okay?"

Her voice pulls me out of my thoughts, and I quickly fill her glass. "Yep, I'm good. Just thinking of what to cook you, that's all." I turn around, walk the three paces to the table and slide the glass toward her.

"I'm not picky. I'll eat almost anything." She pulls the glass closer to her but doesn't drink it.

"What's the matter?"

She leans back in the chair and exhales. "It's nothing that you haven't heard me bitch about before. I'm just tired of it all. I'm almost ready to give up."

"That's because you're still tired, so sleep more, and you'll be ready for a fight. Trust me."

Trust me, what a joke. I'm blowing smoke out of my ass now. Fuck, I'm an asshole. Teagan looks at me with those piercing green eyes like she's on to something. I shake my head and back away, moving to the fridge and pulling out the butter and cheese slices. Grilled cheese it is. It's the easiest and quickest thing I can think of.

"Did you want to fill me in on why Nancy showed up at the shop?"

She picks at her sandwich, taking one deep inhale. "She slapped me with a pink sheet."

I raised a dark brow questionably. "A pink sheet? Explain."

"Oh, sorry. It's a sheet from hell. It's her way of denying my renovations even though it was the city's fault for the damage."

I raise a finger, but she shakes her head.

"I didn't tell her about the room being torn down. The less she knows, the better. And besides, I'm taking it down, not building. It's different."

I chuckle. "I don't think that's how it works. She will find out."

She shrugs and shoves a piece of food into her mouth. I wish I had her outlook on things, no care and dealing with the consequences when they arise. There's no way I could do that. No matter what I do, it seems like a cloud of bad luck is always hanging over me.

"In a way, I hope she does. I have more to say to that stuck-up bitch. She doesn't rule this town. I should have a meeting with the mayor and see what he has to say about all of this. I can't keep looking over my shoulder whenever I want to do something with my shop. It's not fair." She slumps back in her chair. "I'm sorry I don't mean to dump all my shit on you."

"No. It's perfectly fine. That's what I'm here for. Whatever I can help with, I will." Secretly, that's me asking for forgiveness in advance for what I already have cooked up.

"I should get going; John probably needs my help. I kinda disappeared on him."

"Are you sure you are, okay?"

"Peachy, baby. Thanks again for cooking. You're two for two, and I have a lot to catch up on." She stands, grabs our plates, and sets them in the sink.

"Dimples, I wouldn't classify grilled cheese sandwiches as cooking. I think you're safe there."

She turns to me and grins. "How about my place tomorrow? I'll cook. It's not like we have work or anything."

I clutch my chest. "Is this your way of trying to score a date with me? Slow down there, sweet cheeks. This is uncharted territory for me. I'm at a loss for words."

Her laughter rang out. "Shut up, you ass. I asked you out for dinner, not marriage."

"I mean, Mrs. Blackwell does have a nice ring to it."

She's just standing there with her eyes wide open. I can see her throat moving as she searches for the right words to say. I could put her out of her misery, but this is too entertaining. I won't lie; it sounds good, but marriage isn't in my books and never will be. I won't allow another person into my life like that.

"You won't be able to handle me as a wife, Silas."

"I'm beginning to think I can't handle you any day of the week, Teagan."

She walks toward me and pats me on the cheek. "Good. I'm going to head out. I'll see you tomorrow."

I snatch her wrist, pulling her closer. My gaze lingers on her lips; no matter how much I want to taste them, I can't. That's taking things to the next level, and I won't go there. I have to leave my heart out of it; that thing is only a nuisance. I can't let my feelings take over.

"Let me walk you." I force out, jaw tightening with more to say, but I don't.

She doesn't move; she places her hand over mine. "If you don't mind, that would be great. You can hold me back in case Nancy is there."

"I got you, my little psycho." I stand, pushing her backward. "But please, if you plan on killing anyone, let me know ahead of time so I can establish an alibi." I can't help but keep my gaze locked on hers, noticing how the corners of her eyes crease with joy when she smiles and her dimples pop out.

"Understood. No stabbing until we have a plan. But no promises. I can't control what comes out of my mouth."

"Good, I like you unpredictable."

The walk back to her shop is quiet. I can't find anything to say that won't land me in hot water. All my lies are piling up, and one of them is bound to slip, eventually. Once Leroy comes to town, my cover is blown; there is no coming back from that. He'll want to know everything about my life here and those that are in it. I was surprised Leroy didn't ask a million questions about why I needed him for Nancy. He probably wants to see me try to answer his question in person. He knows I'll avoid him if I don't like certain ones.

"Oh, we should do the corn maze. It ends next month, and I never have a friend to go with."

Friend, I was somewhat worried about that word, but I'm relieved she brought it up. It's like a safety net that I didn't have to create for myself, and hopefully, when I inevitably hurt her, it won't sting as much.

"That sounds good, but let's wait until October. Spooky month and mazes work hand in hand."

"Deal."

Let's hope I'm still around by then.

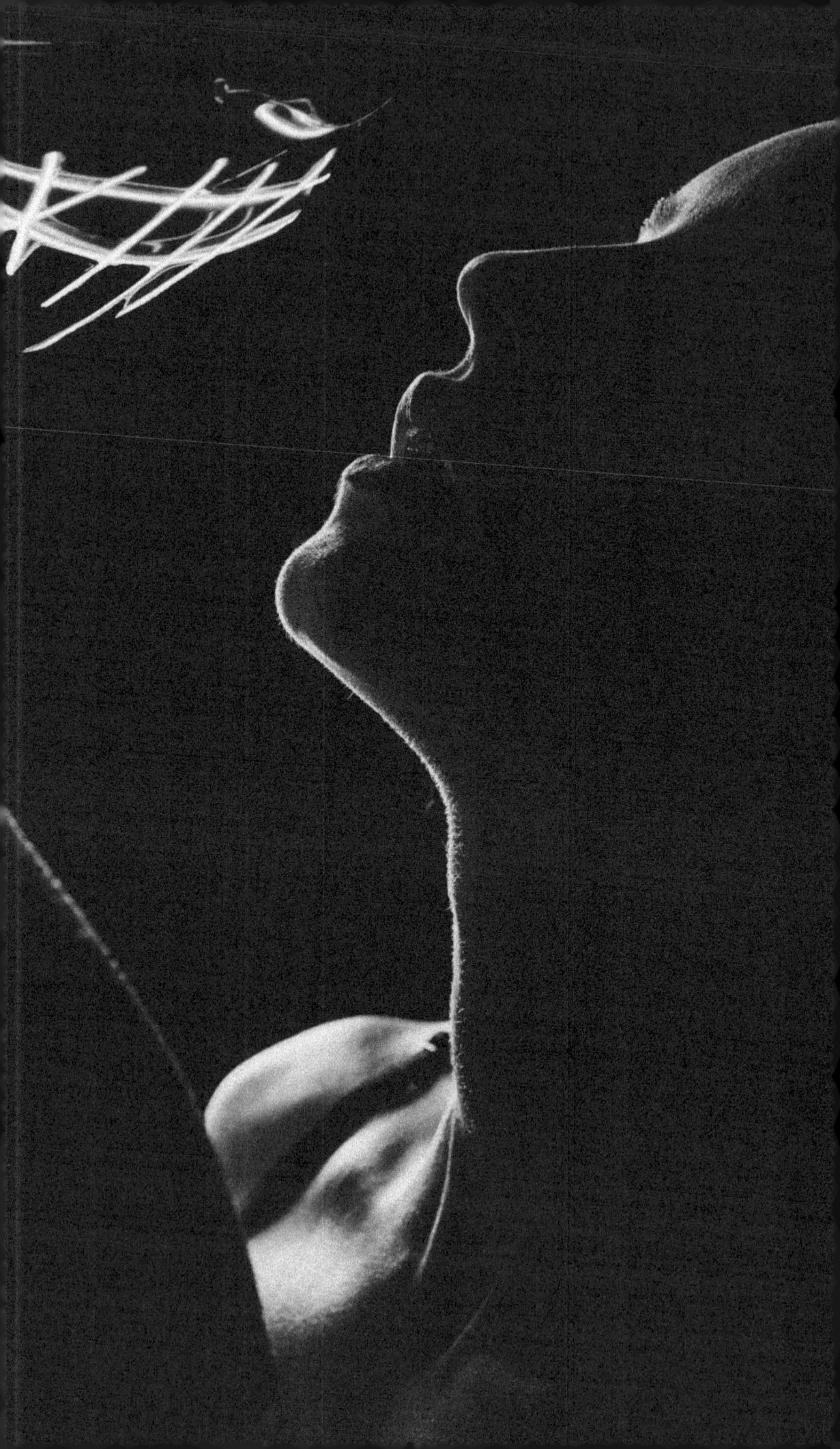

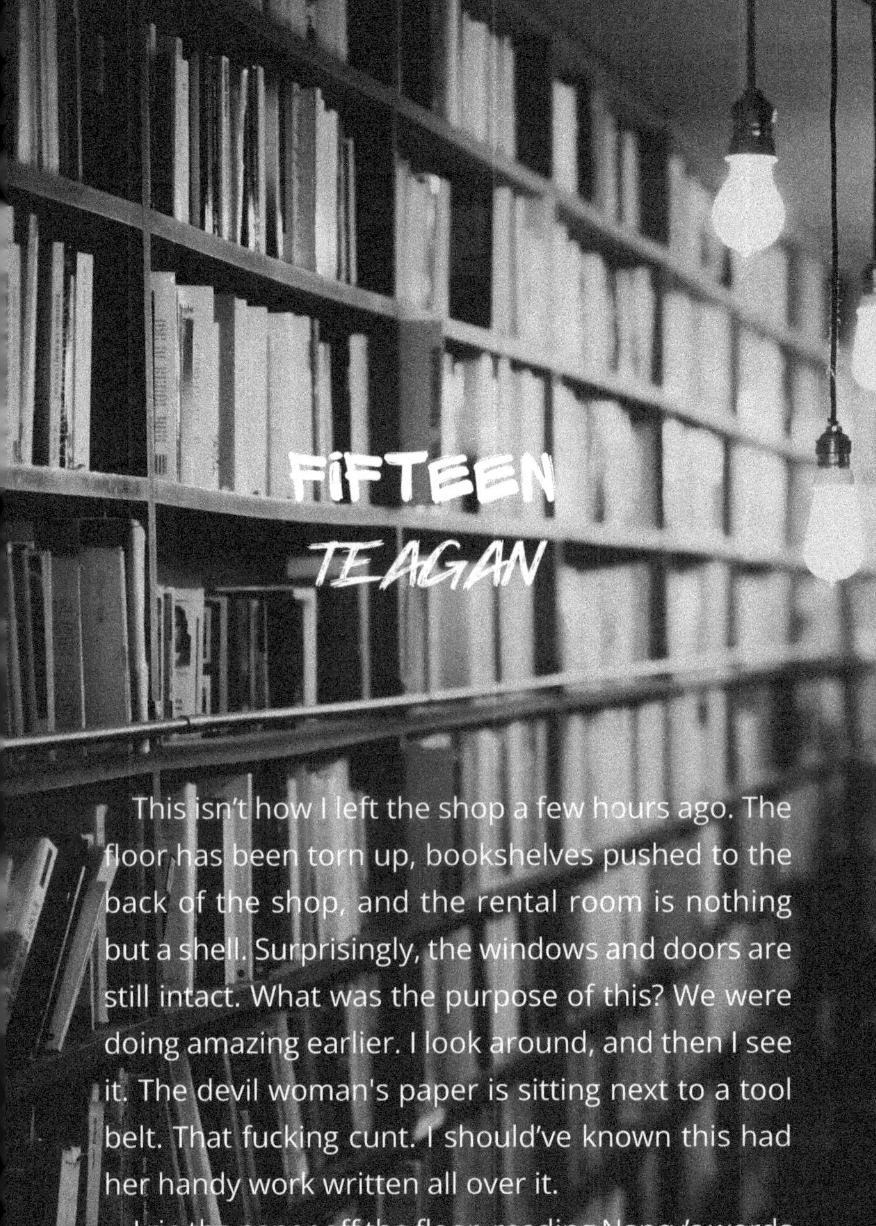

FIFTEEN

TEAGAN

This isn't how I left the shop a few hours ago. The floor has been torn up, bookshelves pushed to the back of the shop, and the rental room is nothing but a shell. Surprisingly, the windows and doors are still intact. What was the purpose of this? We were doing amazing earlier. I look around, and then I see it. The devil woman's paper is sitting next to a tool belt. That fucking cunt. I should've known this had her handy work written all over it.

I rip the paper off the floor, reading Nancy's words of shit wisdom. She shut us down until I get the permit. Surprise, surprise. Why couldn't there be a lawyer in the family? Because I need one. This is bullshit, she can't keep ruining my business.

"John, you and the boys might as well head home. We are officially shut down."

"I tried everything to hold her off, but she threatened to shut my company down. I'm sorry, Teagan."

"No. I would do the same thing. I'll try to resolve this without violence."

John chuckles. "I have bail money if you need it. I'm also a phone call away if you need that too." He whistles to his crew and twirls his finger in the air. I'm mesmerized as they pack up effortlessly, moving in perfect harmony like synchronized swimmers.

I almost wish Silas had stayed, but I thought I wouldn't need him here since construction was ongoing. This is a disaster. But I can't always rely on him to be here for me. Him taking me to his house earlier was too much and something I'd never expected from him.

After locking the shop, I march toward city hall and will make sure she hears from me daily until she understands I'm not backing down. The city is at fault for the damage, and I refuse to obtain a permit for their error. It's complete horseshit that my insurance is suffering because of it. I guarantee she's the reason why I had to go through insurance in the first place.

City Hall sits right in the heart of Holden, sur-rounded by gorgeous oak trees that have been around since the beginning of the town. The brick building also serves as the courthouse, pulling dou-ble duty. The spacious grassy area out front is per-fect for enjoying picnics in the summer months; it's what lies behind the walls that I hate. Nancy Mont-gomery.

My shoes squeak along the tiled floor, and I pity anyone who gets in my way. I'm a woman on a mission. I storm up to the reception desk where Kendall is typing away on her computer. I tap on the desk, grabbing her attention. When she looks up, her smile vanishes when I slam the pink paper down.

"Teagan. How may I help you?" she squeaked.

"Where the fuck is Nancy? And don't even lie to me, Kendall. I know she's here." My body shakes with rage as Kendall glanced away, clearly trying to dodge my question.

"I'm sorry, Teagan. She's in a meeting."

Of course, she is. "Is that the go-to response she tells you to give out? Call her now and tell her I'm about to kill her fucking cat if she doesn't get her ass down her. I'm not playing anymore."

"Teagan, I understand you're upset, but I can't allow you to talk to her when you are this upset."

Laughing wildly, I grab my paper and crumple it. "Kendall, you haven't seen me upset yet. Give the witch a message for me, will you?" I wait for her to grab a pen and paper. "Ready?" Kendall nods.

"Dearest Nancy, watch your back. You don't own this town, and if you think a permit will stop me, you're mistaken. You might want to step up your security at home. Love you, babe. Teagan. How does that sound?"

Kendall shakingly finishes writing the notes before glancing my way again. "The cops will be called. You know that."

"I'm not scared of Taylor; he can't even hurt a fly. I'll see you around the shop once it's reopened."

She nods. "Yeah, sure." Her voice was nothing but a small whisper.

I leave feeling on top of the world. Nancy can suck my dick. This is one small business owner that isn't taking any shit. Now I need a drink, but it's a little early unless I hit up happy hour.

Me: You on call?

Jace: No. Ivory and I are shopping for Halloween. Why?

Me: Want to join me for drinks?

Jace: Oh boy. Is it table dancing or karaoke kind of drinks?

Me: To be determined

Jace: Ivory says she's game, and I guess I'll be getting lucky tonight

Me: You're welcome. The Hollow in thirty, if that works?

Jace: Doable. See ya!

I have enough time to head home and change. And enough time to prep myself for the lecture I'll get for not telling them about Silas. I could only imagine what they would say if I told them about my rendezvous with stalker boy in the park. It would be like the end of the world, and I would be a dirty little hoe, although Ivory would be secretly high fiving me under the table for being a little daredevil. Then, give Jace a dirty look for not doing anything like that to her.

If I had the secret to why and how my stalker found me, I'd spill the beans. But alas, I remain utterly clueless. Maybe one day I'll be able to shake him, but until then, I'm screwed—literally.

The Hollow is the perfect place to drink. Well, who am I kidding it's the only fucking bar in town. But the décor is to die for. The timber rafters are set against the industrial metal, giving a cool mix of textures. One wall is stacked with records, while the other is decked out with taxidermy—just some funky vibes going on.

I grab a booth in the back, facing the stage. When the server comes around, I order a pitcher of margaritas for Ivory and me and a beer for Jace. Leave it to them to run late; I know exactly who to blame.

"Sorry, we're late. Someone had to style their hair." Ivory sits next to me and glares across the table at Jace.

"I figured Miss Beauty Queen had to look his best."

Jace touches his hair. "This is quality work, ladies. It's a masterpiece; don't be knocking the lord's work."

I snort. "The lord's work might need a little more work." I lean in. "Is that grey hair?"

"Fuck off, Tee."

"She's right, babe. Forty is right around the corner. You might want to start dying those luscious locks of yours." Ivory laughs as she pours us a glass of margaritas.

"Watch it, woman, or else."

Ivory grins and raises a dark brow at Jace. The way they gaze into each other's eyes makes it seem as if the entire room fades away and they are the only two souls in existence. Nothing and no one could come between them. I'm glad Jace found his other half; Ivory grounds him, and Jace lifts Ivory. I want that, to be wanted in someone else's life.

"Alright, Tee. Tell us what's been going on. The great flood, how is that going?"

"Noah didn't make it, if that's what you're wondering. Although he probably didn't have issues building his boat."

"Nancy?"

I nod, taking a sip.

"Should we turn this conversation into a drinking game?" He teases.

"Dude. We would be shit faced before I reach the climax of the story. Nancy is such a cunt you have no idea, she pisses me off, and I'm sure the cops are gonna be knocking on my door come tomorrow, so there's that."

Ivory stops mid drink. "Excuse me? What did you do?"

I shrug and turn my head to the stage. "Nothing serious. I just left her a little note that may or may not have been threatening."

Jace groans. "Tee. The fuck."

I whip my head toward him, snap my fingers, and point at him. "Hey, she came at me. This is war, and Sparta will win."

"Easy tiger. We all know how that will end. Are you ready for it?"

On the outside, I'm ready, but deep down, I'm a chicken shit. Nancy can end me. She will drag my name through the dirt to prove she's top dog. I can't let anyone know I'm scared. Once news about any of this hits the streets, I have to act strong. Nancy needs to be ruined.

"I've got this. Now, can we drink so I can forget about my water logged shop?"

"I'll drink to that." Ivory holds her glass up.

I lift my glass, and so does Jace. "I'll cheer to that." I click her glass and Jace's empty beer bottle.

"I'll get another round. I have a feeling it's a karaoke kind of night." He shakes his head.

Ivory leans in. "At least he knows us."

We both fall into a fit of laughter because it's true. Ivory turns to me, looking serious.

"Tell me, any men in your life? This is the time to spill the beans while Jace is away."

I tap my fingers on the table, the subject I knew would come up. I appreciate Ivory waiting until Jace left because it would be a fight. "There might be a guy, but seriously, he's a friend. I hired him to work in the shop. It could get messy."

"Messy, how?"

"I can tell he wants more but refuses to open up about his life. I'm not sure I can date someone with trust issues."

"Teagan. Relationships aren't built overnight. It takes time. Have you ever thought about how he feels trying to open up to you? It's scary to be judged. What if he bares his soul to you, and you run off because he said something you disagree with? Everyone has a past; we aren't perfect humans. Some scars aren't meant to be shown."

"Goddamn woman. What if I pushed him too far away, and he doesn't want to try anymore?"

"What's worst that can happen? You get a no."

Rejection is a hard pill to swallow, and I have so much shit going on in my life I'm not sure I can handle more. I'm afraid Silas and I are better off as friends and nothing more.

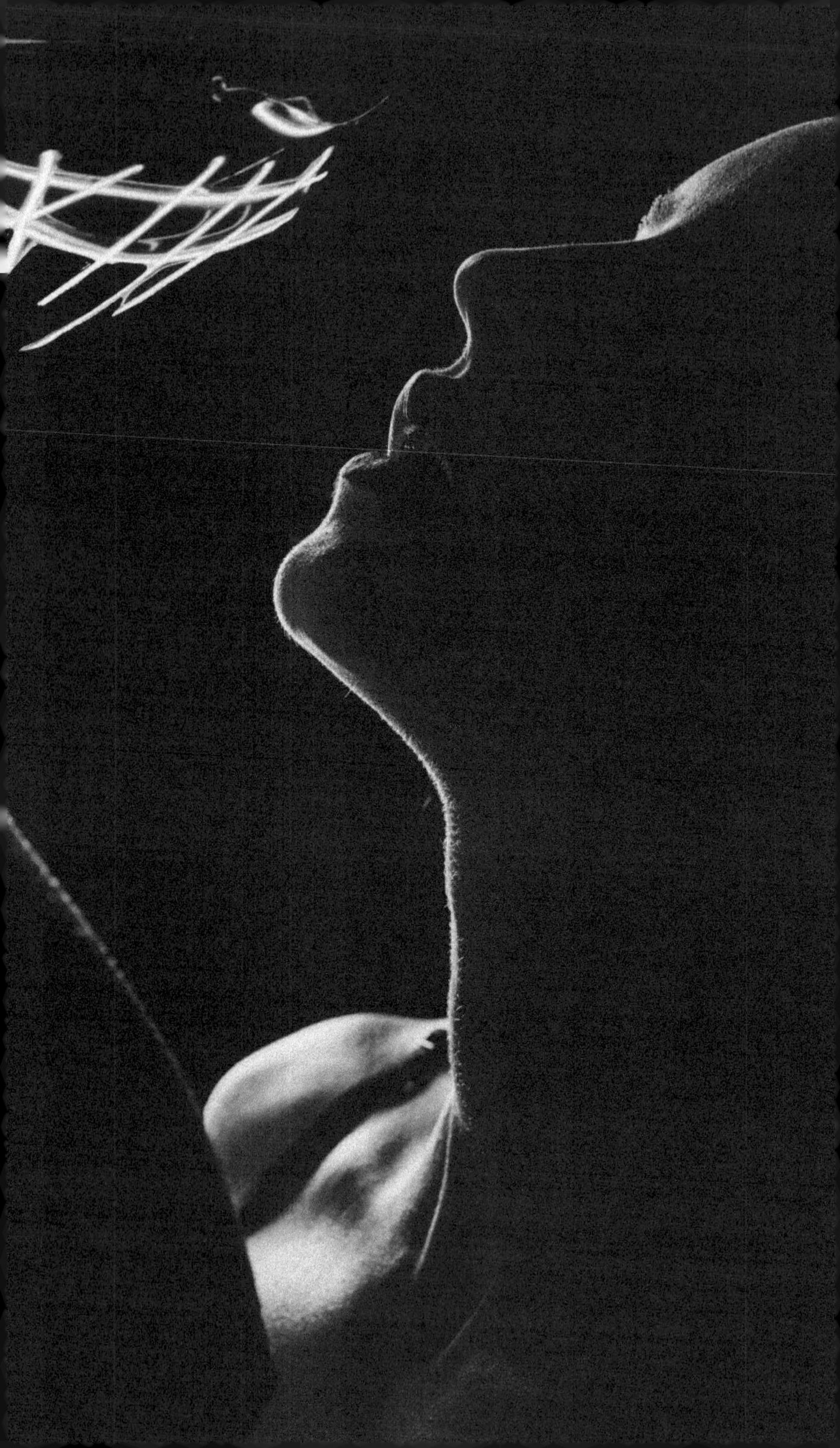

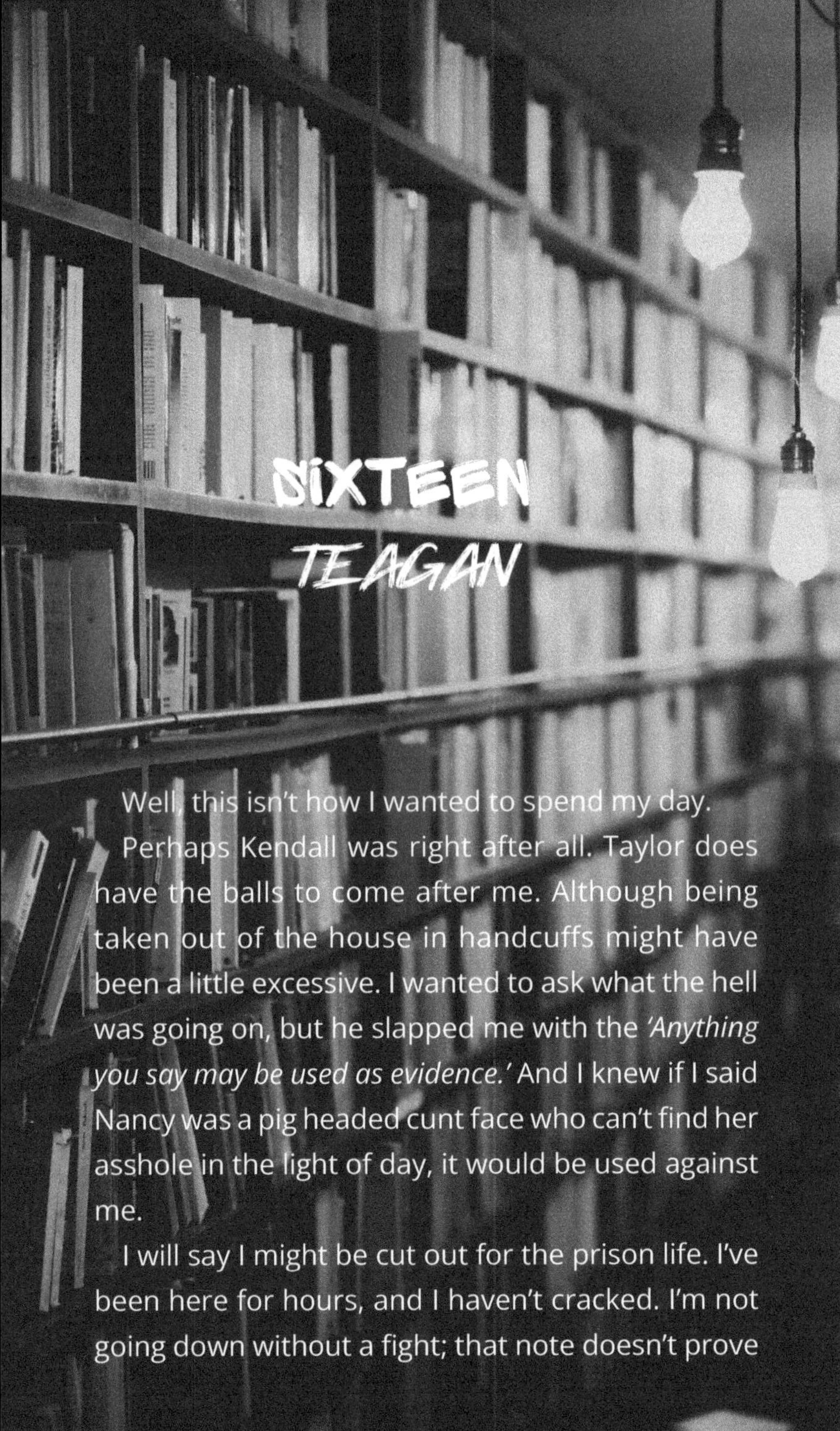

SIXTEEN

TEAGAN

Well, this isn't how I wanted to spend my day.

Perhaps Kendall was right after all. Taylor does have the balls to come after me. Although being taken out of the house in handcuffs might have been a little excessive. I wanted to ask what the hell was going on, but he slapped me with the *'Anything you say may be used as evidence.'* And I knew if I said Nancy was a pig headed cunt face who can't find her asshole in the light of day, it would be used against me.

I will say I might be cut out for the prison life. I've been here for hours, and I haven't cracked. I'm not going down without a fight; that note doesn't prove anything. I've had witnesses who can vouch for the fact that Nancy has been harassing me for years. I'm sure most businesses in town can attest to Nancy harassing them.

Taylor, the prick, wouldn't give me my phone call. I need to cancel dinner with Silas.

I slam my hand on the bars. "Taylor, you asshole. Give me my phone call."

"Teagan, I'll tell you once more. You don't get that privilege."

"You don't understand. I need to call someone. It's life or death."

He sets his palms flat on his desk, tilting his head to the ceiling. "Jesus, Teagan. I highly doubt it. What can possibly be worse than you sitting in a cell?"

"I need to cancel a date." I tilt my head, smile and wiggle my brows.

He glares at me. "Seriously?"

"I know dates are a difficult subject for you, Taylor. But let me explain them to you—"

"I know what a fucking date is." He cuts me off.

I raise my hands in surrender. "Okay, buck. Don't have to chew my head off. I didn't think cops knew how to date is all, since you lack a sense of humour and all."

"What's the number?"

"It's in my phone. I don't know the number off hand."

He grabs my phone and shakes his head. "You should have a passcode. What's the dudes name?"

"I don't need a passcode. I got nothing to hide. His name is Silas. But it's saved under Sunshine."

I watch him pick up the landline and start dialling. My heart leaps out of my chest when he starts speaking.

"Taylor, you prick. I asked for the phone call, not you," I scream.

"Yep, that would be her. I'll tell her the message." Taylor grins. He won't be grinning for long once I get my hands around his neck.

"Your lover says he'll be here in twenty. Hold tight, and don't turn into a psycho."

I smack the bars before sitting on the cold metal bench. I don't want Silas to come here. The whole point of cancelling was to avoid him. Now he'll think I am a psycho once he finds out what I did. Threatening Nancy might not have been my most brilliant move, but now she knows I'm not one to be messed with on the other side of these stupid bars, perhaps. Once I'm free, it's game on.

The chilly bench is freezing my ass off. It must've been at least twenty minutes by now. What's taking Silas so long? Taylor glances at me and shakes his head. He knows I won't try to fight this, and I haven't even asked for a lawyer. The more I think about it. I technically didn't write the note. Kendall did. There is no evidence that I threatened Nancy. It's Kendall's word against mine.

"I'm looking for Teagan Moore."

"Your Silas?" Taylor sounds shocked.

"I am. Is there a problem?" Silas responded with irritation.

I wish I could see what was going on. From the way Silas sounds, it isn't good. I don't need his ass getting arrested. Taylor's shadow falls upon me, and I rise.

"Well? Am I getting freed?"

"You didn't need to be locked up. All you had to do was answer a few questions, Teagan. You made it worse for yourself."

"I didn't do shit, you remember that. And don't act like I don't know where you live and who your mom is."

"Is that a threat?"

"Okay. I think what Teagan means. Is thank you, officer. I would love to head home." Silas grabs the bar and narrows his eyes at me. "Don't you, Dimples."

I take a deep inhale and loudly exhale. "Yeah, what he said."

"Teagan. Get a lawyer. As a friend and not a cop, Nancy isn't one to mess with. It'll be far more serious if I have to arrest you again."

"Nancy can—"

"Nothing, Dimples," Silas says in a stern voice.

Taylor unlocks the door, and I'm free. "I want a restraining order on Nancy. I don't trust her."

Taylor ignores me and walks away.

"That isn't how restraining orders work, Dimples. You need proof that she's threatening you, and you have nothing. Come on, we still have time for our date, and you need to fill me in on your criminal activity."

"It's not a date. It's dinner. And no criminal activity was performed. Don't be a drama queen. Leave that to Taylor."

"Get her out of my sight." Taylor passes me my purse and points to the exit.

"I'm rating my stay a one star; the service was horrible. Couldn't even provide a snack."

As Silas chuckles, he casually slings his arm around me, pulling me in snugly against his side as we leave the police station.

"Teagan, for now on. Leave the criminal acts to the professionals."

"Criminal. As in." I point to him. "You?"

He keeps walking without speaking, which doesn't help my curiosity. I'm like a cat now, and I need to know everything.

"Silas, what did you do in the city?" I ask cautiously.

He digs his fingers into my shoulder. "Teagan, don't push, please. If I wanted to tell you about my past, I would've. When I'm ready, let me tell you."

"Sorry, I can't help it. I'm a pusher."

"I know you are, don't change."

He never lets go of me the entire walk back to my house. Every once in a while, I would catch him watching me from the corner of his eye. God only knows what he's thinking. But if it's him with the criminal past, I feel he can't judge me.

"Silas?"

"Yes, Teagan."

"You didn't kill anyone, did you?"

"No, love. I didn't kill anyone." He presses a kiss on my forehead.

Not murder, maybe break and entry or stealing. The list is endless. It's going to drive me mad, not knowing what Silas did. Does he still do it? When he disappeared for days, he never told me where he went. This is what I mean by not knowing who he is.

I'm not sure I want someone in my life who can't open up; friends are supposed to trust one another.

You're an adult; why do you have to lie or hide the truth? I'm not asking much in return, just a sliver of who you are. But I feel like Silas is hiding so much more. It hurts just thinking about not having Silas in my life. Even though I've only known him for a couple of weeks, it feels like a lifetime.

"What's wrong, Teagan?"

"Just trying to figure out dinner. Since I've been in lock up, what I originally planned won't work." Small lies don't count.

"We can always order something from The Lucky Dragon if you want. I could go for some wonton soup."

"You want the little brain dumpling?"

"Let's do it." He steers me across the street toward Mr. Li & Min. They are going to have a fun time when I walk in and order something that involves an extra person. I can already see Min gasping and Mr. Li rolling his eyes at her.

The bell over the door dings, and Mr. Li's head snaps in our direction. A small smile spreads across his lips when he sees Silas' arm still draped around my shoulder.

"Miss Teagan, how are you?"

"Been better, Mr. Li, been better. How are you and Min?"

He rolls his eyes and waves me off. "Don't worry about us. We good. Business good."

"Do not speak for me." Min pokes her head out of the kitchen, causing Silas to chuckle and say something under his breath, but I couldn't quite make out what it was. "Teagan, I'll get your order. And for the gentleman?"

"Oh, we're together." I watch her eyes go wide.

"A meal for two? Oh, it's a celebration." She claps her hands and moves back into the kitchen.

"Is she always like this?" Silas asks.

"No," Mr. Li answers. "Teagan has always gotten meals for one, always alone."

Silas looks at me, but I try to ignore the look. I've seen that pitying look before, which says, *I feel sorry for you because you can never find anyone to do things with.* I've had that look directed at me one too many times. I don't want to see it coming from the one person that I genuinely care about.

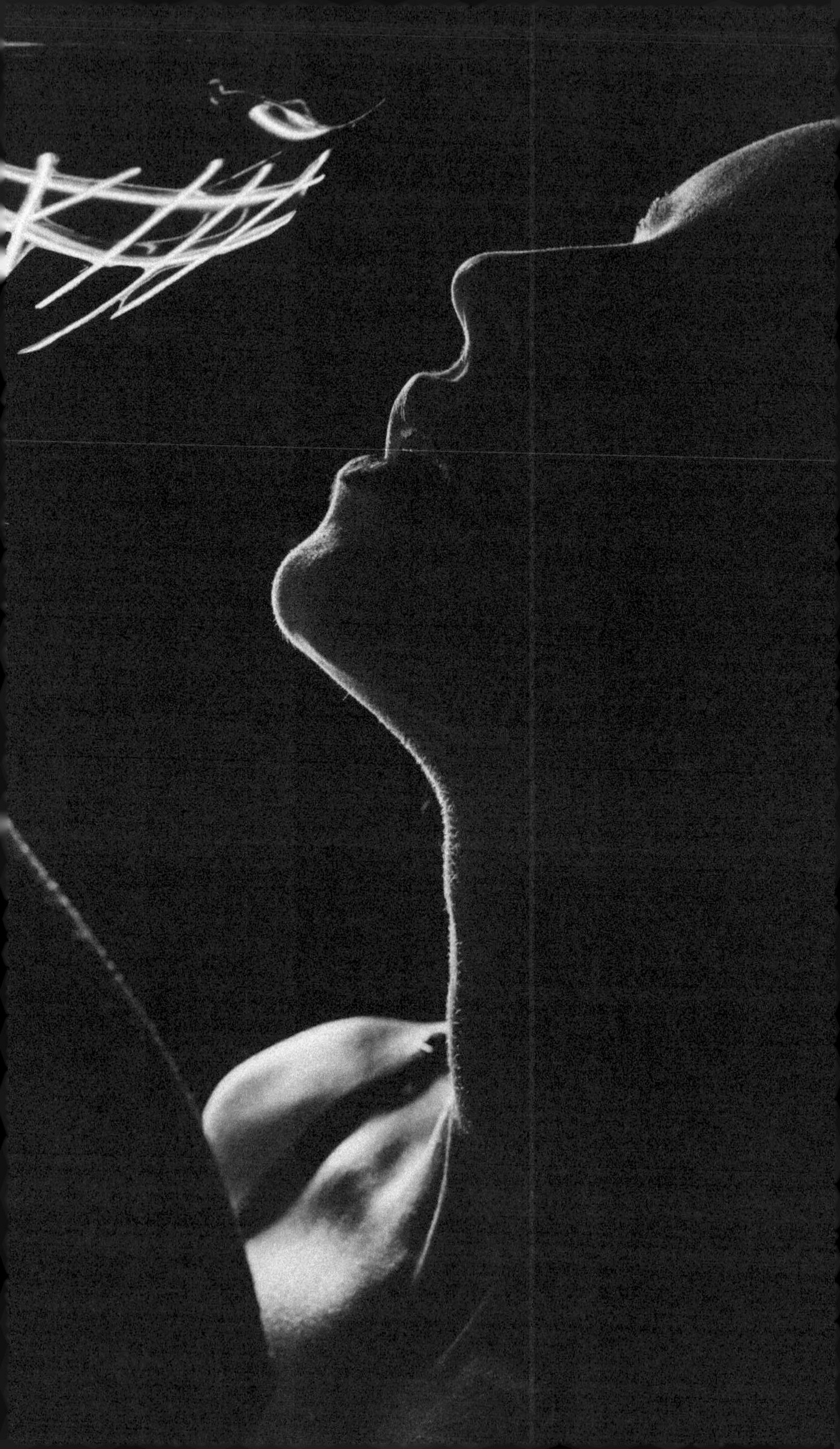

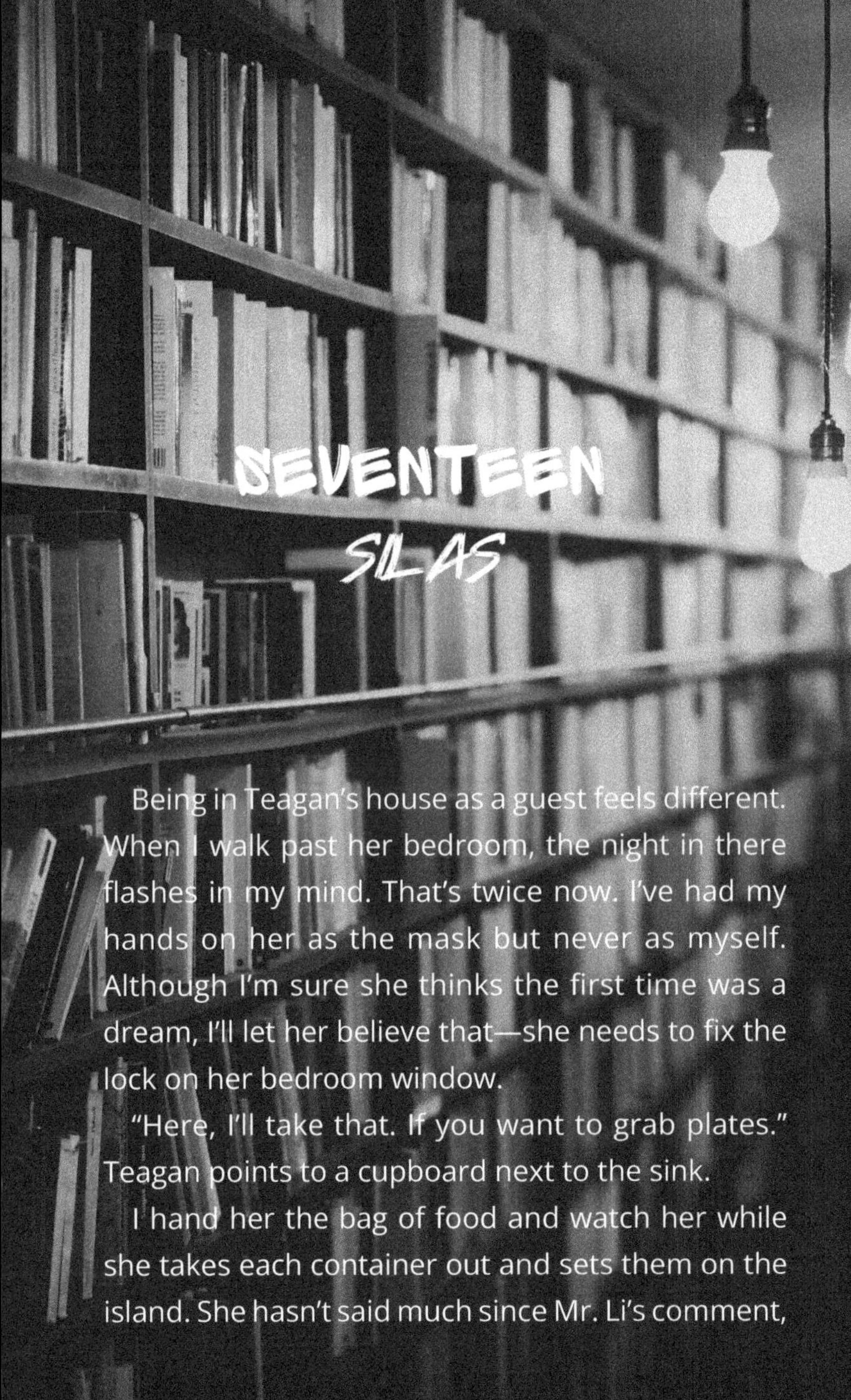

SEVENTEEN

SILAS

Being in Teagan's house as a guest feels different. When I walk past her bedroom, the night in there flashes in my mind. That's twice now. I've had my hands on her as the mask but never as myself. Although I'm sure she thinks the first time was a dream, I'll let her believe that—she needs to fix the lock on her bedroom window.

"Here, I'll take that. If you want to grab plates." Teagan points to a cupboard next to the sink.

I hand her the bag of food and watch her while she takes each container out and sets them on the island. She hasn't said much since Mr. Li's comment, and her mood shifted. I grab the plates, setting one in front of her.

"You doing okay? You had an eventful day. Did you wanna talk about it?"

I watch as she sits across from me, absentmindedly moving her plate. "Not overly. Can we eat, please?"

I know when to talk and when not to. But this isn't Teagan. I feel like she's keeping something from me, and it's bothering me not being able to figure out how to support her. I want to share my past with her, but I'm worried it might cause problems between us.

"My parents weren't there for me when I needed them. They only looked out for themselves; I was just their meal ticket to get what they wanted. I moved out when I was sixteen, and I've been alone since then. I've done some shady shit to get where I am now, Teagan. I'm not proud of it. Don't get me wrong, taking care of yourself is important. But being vulnerable and sharing your feelings can be tough, too." I reach out for her hand. "So many people have screwed me around; I have a hard time trusting others. I don't intentionally mean to block you out; it happens naturally. My walls are built so strong I can't even get over them."

"Silas, I just want to know you more. You can't blame me for wanting to dig into that brain of yours, and I'm sorry for being nosey. I'm trying to respect your boundaries and not ask that many questions, but you are a mystery."

"I answered a few questions."

"You avoid is what you do. It's not your fault."

I let go of her hand and reach for the food, avoiding her. "I don't mean to; it's how I was raised."

She grabs my hand, stopping me. "Silas, I want you to know I would never underestimate you for being honest about your feelings. Your feelings are important to me."

I stare into her dark green eyes, only now noticing how they shift colours depending on the lighting. "Teagan, when you discover who I am, you'll want me out of your life."

"That isn't true. You don't know until you at least try. Why don't you trust me?"

As the person who low-key follows your every move, I fear that confessing my creeping ways will totally derail our vibe. Yeah, that'll definitely go smoothly. I might as well just tell her I'm a car thief for all the luck I'll have.

"Try me."

"Teagan, you're pushing." I feel myself getting annoyed.

"Good. Maybe a little push is what you need to get out of that shell."

I slide out of her hold and position myself behind her. Gently pushing her hair aside, I lean close to her ear and speak softly. "I don't think you want to push me. You might not like what happens."

"I might like it," she whispers, without looking back.

I run my fingers through her hair, intertwining them deeply, and tug her head back. I marvel at how her pupils dilate and hear her take a deep breath. "Are you sure you want this?"

"Yeah. I want anything with you."

I slowly spin her chair and push my legs between hers. With a stroke of her face, I lean in close. "You have two options, Dimples. On the counter or the bed. Either way, this pussy is mine." I release her hair and press it against her clit.

"Silas, I don't care where we do it, just fuck me."

I've been waiting to hear those words, fuck the bedroom. With a swift movement, I lift her and set her on the island. I will always be in awe of Teagan's beauty, and I am constantly amazed by the fact that she still wants to be my friend. It truly warms my heart. But who cares about that now, my mind is preoccupied with more pressing matters.

"I'm gonna finish my dinner now if you don't mind." I push her back and unbutton her jeans. With a tug, she lifts her hips, and I slip her jeans off, exposing her pussy. God, I love that she doesn't wear underwear.

"Silas, can I tell you something."

My hands freeze on her ankles. "Always, don't ever hold back."

She sits up and nibbles her bottom lip. "I um."

I slide my hands up her legs, stopping at her hip. "It's alright. Tell me."

"No one has ever gone down on me before."

Oh, I landed in heaven. "I got you. Lay back, and let me show you what it's all about."

I gently wait for her to completely lay down before carefully pulling her to the counter's edge. Looking up at her, I notice she is staring at the ceiling. "Teagan, eyes on me. Tell me if it gets too much, and I'll stop."

"Okay." She watches me as I move her legs over my shoulders. I slowly lower my head.

The first lick makes her gasp, and her hands grip the edge of the counter; I slide my hands under her ass, pulling her closer to my face. Her taste is intoxicating; I'll never get enough of her, no matter how much I get close.

Her hands weave into my hair, grabbing a fistful when I nibble her clit.

"Silas, fuck."

My dick presses against my jeans, protesting. I slide one hand off her legs and unsnap my jeans. I stroke along the length of my dick with each glide along her pussy. I'm not sure who I'm torturing her or me, but I'm not gonna last much longer. Her hips rise off the counter, her moans filling the room.

"I need you, Teagan."

"Here, take me here," she blurted out.

I gently lift her by the arms, helping her to sit up and face me. Her legs wrap around my waist, and she clasps her hands around my neck. My eyes look intensely onto hers; neither one could escape. Her beauty is something I'll never forget. She slips her hand around my dick.

"Fuck, Dimples. Squeeze me a little harder; I wanna feel you gripping me tight."

I close my eyes and rest my head on her shoulder as she strokes my dick. The sensation is unbelievable; I finally have her hands on me, and it's everything I dreamed of.

"Just like that, fuck don't stop." Her hand moves faster, and I move my hand between her leg, finding her clit. She tightens her grip when I apply pressure with my fingertip. I feel her warm breath softly brushing against my ear.

"Shit."

"You're not coming unless it's around my dick." With a swift motion, I step back and flip her over. Positioning myself, I slip deep inside. Her inner muscles grip me tight, and I have to hold back from coming. "Fuck, love, you're so tight."

She presses her ass back, and I grasp her waist and shoulder, driving deeper. Sweet moans fall from her lips, and it makes my dick harder.

"Where do you want me to finish?"

"Inside, don't stop."

I slam into her hard, making her legs give out. I hold her upright until she squeezes me tight; as she gets close, I pull her into my chest, thrusting faster as she comes.

"Shit, Silas." She groans.

A few seconds later, I find my own release. Feeling a wave of emotion, I gently bring my head to her neck and plant a soft kiss.

"I'm going to go clean up. I'll be right back." She doesn't even look back as she says it, and now I'm just standing here, second-guessing myself. Did I mess up somehow?

Pulling up my pants, I wash my hands in the kitchen sink and tidy up the food, feeling concerned when Teagan hasn't emerged from the bathroom. I move to the bathroom to see what she's up to; I find her sitting on her bed in pajamas.

"Teagan? What's wrong?" I sink onto my knees before her, taking her hands into mine.

"Did we make a mistake?"

My heart drops. "Why would this be a mistake?"

"Because, Silas. We're friends. This is going to change how we see each other now."

"No, love. Nothing will change. I'm still Sunshine, and you're still Dimples. Nothing will change. You can still yell at me when I don't do my job correctly if that makes you feel better."

She laughs. "If my shop ever opens again."

"You still have to tell me what happened."

She pulls my hands away, falls back onto the bed and groans. "Please don't. I wasn't thinking and didn't think Taylor would arrest me. He's such a pussy."

I climb on the bed, pulling her into my side. "Yeah, but I like your pussy more."

She slaps my arm. "Don't start."

"I can finish if you want." I run my hand down her stomach, but she stops me.

"Can we just sleep?"

"Of course." I pull the blanket over us and smooth her hair.

No matter how often I reassure her, I can't shake the feeling that this has altered our relationship. Perhaps it was easier when I wore a mask and stayed a stranger.

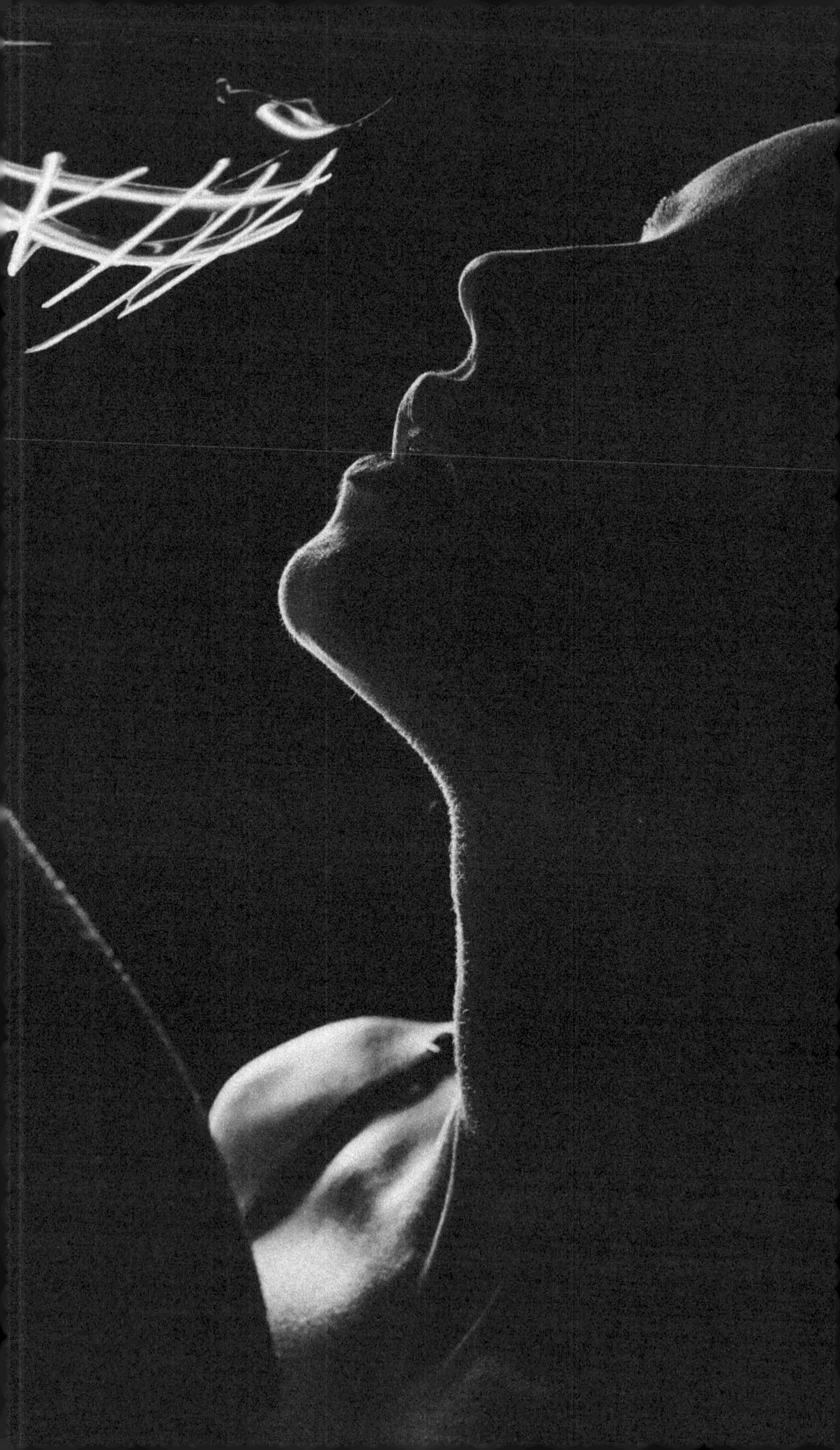

EIGHTEEN
TEAGAN

I should've stopped it, but goddamn Silas was amazing. And now I'm suffering the consequences. Then again, it's what I deserve. Friends and sex don't mix. This is why I have stayed single all this time. It's not worth the heartache.

I woke up alone. Which honestly doesn't surprise me. I knew sleeping with Silas would change things, even though he said it wouldn't. But why wouldn't it change? Sleeping with a friend can complicate things when you're not in a committed relationship. I let my emotions seep into this entire thing, and I'm unsure how I can pretend otherwise now.

The only thing I have left to do now is drag my ass back down to my shop and see if John is down there. And probably call my parents and explain my stint in jail. Maybe I'll call them as I walk, blow off steam, and no one can bug me. AKA Elma, she can't say anything if she finds me.

I dial my parents and the ancient contraption known as a landline shrieks for attention, much to my dismay. Naturally, my parents are the proud owners of this relic, clinging to the past with their refusal to embrace voicemail. Go figure. I swear, trying to track those two down is a task of its own.

Me: I need to talk to you and Mom. Call me

If that doesn't work, I have no clue what will—maybe getting Mom a cell phone.

As I approach my shop, a wave of joy washes over me. Even with the renovations, I still adore being here. I only hope it has a chance of reopening. With the amount of blood that is being poured into it, The Dancing Goat will dance once again.

That joy flew out the window when I noticed John wasn't at the shop with his crew. He should be here ripping up the place, permit or not. I fumbled to find my phone and dialled him.

"John, what's going on?"

"Teagan, I couldn't get a hold of you yesterday. We got called away for another job. I'm so sorry. We won't be able to get to your shop for a few more days."

"Yeah, sorry about that. I sorta got arrested." I unlock the door and step in. As I venture deeper into the shop, the scent of wood hits me square in the nose.

I swear, I can practically hear John touching the bridge of his nose. "Teagan." He exhales. "Stop pestering Nancy. We can't work with you in jail."

"Well, technically, you can. It would only make your job harder."

"Teagan, no more jail."

"Promise," I tell him with my fingers crossed. "I'll let you get back to work, and I'll do something."

After hanging up the phone, I look at the checkout desk and find something interesting. I see a small black box with a red bow. Could it be something one of John's crew forgot to take with them? Naturally, I can't resist picking it up to see if there's a name on it. But as soon as I find the name tag, I quickly drop it in surprise.

The words *To: Sweets* stare back at me in messy handwriting. Only one person has ever called me that. I'm unsure how he got into my shop or when, and now he's leaving me gifts. What am I supposed to do with this? There's no way I can keep it. I snatch it off the floor and storm to my office. I reef open the top drawer and toss it in. It can haunt me from there.

I hadn't seen my stalker since that night in the park, but I figured he got what he needed and left. Gifts are a whole new ball field. I don't like how this is shifting. The sound of my cell phone ringing makes me jump. Jesus, I need to get out of my head.

"Hey, Dad."

"Hey, Small fry. You sent a message. Where's the fire?"

"You haven't heard?"

He groans. "What did you do?"

"I'll explain. Did you and Mom wanna meet at Holden's for a bite to eat?"

"That can be arranged. Try not to do anything stupid in the meantime."

"I can't promise. I'll see you there."

I hear him moan as he hangs up. If Mom doesn't keep him on his toes, I have to. I stare at the desk drawer one more time before leaving the office. Walking to the back, I double check that the door is locked. It had to be the front if he didn't come through this door. But I unlocked it. Don't tell me my stalker is a master at picking locks.

I could change the locks, but let's be honest, my shop is still not safe from him. My boundaries don't exist. I lock the front door and take off to The Holden

Restaurant. I'm not sure how much more stress I can take, but talking to my parents about threatening Nancy and being arrested has to be at the top. I'll stand by what I did. Nancy had it coming. It was about time someone gave her a taste of her own medicine.

I only want Nancy to fall off that high horse; where is karma when you need her? Work that magic already.

As soon as I walk into the restaurant, it's like the room falls silent. The gossip has clearly made its way around, but somehow, my parents are none the wiser. That tells you that they never leave the house that often. I ignore the stares and find a seat by the window.

Jace: A little birdie told me some news

Motherfucker.

Me: Did this little birdie happen to be 5'5", have grey hair and don't know how to stay out of people's business?

Jace: That would be the one

Me: Whatever you heard could be true

Jace: Tee, I'm not sure what Elma is saying is true because we both know how she likes to add her twist onto things, but you need to sort her out. I don't need your reputation being spread through the mud over nothing.

I knew this would happen. Elma has a way of twisting everything she talks about. She once said Mr. Campbell ran a stop sign and hit a kid riding a bike. The entire town turned their backs on him until the police report came out and said the kid rode his bike into him when Mr. Campbell was stopped at the stop sign. She turns everything into a bad situation. It's sad, but Mr. Campbell was never able to bounce back from that rumour. Nowadays, he hardly ever steps foot outside his house. Elma doesn't appear to be bothered by the fact that she essentially destroyed his life, and the folks in town seem to have no problem letting her off the hook.

"Teagan, hunny, why the sad look?" Mom says as she scoots into the booth across from me.

I raise a questioning eyebrow, waiting for her to mention anything. I look at Dad, but his face is stuck in the menu.

"Leave her be, dear. Let's order first, and then we can talk business. I'm hungry."

"You're always hungry, Dad."

He pats his stomach. "I'm a growing boy. What can I say?

Mom nudges him. "Oh, we both know that."

When the server comes by, we all place our order, and the silence between us is deafening. I know I should mention something, but I don't want to bring it up. How does one mention that their daughter is a felon? Am I a felon, though?

"How's the renovations coming along? Mom asks.

I stare out the window and answer her. "They aren't. John got called away on another project, so my shop is waiting."

"That's too bad. I'm sure they'll work extra hard to get you back in running order once he's back."

"I hope so. I'm unsure what to do with all my spare time. I feel lazy just sitting around."

"How's that boy been working out?" Dad asks, skeptical.

The phantom of Silas. I haven't heard a peep out of him today. And if I'm being honest, I'm not reaching out to him. I'll likely hear some made-up story about why he left, and then I'll be left questioning whether it's the truth or not.

"I'm not entirely sure he works for me anymore."

"Oh? What happened there?"

I shrug because who wants to tell their parents they slept with a friend who turned into an employee, and then he what—ditched me? Maybe I'm reading too far into it, and he didn't ditch me? Perhaps something happened, and he had to leave.

"What's the point of working for me when I don't have a place of work."

"I'm sure he'll still work for you when you reopen." Mom smiles at me.

Our food arrives, and I know this is the time I have to spill my guts. I wait until they both take a bit and swallow it. I don't need them choking and dying on me.

"Mom, Dad. I need to tell you something."

They look at me with worry.

"What is it, Small fry?"

"I was arrested yesterday." My voice tapering off toward the end.

Mom looked away, her short blonde hair swaying as she closed her eyes and gave her head a gentle shake. Dad takes a bite of his sandwich and chuckles.

"Seriously, Caleb. This is no laughing matter. Our daughter was arrested."

"Yes, Janette. I'm aware and sure the story behind it will be funny. Teagan. Fill us in."

And so I fill them in, from the letter I left for Nancy to being arrested by Taylor.

"What. How did you get out?" Leave it to Dad to ask the only question I didn't want to answer.

"Um, Silas."

"You called some boy instead of your parents? Why didn't you call Jace?"

I rub my forehead; I hate having these conversations. "Because. Now, can we finish eating?"

"No. Stop dodging the question." He let some of his frustration seep into his words.

"Oh my God, Dad. Because we had a date and I needed to cancel. Anything else you would like to know about my love life?"

I swear he has to be the only father who needs to know everything about their daughter. I hope he's satisfied about his answer.

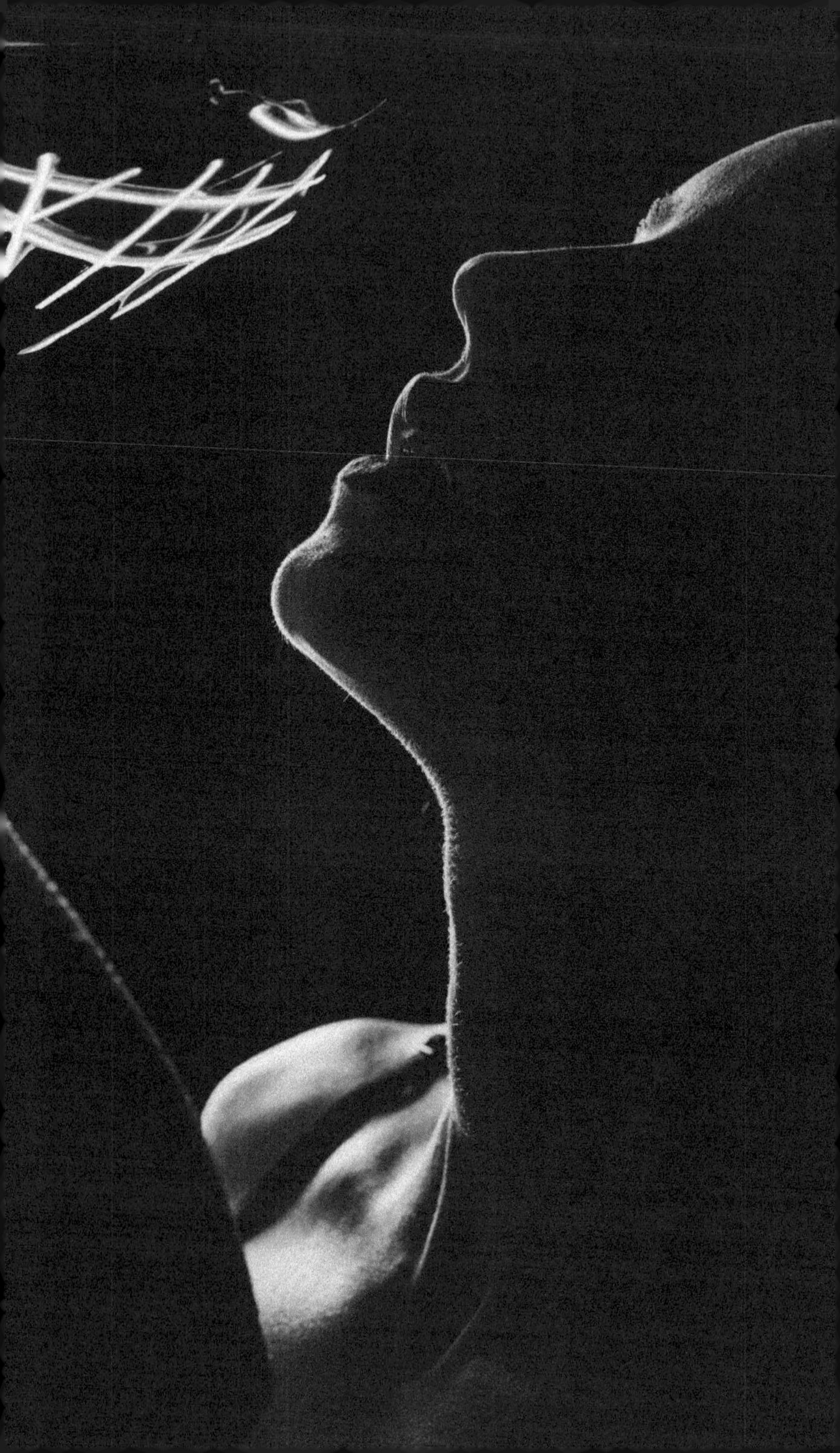

NINETEEN
SILAS

All I wanted to do was wake up to Teagan, maybe have morning sex and go for breakfast. That would've been the highlight of my fucking day. Instead, I ended up in the city because of Leroy. He played the I'm doing you a favour, so you do me a favour card. Yet he hasn't even done his share of the favour yet.

Asshole.

I find it strange that Teagan still hasn't messaged me. It's already past lunch, and I haven't heard a peep from her. I can't blame her. She's probably pissed at me, and I don't blame her; I left in the middle of the night. I'm on the fence about reaching out to her. The way she spoke, it sounded like she already knew how things would turn out. I'm not sure she can handle friends with benefits.

Maybe I'll just keep my distance as myself and only return when I'm wearing my mask. It just seems like the best way to stay safe. Eventually, she'll move on from me, and I'll do the same in time. I shouldn't have become friends with her; being her stalker was safer.

"Blackwell, get your head in the game. This is a serious job."

Every job is serious. I swear Leroy is a drama queen. When he called, he made it out to be life or death, and I had to be out here pronto.

"Yeah, got it. Only been sitting here for hours." Annoyance floods me. He should've figured this shit out before calling me.

He pushed me up against the brick wall, getting close to my face. "Listen here. The only reason why I keep you around is because you still owe me. If it weren't for that, I would've tossed your ass long ago."

I push him back. "I don't owe you shit. I paid you back tenfold. You can't find anyone stupid enough to keep doing this with you, and that's the only reason you keep calling me."

He points his finger at me, narrowing his dark eyes. "Watch what you say, or you'll find yourself in more trouble than you're worth."

"And you're an asshole. Where's the car you want stolen?"

"We need the black Cadillac Blackwing." He nods to the blacked-out car across the street.

In this area, only a specific group of people drive this particular car. I'm not too fond of being shot or stabbed when I try to steal a drug dealer's car. I would say this is the first time stealing a drug dealer's car, but it isn't and sadly won't be the last. I have a hard time saying no. And honestly, the money isn't bad.

"Leroy, who's car is that?'

He scratches his chin. "It's um. Wolf's."

I turn to him. "Are you shitting me? You want me to steal from Wolf. Nope. I'm fucking out. You're on your own."

"Silas, seriously. Grow a pair. That asshole owes me. Steal his car, and I promise to never call you again for a job."

"And if I get shot?"

"Won't happen. Now finish the job."

There's no point in arguing anymore; it's like talking to a toddler half the time. I point to the tow truck so Leroy gets the hint that I'm ready to go. There's only one way to steal a newer vehicle, and that's to do a fake repo—no one questions when a tow truck pulls up and hooks up to a car.

Pulling up enough that the tilt bed has enough space to touch the tires. I leave Leroy in the cab while I get to work, hooking up the axle to the winch. I hate crawling under such low cars, but I'm also glad I'm not overly tall. When I press the button on the truck deck, the winch slowly pulls the car ahead. I feel that with each passing minute, Wolf and his crew will come crawling out of the building next to us and shoot without questions.

I shoot daggers at the back of Leroy's head as he sits sheltered in the cab; the sooner this is finished I'm out. Then he owes me for once. The winch comes to a halt, and I press a different button to raise the flatbed. I quickly climb onto it and strap the car down. I don't know why, but I'm feeling super on edge as I hop back into the cab.

"About damn time. We need to leave, that there is a member of Wolf's crew." Leroy points to a guy standing a few feet across the parking lot, having a smoke. Surprisingly, he hasn't noticed us yet.

I knew something wasn't right.

"We can't get away without drawing attention."

"Either way, we're attention seeking whores, Blackwell. We've got a six-figure car loaded on the back of this bad boy. What do you suggest we do?"

Fuck. No matter what we pick, shit is about to go down. But driving away seems to be the safest option, and if we do it fast enough, we can be a reasonable distance away before the crew tries to find us. Slamming the truck into gear, I step on the gas. The truck rocks forward and roars to life. The little prick comes running toward us, phone to his ear. I glance at the passenger side mirror and notice the door swinging open to the building with Wolf sprinting towards us, frantically waving his arms.

"I think he knows we stole his car." I chuckle, turning out of the parking lot and onto the street.

"Good, now fucking drive like you stole it."

I roll my eyes. What a lame response. Then again, Leroy is older than dirt. I turn the corner and relax.

"I swear, Leroy. I'm never doing your shady business again. You need to find someone else."

"Don't be such a pussy, Blackwell. You act like you were shot at."

The sudden sound of gunshots causes me to swerve into oncoming traffic; I crank the steering wheel hard to the right, slamming into an SUV. Another round of gunshots ping off the side of the truck. As I glance into the side mirror, I spot an

SUV beside me and a man in the passenger seat sticking a gun out the window. Suddenly, the mirror explodes as a bullet hits it.

"Leroy. I blame you." I glare at him.

"I didn't cause this. You were slow." He pulls a gun out of his waistband and leans out the window.

I try to control the truck and ensure they don't shoot a tire. That'll be my worst nightmare.

"Hold on, I have to ram this asshole." I jolt left into the SUV, making them lose control and drive into the pathway of a semi-truck. My bad.

"Good job. Now it's just this prick, and he's fighting me."

"Well, aim for their fuckin tire or the windshield. Jesus. I can't keep driving like a prick."

"What the hell do you think I've been trying to do? It looks easier in the movies, you know."

I would like to see him drive while being shot at. Not so easy.

"They haven't shot the car up, have they?"

Leroy groans. "I hope not, but if they did, oh well. Bullet holes in a car are an easy fix."

A bullet to my brain, not so much. I jerk the truck to the right and slam into the SUV, making them smack into a parked car.

"Just get the job done, Leroy. I'm not dying on your watch."

He sits back in his seat. "I was getting to it. You have no patience."

I'm glad he's finally figuring that out; if only he realized it sooner. I'm only patient with a few things in life, and this isn't one of them. I need to promise to myself that this is my last job; this shit isn't worth it. I thought being in Holden was it for me, but I'm sure I burnt that bridge.

Leroy directs me to the drop off, another shitty warehouse, which doesn't surprise me. The cops look for clean and busy locations. This ain't it.

"I'll help you with your problem next week if you want."

"Yeah, that would be great. It needs to be dealt with smoothly, and I mean it."

He waves me off. "Yes, so you've told me. I'm not gonna fuck it up. Have some faith."

Faith? Not in this lifetime. That went out the door when Leroy told me I would never be shot at when I did a job. I've lost count.

I climb out of the truck and toss the keys to some rubberneck. My hands are done here, I follow Leroy into the warehouse because I still don't trust him enough not to stiff me with my payout. And this payout will be the best one yet and stealing a six-figure car high up there. They can turn it around fast if they want, but if they were smart, I would sit on it until Wolf calmed down.

I check my phone, and still nothing from Teagan. I'm unsure if I should reach out. Should I give her a few days? Or head back tonight and watch her. That is more appealing to me, and deep down, I know she enjoys it, too.

If I can keep up that charade, things will be better.

"Blackwell, head out of the sky." Leroy tosses me an envelope.

I casually open it up and flip through the crisp one-hundred-dollar bills, ensuring my cut is accounted for. When I'm satisfied, I slip it into my back pocket.

"I'm out. I'll call when I'm ready for you." I salute him and walk out.

Now that I'm done, I'm not sure where to go. If I head home, Teagan will know I'm back and wonder why I'm avoiding her. Do I want to become a hermit during the day, just to be an avoidant?

I also wonder if she liked the gift that mask left behind in her shop. I want to see if she found it; her shop isn't being touched, so I'm not even sure if she would go there today. Maybe I should've left it in her house. But that might have freaked her out too much.

I'm somewhat surprised Teagan never brought up her stalker to me. Is she scared to mention it, or does she not think it's serious enough?

It's time for a little more fun.

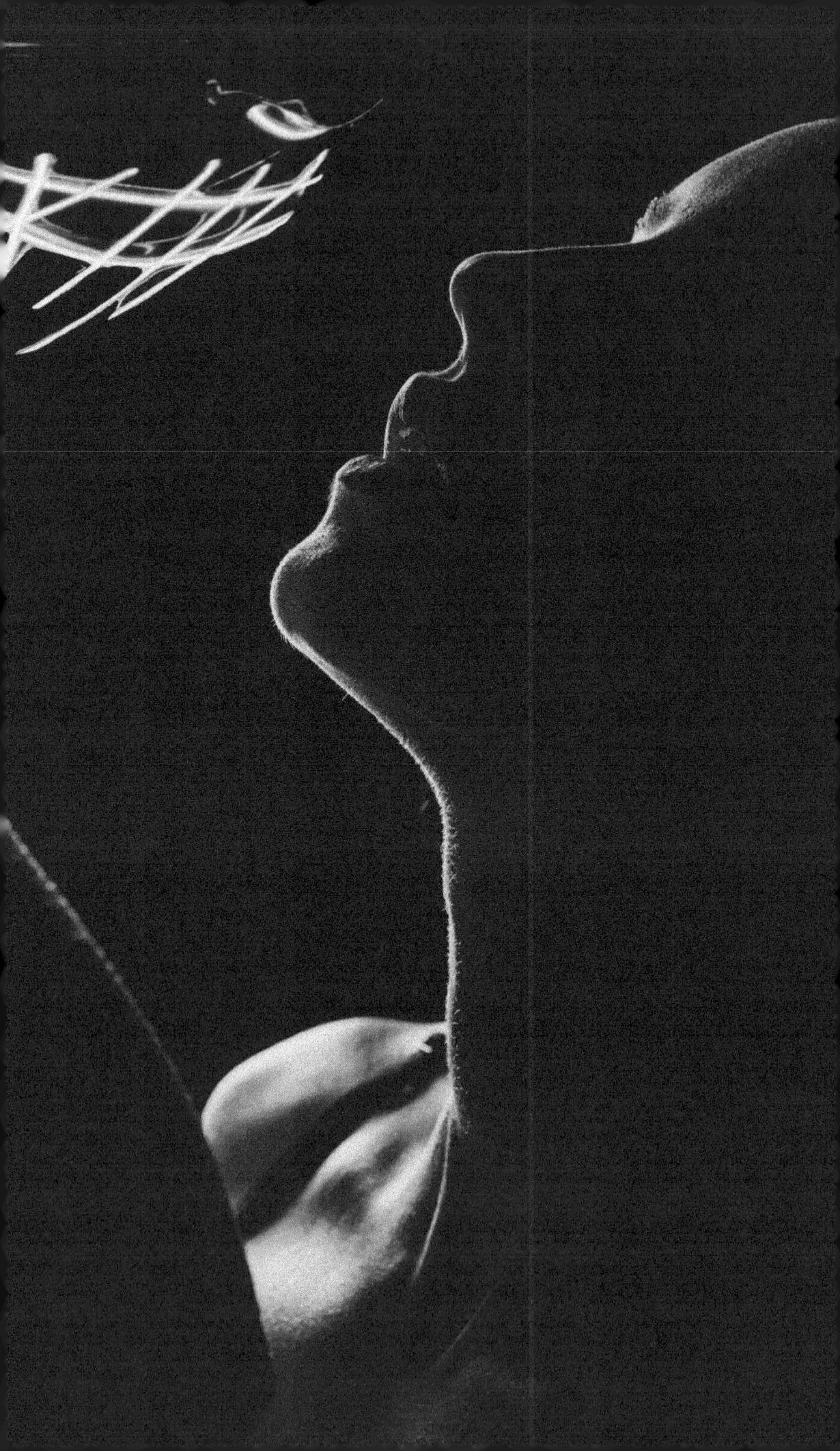

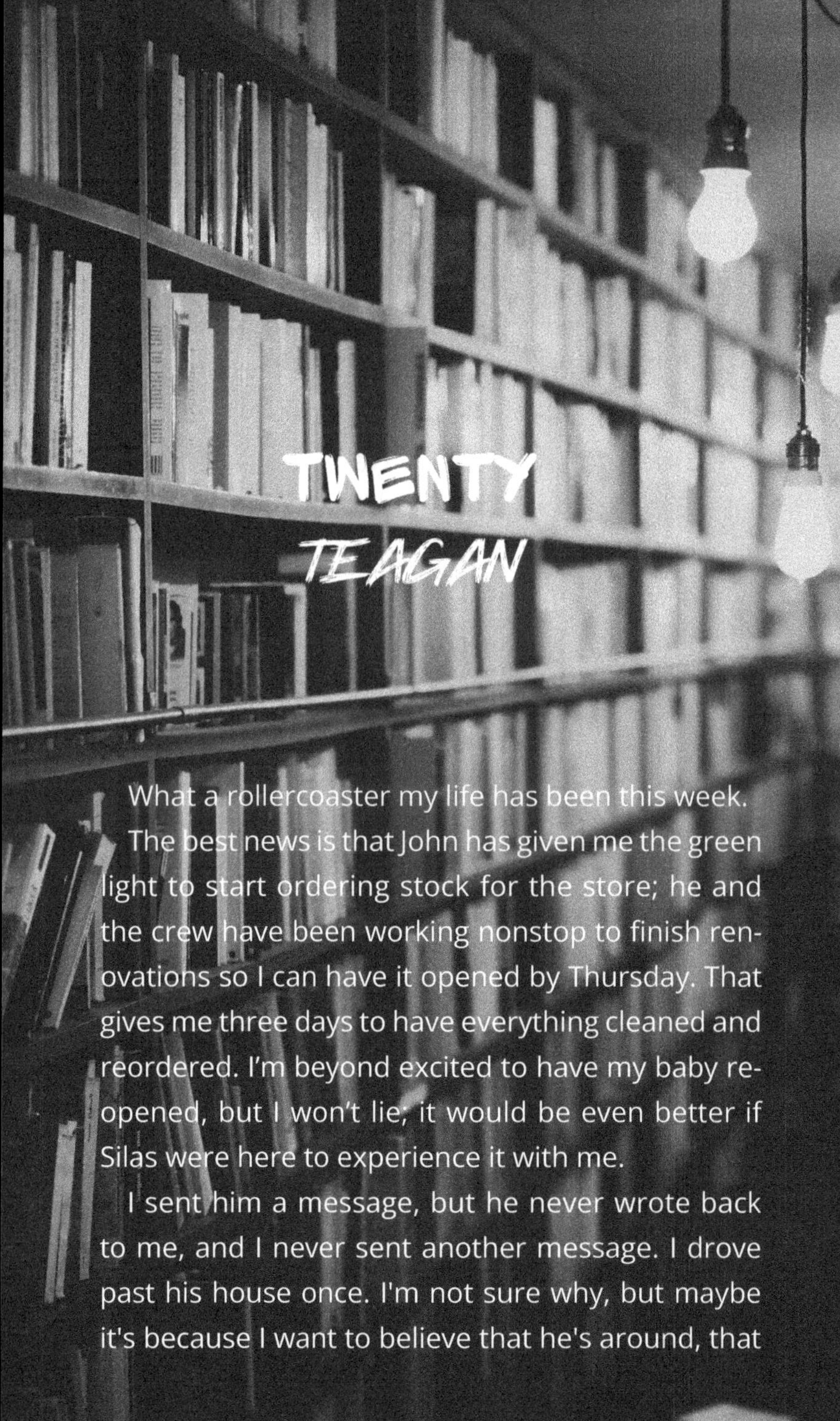

TWENTY
TEAGAN

What a rollercoaster my life has been this week. The best news is that John has given me the green light to start ordering stock for the store; he and the crew have been working nonstop to finish renovations so I can have it opened by Thursday. That gives me three days to have everything cleaned and reordered. I'm beyond excited to have my baby reopened, but I won't lie; it would be even better if Silas were here to experience it with me.

I sent him a message, but he never wrote back to me, and I never sent another message. I drove past his house once. I'm not sure why, but maybe it's because I want to believe that he's around, that

I might catch a glimpse of him and finally have the chance to talk to him.

I should leave it alone, chalk it up to that I'm no good and he got what he wanted from me. I was his hump and dump and nothing more. Now I know why I don't open up to anyone; it only ends in breaking my trust.

But luckily for me, I have Nancy bullshit to deal with. She's charging me with harassment. I've been meeting with my lawyer on and off this week, trying to determine my next move. I should've punched her in the face, and we could've added assault to my list of charges because it would've been worth it.

My lawyer told me that if Nancy tries to come near me, it's best to have some people around as witnesses. And if she shows up at the shop and I see her in time, I should lock the door. This will never happen; I'll be busy once I'm open again. Since my one and only employee ditched me.

My phone lets out a little ping from beside me on the kitchen island, where I've been camped out all day, hustling to get all my orders in before the deadline.

Jace: Stop pouting. We're coming to grab you, and we're hitting up the corn maze

Me: I'm not pouting dickhead. I'm stressing. BIG difference. Why are you doing the maze at night?

Jace: ;) I'm sure you know. Gotta keep my girl on her toes

Me: I am not third wheeling while you have sex in the corn, Jace!

Jace: You have to get out of the house Tee. It's officially Spooky Season!

Me: Fine. But I'm getting lost so don't search for me. I'll meet you there

One thing about Jace is you're better off agreeing to do shit with him, or he'll keep nagging. He has a way of pulling you out of a dark spot, even if you don't quite know you are in there. I'm glad he's my best friend. Even if we don't hang out all the time, when we do, it's the best. Now that he has Ivory, it makes it even better.

I try to get these orders finished. With Halloween coming up, I want to order some spooky reads and have them in the shop. But leave it to my mind to wander where it has nowhere to go. Silas. I wonder if he even thinks about me like I am him. Does he even give a shit that he hurt my feelings? Why should I even care this much? Maybe it's a good thing I'm getting out of the house; a distraction is what I need.

Holden's corn maze is the main attraction in the fall and its date central. Or, in my case, it's third wheeling central. I park my car, throw my wallet into the glovebox, and tuck my keys into my hoodie pocket after locking the door. I take my phone out and shoot Jace a quick text saying I made it and I'll be hanging out by the main gate.

I try to ignore some of the looks I get, but I know what they are from. I've been avoiding Elma. I can't look or speak to her. Between her and Nancy, I feel like they are turning this town against me. Unless you're a business owner, you wouldn't understand what it feels like to be attacked by Nancy.

Lost in my thoughts, I am unaware of the presence sneaking behind me. Swiftly, a pair of hands abruptly cover my eyes, plunging me into total darkness.

"Get excited, girl," Ivory's soft voice whispers in my ear. She removes her hands and steps to the side, giving me a bright smile.

"Don't do that." I swat at her.

"Yeah, baby. Tee here is a scaredy cat." Jace chuckles, pulling Ivory into his side and placing a kiss on her forehead.

A tinge of jealousy runs through me; I want to have that in my life. I don't think it's too much to ask for, but maybe my expectations are too high. I'm unsure what's worse, following or leading two love birds. Their whispers and giggles make me wanna gag, and not in a good way.

I make a random turn, leaving them behind me; I'm sure Jace is thankful. He and Ivory can do their own thing. His invitation was only to get me out of the house; we both knew I needed it, but I didn't need them to hold my hand.

The hairs on the back of my neck raise. I peek behind me, but there isn't anyone there. I remind myself that it's the fact that I'm in a corn maze, and it's dark out. My mind is playing tricks on me. Nothing more. The more I walk, the more I can't shake the feeling of someone following me. It was the same feeling I got when my masked stalker was around.

I stop, and a dark figure is a few feet behind me when I turn around. He holds his hand out, and a small black box rests in his palm. Fear twists deep in my gut when I realize what black box it was. It's the same one that was left in my shop. I tossed it in my desk drawer. I look back at the dark figure when his face lights up.

My masked stalker.

How did he find me? Has he been following me this entire time? I drove out here; I never noticed a random car following me. Then again, I never took notice of anyone behind me. I didn't think I had to. But I've been in denial and stupid not to take in my surroundings. Just because he isn't around me all the time doesn't mean he isn't there.

I slowly step to the side, where the path takes a fork. I'm unsure what he wants, but I don't want anything to do with him anymore. Or that's what I tell myself because I'm stupid enough to be here still. He shakes his head and steps forward, shoving his hand toward me. Can't he understand? I don't want it.

"I'm not taking your gift."

His fingers curl around the box, and he marches for me. I stumble backward, not expecting him to move so fast. His hand wraps around my bicep and drags me into the corn until the pathway disappears. I try to block my face from being smacked with cornstalks, but it's pointless, and I can't block them fast enough.

"Can you stop?" I try to yank my arm free, but he squeezes tighter. "Look, I don't want your stupid gift."

He stops and swings me around, and I bump into his chest. He jams the box into my chest, making me flinch. I reluctantly place my hand over it, whatever is in this box must be important to him. And once I open it, it'll be the end of me.

I take the box, and I stare at the words again. *To: Sweets.* With a deep inhale, I pull the lid off. Inside is a heart-shaped necklace with red liquid. A necklace, that's his gift.

"What's this supposed to mean?"

He reaches inside his hoodie and pulls out an identical necklace. "Your blood, my blood. Forever mine."

Oh, fuck this. I drop the necklace and run. I need to find a way out of this maze. The last thing I need is for his delusional ass to think we're meant to be together. I don't know him. I made a mistake in the park and now this is me paying for it. No matter how good it felt, it was a mistake.

I try finding an exit from the stalks, but it's useless. I feel like I'm running in circles, and who knows, maybe I am. Laughter rings out to the left, and excitement runs through me. That means people are nearby. I dart to the left, and the wind flies out of my lungs.

I land on the ground with a hard thud, cornstalks breaking around me, and pain shoots up my ankle. I attempt to stifle my cries of agony as he forcefully clutches my ankle while flipping me onto my back.

No matter how much I tried to fight him off, he still climbed on top, pinning me to the ground. He lifts his hand, and the heart-shaped necklace tumbles from his fist.

"I'm not wearing that. You can go to hell."

"You will." He grabs me by the neck, pressing hard.

Everything around me starts going fuzzy, and no matter how much I try to pry his hand off, nothing works. I can feel my energy fading. He lets go, bringing his mask close to my face. The bright light from his mask blinds me. His hands work around my neck.

"Mine."

I bring my hand to my neck and touch the necklace.

"I am not yours, and I will never be yours. Leave me alone." I shove him backward, but he doesn't budge.

His hands dance beneath my sweater, causing my body to tighten with anticipation. His hand moves higher up my chest, squeezing my boobs. Tears gather in the corner of my eyes, and he buries his head in the curve of my neck. I don't care if he's obsessed with me or not; today is not his fucking day. I reach up and grab the back of his hood and rip it off and bring my knee up and ram it into his dick.

"Suck on that, you cocksucker. Find another girl." He jerks his hands out from under my shirt when I go for his mask.

"Touch it, and you'll be punished." His hand wraps around my wrist.

"Try me, asshole." Using my other hand, I slam into his face, causing his mask to move and expose a black balaclava. His eyes, a deep shade of green, lock onto mine in surprise. I'm surprised, too, but with the look in his eyes, I'm afraid of what's to happen next.

TWENTY-ONE

SILAS

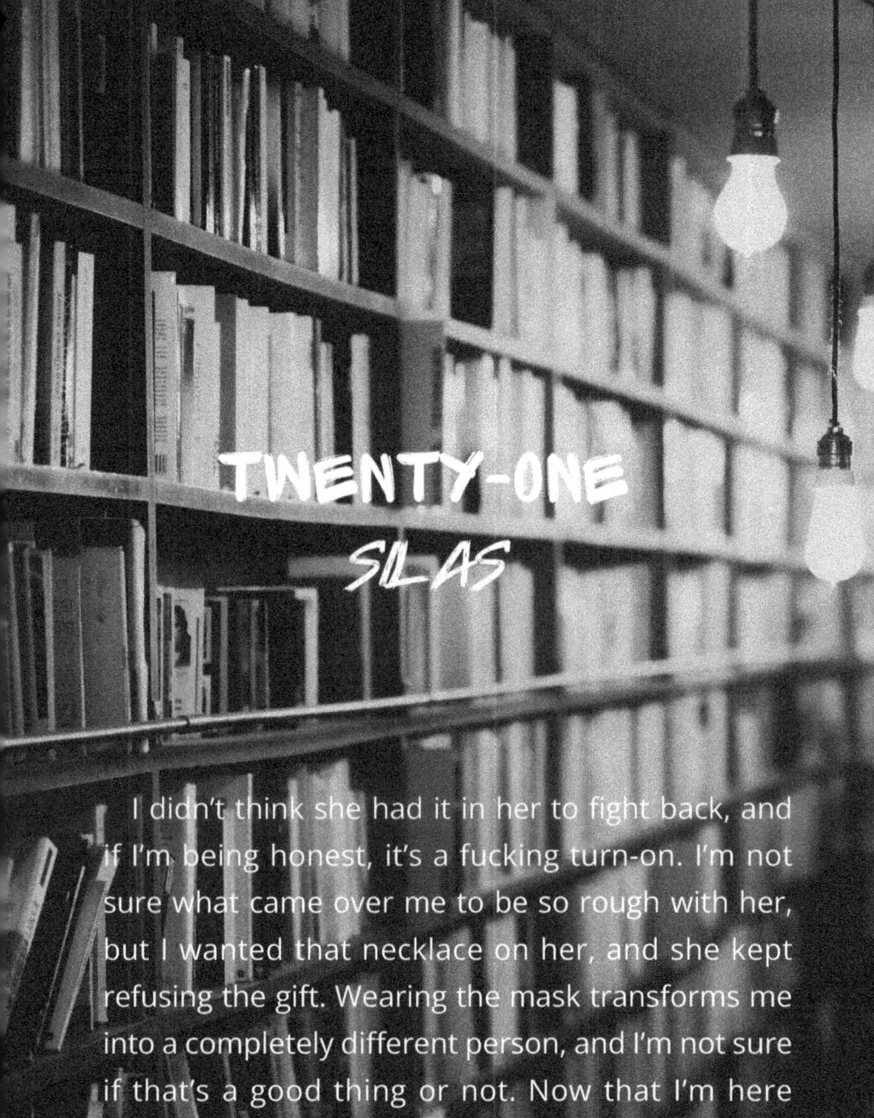

I didn't think she had it in her to fight back, and if I'm being honest, it's a fucking turn-on. I'm not sure what came over me to be so rough with her, but I wanted that necklace on her, and she kept refusing the gift. Wearing the mask transforms me into a completely different person, and I'm not sure if that's a good thing or not. Now that I'm here with Teagan, I don't think I want to wear the mask anymore, but I'm unsure how to remove it.

I grab her hands and lean into her, pressing my hard-on into her. I need her to know what she does to me.

"You're a pig." She spits in my face.

There's so much I wanna say to her, but the more I talk, the more I'll give myself away. The constant push and pull is getting to be too much. I'm going to crack sooner or later. There is nothing I want more than her.

I need her to know that I'm not going to hurt her; I sit up and fix my mask. Taking hold of one of her hands, despite her resistance, I guide it to my chest. With determination, I gently press her hand flat against my chest until she can feel my heartbeat.

"I don't care that you're a human under that mask. Let me go."

"No." I shove her hand down, feeling her hand gripping my dick through my pants.

"Is this what you want, you sick fuck."

I groan when she squeezes harder; I wouldn't put it past her to hurt me. I stand and grab her by the shirt, bringing her face next to my dick.

"Open my jeans."

Teagan remains still; I draw a deep breath, then swiftly grasp her hair and shake her until her hands reach out, grabbing hold of my thighs.

"Stop, you're hurting me," she yells.

"Do it." I hold the bottom of my hoodie up.

Her shaky hands work their way to my waistband and slowly undo the button. "I hate you. I'll never forgive you, and I hope I never see you after today." She mutters as she pulls my pants down.

I'm afraid that my masked days are going to be behind me. Teagan will never trust it again. But right now, that's the least of my concerns. I push her head closer and hold my dick for her, running it along her lips. As I look into her eyes, she glares up at me, and I gently pat her cheek with the tip of my dick.

"Suck." I tap on her lips, waiting for her to open.

She opens wide, and I slip in, feeling the warmth of her mouth. Holding her head, I thrust deep, listening to her gag; her hands push against my thighs the more I fuck her mouth. I pull out and watch the drool run down her chin. Once she sucks in a deep breath, I push back into her mouth again. I press her face to its limit until she gags again. Fuck, this feels amazing. I pull out, and her hand circles around my shaft, stroking it slowly, almost painfully slow.

I let go of her hair and gently run my fingers along the curve of her jaw. I can't help but be captivated by how beautiful she is. With care and gentleness, I tilt her head back and bring my face closer, allowing my mask to brush against her forehead lightly. I switch off the light, enveloping us in darkness. Her hand tightens around my dick, and her breathing picks up.

"Shh, you're safe." I try to reassure her. I'm at the point where if she figures out who I am, I wouldn't care. When her breathing goes back to normal, I thrust my hips forward.

"Do you have something with getting off in public?"

I'm beginning to think it's just being with her that gets me off; it doesn't matter where I am. It has to be with her and no one else. And if I didn't know any better, she also has a thing for public play. I push her backward onto the ground and slowly sit up, moving my hands to her waistband. She snatches my hand, stopping me.

"I don't want to be fingered." I cock my head to the side, somewhat confused. "I want more."

She has been opposing me throughout this whole time, and now she is demanding more. Talk about whiplash. I unsnap her jeans and pull them down to her thighs. Lifting her legs onto my shoulders, I move in closer. I didn't wait for her to be ready; I drove into her, sinking deep with one firm thrust.

She clutches my hoodie, dragging me closer. She moans when I hit her g-spot; I withdraw inch by inch and drive in hard, making her back bow and her muscles clamp down.

"Keep it down, Sweets." I pull out and slam in again. She bites on her bottom lip, trying to keep quiet.

As I lower my hand next to her head, pushing her legs even further back, and my knees press into the dirt below me. Feeling her breath on my neck through the balaclava, wishing I could feel her skin against mine once more. Voices grow louder to the left, and her body stiffens.

I pick up the pace, and when her moans start, I cover her mouth. I'm ready to blow, but I need Teagan to finish first. Running my hand down her thigh to her pussy, I find her clit and rub; with a powerful breath, she inhales the skin of my hand as her moan is muffled. I press my thumb firmer, making her walls clamp down on my dick. I keep a steady pace of thrusting and rubbing. Her eyes clamp shut, and her thighs shake as she comes around my dick.

I quicken up my movements when I feel myself close. I drop her legs, slip out of her pussy and, wrap my hand in her hair, pull her face up.

"Open." She opens her mouth, and I slip in and come down her throat. "Good girl." I wipe her lips and, sticking my finger in her mouth, she sucks it clean without me saying anything. I stand, tucking myself back into my pants.

"Don't fucking leave me alone in the dark again, you asshole."

I turn around, ignoring her. If I hang around, it's harder to disappear. Doesn't she understand that? You can't be a stalker and be a gentleman. I casually weave through the cornstalks, eager to create a bit of space between us. Once I feel like I'm safely out of reach, I smoothly remove my masks and casually flip up my hood.

After successfully escaping the maze, I head directly to my car, waiting for me at the far end of the parking lot. I sit and wait for Teagan to come out. I know she headed in with friends; that shit goblin is lucky he had his arms around a different woman. I wouldn't hold back from beating the shit out of him if he touched Teagan.

I'm not sure what I'm supposed to do now, I can't show my face at her shop come morning. I have no excuse; she'll want to know why I left her, but telling her scares me, which should be the least of my worries. I shouldn't be afraid of talking to her or telling her anything. I'm fearful of her not wanting me after she finds out about my past, and most definitely when I take off the mask.

Movement at the exit drags my eyes back. It's fucktard and his woman, followed by Teagan. In a posture of defeat, with her head bowed, shoulders weighed down, and with a slight limp, she appears to be carrying the weight of the world on her shoulders. She doesn't exude happiness; instead, there's a palpable sense of sadness and confusion radiating from her. And it's my fault. I did that to her.

I touch the necklace, the one other piece I have of her. The other piece is the bell I stole from above the door of her shop. The smartest thing I'll ever do in my life is to let her go. I watch as she waves goodbye and heads to a red Mini Cooper. She stands next to the driver's side door, looks down and leans against the door. She finally opens the door and gets in. The headlights illuminate the car in front of her before she drives away.

I resist the urge to follow her; instead, I wait ten minutes before leaving and returning to my house in defeat. I'm such a pussy for not doing what's right. I make a pitstop at a liquor store; tonight needs some alcohol in the system. Drinking your sorrows is entirely normal, or the liquor stores wouldn't be in business.

I can't wait to get home. I crack open the bottle of vodka and take a big gulp. The clear liquor engulfs my stomach in warmth. The only warmth I can rely on, the only thing that will always be there. I drive around, not ready to go home yet. The silence of the house will haunt me. I still hate Holden, no matter how much time I spend here.

I end up in the rich part of town, the one area that I haven't ventured before. Rich pricks. I don't feel guilty about stealing their cars. They can afford to replace them when they live in houses like these. I take another drink, cursing the stupidly rich fucks.

I roll my window down. "Fuck you all!" I yell into the darkness. With a swift motion, I hurl the bottle of vodka out the window, hearing the satisfying crash as it collides with the front door of a random house. I hope they enjoy their little gift.

My head is slightly fuzzy, and in the back of my mind, I know I should head to my house, but I can't. I turn down her street, parking a couple of houses down. I grab my mask and stumble out of the car. Holding onto the door when the world spins, I re-think my plan. Maybe coming here half-loaded isn't the brightest. Then again, my brain isn't working at full capacity.

Carrying my mask in my hand, I stumble along the street until I find myself in front of her house, barely able to keep my balance. I try to place my mask on, but I can't figure it out; I throw the thing on the grass and stagger to the front window.

Her curtains are closed.

All of this was for nothing. I feel closed out, as if Teagan doesn't need me in her life anymore. Now what the fuck am I supposed to do? Head home and wallow? I lean against the window, only wanting to be close again. Why can't I let her go?

Is she struggling like I am? I hope not. I hope she can move on without me.

"I'm sorry, Dimples. You need to find a better man, one that isn't a fuck up." I grip the necklace, praying she finds someone better.

I slowly walk back to the car, taking in the quietness. Once I'm back in the city, I'll never hear peace or my thoughts again.

TWENTY-TWO

TEAGAN

Jace and Ivory looked happy when I found them in the corn maze, and I couldn't be happier for them. And I felt like a wrung-out wet cat. Just when I thought things couldn't get worse, my lawyer called this morning for an early morning meeting. I lie in bed praying it's nothing serious, but shit with Nancy isn't easy, and I should know better.

I slowly hoist myself up and glance around my room. Perhaps it's time for a bit of change. I've been doing the same thing almost daily; I feel stuck in a hamster wheel, never going anywhere. Maybe reopening the shop wasn't a good idea; perhaps

I should've taken that vacation when I had the chance, not causing a shitstorm.

Now, I'm afraid it's too late. I dug myself a grave and now have no choice but to get out of it: me and my big mouth. I eventually move to the closet and try to find something decent that doesn't scream. *I work in a bookstore, and I'm lazy half the time.* You don't realize your wardrobe is lacking until you need to find professional wear.

I grab a black dress since you can't go wrong there. It's classy and screams I'm not one to be fucked with. I pull off my nightgown, and the necklace falls against my chest. I touch the heart that's filled with his blood. It's the creepiest gift I've ever received. I reach for the clasp and stop. Something in the back of my mind screams at me to stop. What if he catches me again, and I don't have it on? I'm over his grabs and fucks. I swear, next time, his balls will meet my fucking knee. Who are we kidding? I damn near begged him last night like an idiot. I crumbled so fast. But the sex—goddamn, it was hot.

I hope my lawyer has good news because I don't know why he would want to meet with me. I've done everything he suggested, even though I've secretly hoped for a run-in with Nancy. I grab my bag off the island and my car keys.

I was so caught up thinking about the meeting I almost didn't notice the dark object on the grass in the front yard. I swear, if it's kids throwing trash on my grass, I'm going to be pissed. The closer I get, the more confused I am.

The mask is flipped over, revealing the cushioned foam on the forehead, an adjustable strap, and a cord leading to the battery pack. If this is what I think it is, that means he came here last night. I kick the mask over, revealing white LED stripes. Like, I figured it was the mask.

I look around, wondering if he's out here watching me now. I scan the neighbourhood as I slowly back up; deep down, I know he won't show his face during the day, but secretly, I want him to. I want to know who is behind the mask. I thought I was close last night when I smacked his mask off; if only he weren't wearing that stupid balaclava under it. I can't quite make out his voice, and it's so muffled that I can't tell if I recognize him or not. That's what bugs me; his speech pattern is just not familiar.

Opening the car door, I take one more peek at the mask; shivers roll down my spine. I can't think of him today. I have Nancy bullshit to deal with. I back out of the driveway like a mad woman, trying to add distance between me and that mask. That's a problem for afternoon Teagan.

Fredrick and Jason Law Office, a quiet office tucked behind the only grocery store in town. The building's exterior is all classic red brick, but you're immediately surrounded by luxury when you step inside. The floors are white tile, the walls are white, and there's sleek black leather furniture for clients in the waiting room. It's quite the contrast, but it works.

The lawyers here are cunty as fuck, but they come with a considerable price tag. Unfortunately for me. My lawyer, Sam, comes strolling into the waiting room with my folder tucked under his arm. When he sees me, he shakes his head.

"Teagan, good morning."

"Morning, Sam."

He nods for me to follow him, time to get this over with. Whatever happens, happens.

"I got a disturbing phone call from Tom, Nancy's lawyer, and I figured we should get together before cops were involved," he says when we enter the small office.

"Why? What did she do?" I take a seat across from him.

He places the folder on the desk, opens it, takes a piece of paper out and slides it toward me. I grab it and try to read lawyer talk.

"I'm not following; what does this mean?"

"It seems some vandalization happened at Nancy's house last night, and she's accusing you."

"Hold the fucking phone. I was at home. Does she even have proof that it was me, or is she just saying this because she hates me and cause I may or may not have threatened her cunty ass?"

Sam grins. "She's saying you threw a bottle of liquor at her house last night."

"The fuck. I have better shit to do than waste booze on her. What does this mean now?"

"She's becoming unhinged, and I shouldn't say that, but it's true. I'm unsure why she has it out for you Teagan, but I would be careful. I wouldn't put it past her to push you so she can get a restraining order. Don't get violent. That's all I can say."

"Great, so I have to watch myself while she goes on her merry way, tormenting people still. How is that fair?"

He shakes his head. "Life isn't fair, but jail isn't where you want to be."

Perfect. I get punished for something I haven't done, and Nancy gets away with being a dick. This isn't how I was expecting this morning to go. At this point, I might as well try and grow eyes on the back of my head because, at this rate, I'll never survive.

"Anything else I should be aware of?"

"Yes. Nancy's lawyer says if she complains one more time, he'll go straight to the cops. I'm doing the best I can, but my hands are tied. It's the note you wrote that isn't helping."

"Allegedly. It's in Kendall's writing, not mine. You still don't have proof I said it."

"You do know Kendall came forward and said you told her what to write."

"Snitch. There was a reason I never liked her." What a bitch, what happened to girls helping girls?

"Teagan, no more threats," Sam warns.

"Sure. Is that everything? I need to head to the shop."

"That's everything. If something comes up, I'll call." He stands, walks to the door and opens it for me. "I mean it, no more threats. Nancy isn't one to be messed with. I can't help if you dig a deep grave."

"Thanks, Sam." Everyone is afraid of that deep grave of Nancy's wrath. I should've known even my lawyer was afraid of Nancy. What does that say about her power in this town? I need to find some dirt on her before I end up in the dirt. She probably smashed a bottle of liquor and blamed me, and I wouldn't put it past her to go to such lengths just to get me off her back.

Two more days and the shop will officially reopen. The nerves are getting to me. What if Nancy does something then? I leave the office feeling defeated. I can see where Sam is coming from, telling me to cool my jets, but that woman irritates the living shit out of me. I have a sneaking suspicion she will show up on opening day and cause trouble, and I don't have any backup unless I call Dad to man the door, but then it looks like security is needed. It's bad enough that people are talking about my name; do I want Dad to be dragged into it?

I've got a lot on my mind, but asserting my dominance over Nancy's is at the top of my priorities. It's time to show her who the real boss is.

Being back at my shop, I'm over the moon; John and his crew have outdone themselves. The space is more open without the backroom blocking most of the space. I'm in love with it, but now I'm not sure I want to add the coffee bar; maybe a tiny retail space filled with bookish items would be perfect.

The only thing missing is someone to celebrate this with. When I talked about renovations, it was with Silas; he was supportive, and I looked forward to sharing this moment with him. Fuck it. Grabbing my phone, I find his number.

Me: I know it's a long shot, and you probably stopped talking to me for a reason, but the shop is reopening in two days, and I want you to be here when it does. Don't feel obligated to just because I'm messaging you. I hope everything is okay with you. Anyway, take care Sunshine.

If he chooses to ignore me, it was worth a shot. I'll finally get my answer and be able to move forward.

I step into my office to a complete mess, paperwork scattered from one end to the other across my desk, boxes of books piled in the corner. I have a delivery coming tomorrow, and I still need to clean this entire place from top to bottom.

At least cleaning will help distract my mind.

I'm working on wiping down all the bookshelves when a knock on the door startles me. I peek around the shelf and see Elma's face squished against the door, trying to look inside. I see her eyes lock onto mine, and I know I'm fucked. She greets me with a wave, looking so happy, like she hasn't been spreading rumours about me.

"Teagan, open up. It's been ages, Hun." She knocks again and pulls on the handle. Thankfully, I locked the door.

Is it too late to pretend I didn't see her? She knocks once more. I drop my rag in the water bucket and slowly make my way to the door. She won't give up, and god knows what she has to say. I turn the lock, and she pushes the door open.

"About time. It's getting cold out there for an old lady like me. You won't believe the news, I have to say. I feel like it's been ages since I've told you some juicy gossip. Where have you been hiding out?" She waves me off and walks further into the shop, leaving me behind. "Doesn't matter; let me tell you what I heard."

"Elma, can't this wait? I have a lot to do before I reopen."

"Nonsense, this won't take long." She looks around the empty shop before facing me. "I heard some folks were caught having intercourse in the corn maze."

My head felt like it was going through a tunnel, and I didn't hear her correctly. "I'm sorry. What?"

"A group of teenagers took pictures of a couple in the middle of—"

I hold my hand up. "Got it. Who was it?" Sweat forms on my forehead, praying it's not me.

"I'm not sure; it was dark, and they didn't have the flash on. Who would choose a public place to have sex? You have to be sick in the head."

"Some people like to have fun, Elma. Even if it's in public, was this the juicy gossip you were in dire need to tell me?"

"No. I heard no one is coming to your reopening. They are upset about what you did with Nancy."

"Gee, I wonder where they heard that little tidbit of news?"

"I only tell the people what they should know."

"Well, your facts are out to fucking lunch, Elma. Next time, go to the source for everything before you ruin their livelihood. So, if you don't mind, there's the fucking door. Don't come back until you learn your place in this town."

She places her hand on her chest, and her eyes grow wide. "Are you threatening me?"

"No, Elma. I'm tired of you spreading rumours about me." I point to my chest.

"I'm sorry, Teagan. But that's how things work."

I shake my head. Unreal, I step back, opening the door. "Then you can leave. Our friendship, or whatever you think it was, is over. Don't come back."

Elma brushes past me without another word. If someone prefers spreading rumours over building friendships, they're not someone I want around.

I already have enough drama to deal with for a lifetime.

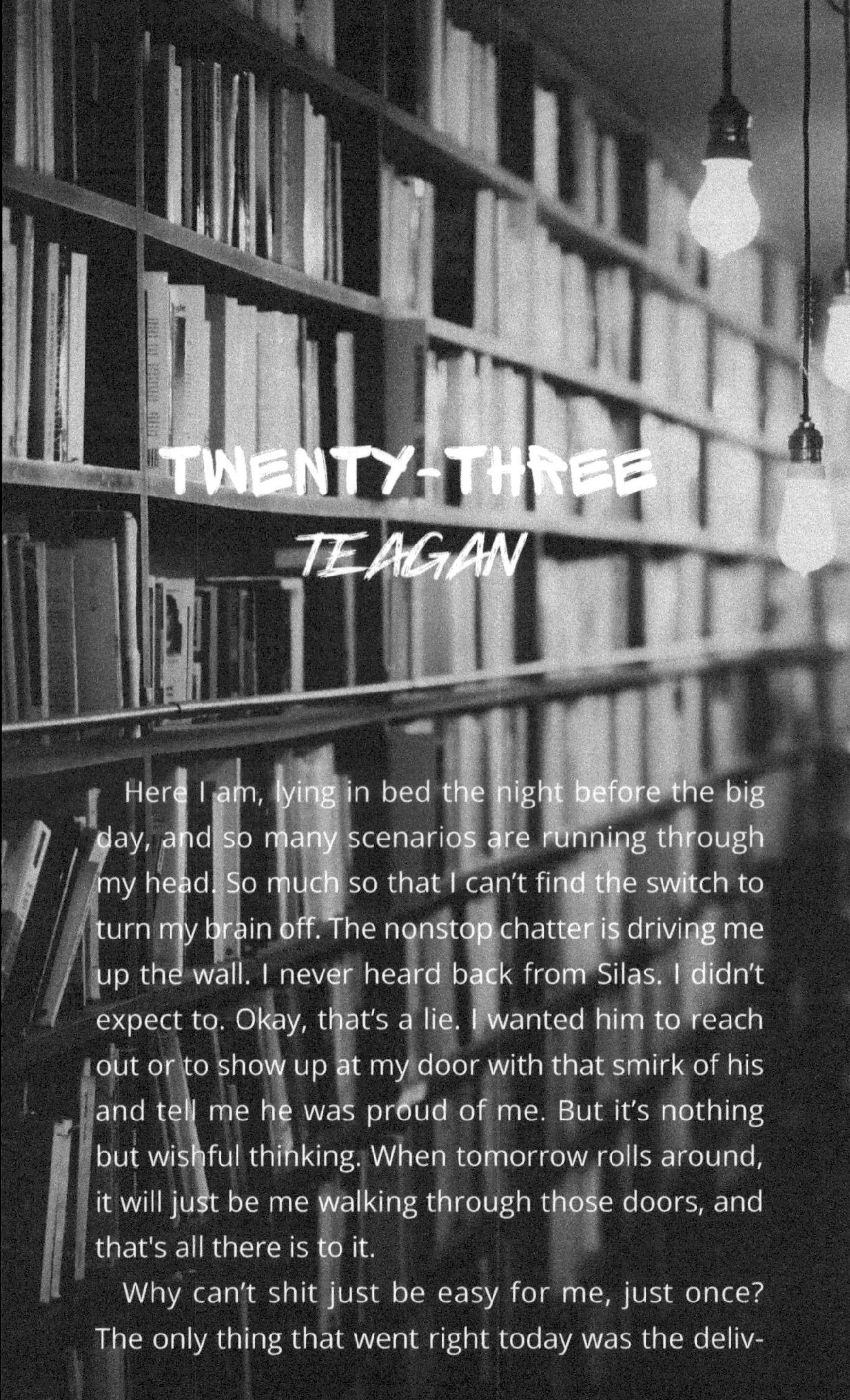

TWENTY-THREE
TEAGAN

Here I am, lying in bed the night before the big day, and so many scenarios are running through my head. So much so that I can't find the switch to turn my brain off. The nonstop chatter is driving me up the wall. I never heard back from Silas. I didn't expect to. Okay, that's a lie. I wanted him to reach out or to show up at my door with that smirk of his and tell me he was proud of me. But it's nothing but wishful thinking. When tomorrow rolls around, it will just be me walking through those doors, and that's all there is to it.

Why can't shit just be easy for me, just once? The only thing that went right today was the delivery. Thankfully, everything I ordered came in, and I worked my ass off stocking the shelves. I should be beyond tired and yet I can't fall asleep. I swing the blankets off and head for the kitchen. Maybe ice cream and true crime will help me fall asleep.

I've done this all before, including ice cream and true crime. My life feels stuck on a never-ending loop, going round and round with no progress in sight. That damn hamster wheel won't stop spinning long enough for me to step off.

I startle awake when the TV volume increases. I can hear my heartbeat in my ears; I try to calm down by placing my hand on my chest. It's almost like déjà vu. I slowly get up and walk to the front window. Grabbing the curtain, without thinking, I fling it open fast, hoping to scare whoever is out there. But there's no one there.

All that's there is the mask that I left in my yard. I couldn't touch it again; honestly, I thought he would return to grab it. I guess I couldn't keep a stalker around, either. I close the curtains, shut the TV off and head to the bedroom. It's going to be a long night.

I stare at myself in the bathroom mirror; my hair is a mess, and the bags under my eyes are a dead giveaway that the sleep never came. I can't give myself a pep talk because I'm too busy being a Debbie downer. The words that Elma said are going through my mind. What did she mean by saying that everyone was upset with me? Is today going to be a complete bust?

I run a brush through my hair, contemplating my next move. At this point, I really couldn't care less. If people show up, they show up. There isn't much I can do about it. Elma ruined things for me; even if I dug the grave, she opened her mouth without all the information.

"You've got this, you're a bad bitch, and no one can ruin this day." I nod at myself and finish getting myself ready.

The walk to the shop was refreshing and what I needed. But that fizzed out when I turned the corner and noticed a blacked-out Land Rover parked outside the shop. I stop dead in my tracks and turn around. I'm not dealing with that witch. I take the alley and find my phone.

"What's the matter, Tee?"

"Where are you?" I demand, ignoring his question.

"What's wrong?" Jace's voice raises a notch.

"I'm at the shop, and Nancy is waiting out front. What should I do?"

I hear a door slam and some yelling. "The boys and I are coming. Go through the back and stay in the office. Don't open any door until I call you."

"Okay." I rush down the alley, trying to dig my keys out of my bag. Why would she be waiting? Is she trying to bait me into doing something, or does she want something from me? Struggling to insert the key into the lock, my trembling hands refuse to cooperate. My heart pounds with uncertainty, dreading the possibility of Nancy suddenly appearing around the corner.

I feel such a sense of relief as I slide the key into the lock. Once inside, I immediately lock the door behind me. My whole body is shaking, and I'm on the verge of crying. I have to pull it together. I haven't broken down yet, and I can't start yet. I slip into my office and wait for Jace to call. Without thinking, I text him.

Me: Silas I know you don't wanna talk to me, but I'm scared.

I don't know what made me reach out, but I'm unsure what could happen with Nancy sitting outside. I hold my phone close to my chest and lean against the door. I jump when my phone dings.

Sunshine: What's going on? I'm calling pick up the fucking phone

The phone hardly rings before I accept the call.

"Silas."

"What's going on, Teagan?"

God, it's so good to hear his voice "Nancy is waiting for me at the shop."

"Dimples, it'll be alright. Are the doors locked?"

"Yeah, I'm in my office. I called Jace. He and the guys are coming, but I'm scared she might try to force herself in." I feel my voice cracking and tears welling up.

"That's good, love." His voice softened. "Don't leave that office; stay there until Jace shows up. I'm sorry that I can't be there."

I stay silent to avoid breaking down in tears. I nod, sniffling. "You left me."

"I know. I'm sorry."

"Why?"

He's quiet. "We aren't having this conversation right now. We can talk when you are safe."

"Okay."

"Where is Jace?"

I check my phone even though I would get a notification. "I'm not sure. Jace said he would call." I feel a tear slipping down my nose, so I quickly wipe it away while sniffing a bit.

"It's okay, breathe. He'll be there shortly. Stay on the phone until then. Can you do that?"

"Yeah."

"Perfect, love. Tell me about the shop. How does it look."

I smile; the shop is beautiful. "It's amazing, Sunshine. You can't tell a stupid fire hydrant took it out." He chuckles. "The shelves are all stocked, and I decided not to do a coffee bar. I'm going to turn it into a small retail spot instead; I think that would be better."

"Sounds perfect. No more screaming demons is even better in my books."

"Oh, tell me about it. My books will be safe now."

I missed talking to him, and I'm trying not to think about when I have to hang the phone up and our time will come to an end. I want to ask so many questions, but I know it would be pointless. He'll never answer them.

A deafening bang echoed from the front of the store, sending waves of fear coursing through me.

"Teagan?" Silas yells. "Teagan, answer me. What the fuck was that?" calls again when I don't say anything.

"I...I don't know." I could barely force the words out.

"Lock the office door. I'm coming back to get you, Dimples."

I try to calm my breathing when I hear voices I don't know in the shop. "I'm so scared. What do I do?"

"Hide, call the cops. I'm hanging up. Call the cops. Teagan."

The line goes dead, and I stare at the wall. I'm slowly losing my will; this was supposed to be my happy day, but now it's becoming a nightmare. I'm on autopilot at this point as I hit Taylor's number. I barely remember what I said to him, but I re-member something about the shop and Nancy. I'm sure he'll blame me. The voices continue along with banging and destruction.

I sink down between my desk and the wall and bury my head in my hands. And the tears finally fall. I wipe them away so I can see the screen on my phone.

Me: Where the hell are you?

I shouldn't have to ask Jace where he is. It never takes him this long unless he's out on a call. I close my eyes and try to escape, but it's not enough. I'll never get that sound out of my ears. I want to call Dad, but I don't need to get him mixed up with whatever is happening out there. I cover my ears when I hear the bookshelves being pushed over.

Nancy must've called in people to do this because I've had loyal customers for years, and I know they wouldn't do this to me.

I'm unsure how long time has passed until a knock on the door had me jolting away from the desk. I don't say a word. All I can do is stare at the door, waiting for someone to kick it down.

"Tee, baby, it's me. Open up."

"Jace?"

"Yeah, it's me. Can you open the door?" His voice is muffled, almost like he is pressing his mouth against the door.

I grab the desk, lifting myself. I'm so exhausted and scared to see what lies behind the door. As I unlock the door and cautiously open it, my heart races in anticipation. Jace stands there in his firefighter gear, and I can't hold back my tears of relief and gratitude. With a swift motion, he swings the door wide open and pulls me into his strong embrace.

"Shh, I got you. I'm sorry it took me a while. We tried to get here sooner. I'm sorry." I grip him tight, smelling smoke on his uniform.

"I'm scared, Jace. What happened?"

"Don't worry about that. Are you okay?"

"I don't know what to think. Today was supposed to be the best day. All that hard work went into this day, and for what? Nothing."

He hugs me tighter. "It wasn't for nothing. This shop is your passion, Tee. Don't let some assholes take that away from you. Can I take you home?"

"What about the shop?"

"The guys are dealing with it, and Taylor is here. He'll want to talk with you, but I'll have him stop by your place afterward. You need to get out of here."

"Thank you."

I'm not sure I want to be home alone. What if something happens there?

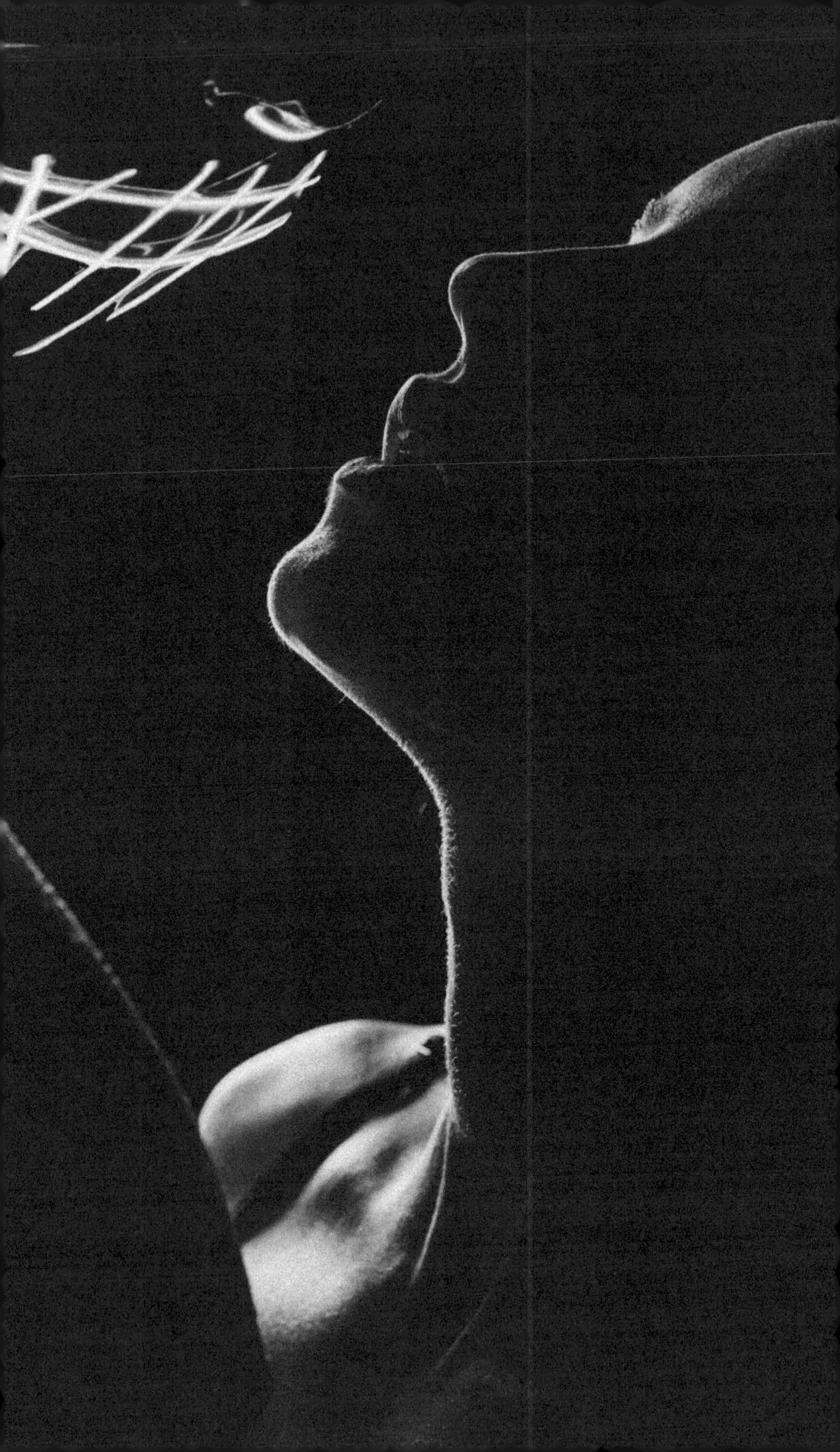

TWENTY-FOUR
TEAGAN

I stare out the fire engine window as we drive through the town. Every business we pass is open, and customers are happily shopping. A tinge of jealousy rushes through me. That should've been me today. But it was taken from me. Jace wouldn't let me see the front of the shop, and if I'm being honest, I'm not sure I could've handled it. I'm nervous when the time does come, the first time around was bad enough, but this I'm not sure I'll be able to handle it.

Luke parks in front of my house, and Keegan opens the door for me.

"You doin' alright, Teagan?" Keegan asks as he helps me out.

"Eventually. Thank you for coming today."

"Anything for a friend." He squeezes my shoulder.

I'm grateful to have this group of guys around; they've helped so much that I'll never be able to thank them. Jace meets me at the edge of the truck, wrapping his arm around my shoulder and walks me to the curb of my front yard.

"Did you want me to come in?"

"No, I'm gonna call Mom and Dad." I would tell him Silas said he would come, but I'll believe it when I see it.

He pulls me in for a hug. "If anything happens, call me, and I'll be here. I can always send Ivory over for a girls' night if that makes you more comfortable. I don't want you alone tonight."

"Thanks, Jace. I can always go to Mom and Dad's."

"Or the fire hall. Don't be afraid. You have a team behind you, Tee." He squeezes me tighter, lifting me off the ground until my back cracks. "Get in the house. We'll leave once you're inside."

I walk across the grass, disregarding everything around me. I find my keys and unlock the door. I step inside and barely close the door when a hand covers my mouth. Startled, I drop my bag, letting out a muffled yelp. I quickly reach up to pry the hand away.

"Shh, Dimples. It's me." Silas drops his hand, and I burst into tears. "Love, come here." He pulls me close, wrapping his arms around me and gently caressing my hair. Feeling the aroma of his earthy cologne engulf my senses, I draw him nearer.

"I've missed you, Sunshine."

"I'm sorry about today. I promise to find out who did this to you and make them pay. You didn't deserve any of this. I should've been here today." With a gentle touch, he lifts my chin, causing me to tilt my head back. His face is concealed in his baseball cap, making his deep green eyes seem even more intense.

"It's fine. You had your reason for leaving. I need to call my parents. Excuse me." I grab my bag off the floor and leave Silas by the front door. I slip into my bedroom and close the door. I can't believe he showed up. I only wish it didn't take me being scared out of my mind to get him to come back. Why couldn't he come back when I asked him before? I'll never understand him. Sitting on the edge of the bed, I grab my phone. I hope that the news hasn't broken within the town yet.

"Hi, hunny. How's your day so far?" Mom asks in her bright and cheery voice.

I pinch the bridge of my nose when I feel the tears starting. "Mom." My throat grows thick with emotion.

"Teagan. What happened? Caleb!" She yells for Dad. "Hold on, I'll put you on speaker."

"What's wrong, Small fry?"

I try to find the words without crying. "The shop, it's um." I stare at the ceiling when the tears well up. "It's gone."

"What do you mean it's gone? What happened to it?" Mom rushes her questions.

"Are you okay? Where are you?" Dad adds.

I wipe the tears away and wipe my nose. "I'm at home. Nancy was waiting at the shop."

"Fuck her." Mom cuts in.

"Janette," Dad scolds her. "Let her talk first, and then we can bash that stupid witch."

I would laugh if it were under different circumstances, but just thinking what Nancy had done turns my stomach. The door to my bedroom slowly opens, and Silas approaches me, sinking to his knees in front of me. With a tight grip, he holds onto my knees.

I stare into his eyes and try to focus on this morning. "My shop is destroyed. From the little info Jace told me, they broke the windows to get inside. Trashed all the shelves and." I close my eyes, and

Silas tightens his grip. "And hauled the books out and lit them on fire." I clutch the edge of my mattress at the thought.

I think that's the worst part. They burnt my books. Jace wouldn't tell me who was involved. He didn't want to ruin Taylor's investigation and questioning with me. This entire thing goes beyond a threatening note to Nancy McCunt face. Now she's getting personal.

Mom starts crying, and I can hardly make out her question. "My God, Teagan. Are you okay? Are you hurt?"

"I'm okay or will be, eventually."

"Are you alone? I don't like the thought of you being in that house alone. What if they tried to do something." Dad's voice was calm, but there was an underlying urgency there.

I look at Silas. "I'm not alone, and I think Taylor should be stopping by sometime to ask questions. Jace wouldn't let him earlier."

"That's good. Small fry. If you want, we can come by."

"No, it's okay, Dad. I might try to take a nap. I'm exhausted."

"That's a good idea, hunny. Call if anything changes. We love you."

"I love you guys, too."

Silas and I sit there in silence. He rubs his thumb along my knee and reaches his other hand for mine, which is still clutching the mattress. He tenderly brings it to his mouth, gently laying a kiss on my knuckles.

"I'm proud of you. You did everything you could today. The shop doesn't define who you are; remember that. Don't let this stop who you are. You didn't let a little water damage stop you, right?"

"Yeah." I nod.

He stands up, pulling me with him. "Let me make you something to eat, and it'll make you feel better."

I can't help but laugh. Only Silas will be thinking about food. "There's leftover chow mein in the fridge."

"Dibs." He drags me out of my room. I can feel my mood lifting already, but I'm afraid he'll take the joy with him when he leaves. He's like a little kid when he opens the fridge and finds more food than expected. He pulls out the container of ribs and grins.

"When's the last time you ate?"

He shrugs. "I've been busy." He leaves it at that and grabs a plate. "Want some?"

"No, I'll find something, you enjoy." I open the fridge and grab the chow mein. I'm about to place it in the microwave when the doorbell rings. I turn to walk out when Silas grasps my arm and shakes his head.

"I'll get it. You stay here."

I watch as he peeks through the peephole, his shoulder dropping. He unlocks the door and opens it. Taylor stands there with his hand on his gun, looking ready to shoot up the place.

"Can I speak to Teagan, please?" Taylor looks at me with no expression on his face.

Silas doesn't move; he tilts his head, looking at me, eyes on mine, silently asking me if it's okay.

"It's Okay, Taylor. You can come in." Silas crosses his arms but still doesn't move far from the door. Taylor squeezes past him but doesn't move from the entryway.

"Can I ask you a few questions about today?" He pulls a notepad and pen from his jacket pocket, clicking the pen open.

"I'm sure you are dying to blame me somehow, so get on with your questioning, Taylor." I cross my arms and widen my stance. I'm not going down without a fight.

Taylor exhales, shaking his head. "It's going to be like this then. Okay fine. Where were you last night?"

"Here."

"Do you have an alibi?"

"Yes. Ben and Jerry."

He looks up from his pad. "Who?"

"Ice cream, Taylor. You would know this if you had a girlfriend. If you must know, it was chocolate flavour and to top it off I watched some true crime. And yes, I know how to hide a body."

"Can anyone collaborate on this?"

"I can," Silas says.

Taylor turns to Silas. "And you are?"

"Her boyfriend. Silas Blackwell. We were here all night, eating ice cream, watching true crime, and then I fucked her on the couch. Any other questions?"

My face heats up; I can't believe he would lie to a cop. Taylor looks at me, raising an eyebrow. Can he sniff out a lie?

"This morning, Teagan. What time did you arrive at The Dancing Goat Bookshop?"

"I arrived just before nine."

"And you went through the front door?"

"Jesus Christ, Taylor, you know I went through the back door. Cut the crap and tell me what Nancy and her minions did to my shop?"

"Listen, Teagan. I'm not here to start a fight. Only answers."

I rub my forehead. He's giving me a headache. I bet everything I owe, he's in Nancy's pocketbook. "Then ask the question you are dying to ask, Taylor.

Did I or Did I not provoke Nancy? That would be a no. When I arrived, she was waiting at the shop, and I turned around. I called Jace and asked if he could come down, and then I texted Silas, telling him I was scared. He called and talked with me through the entire thing. He heard when the windows broke, and that's when I called you. So, if you don't mind. Do your fucking job."

When Silas approaches me, he gently puts his arm around my shoulder and pulls me close to his side, making me feel safe and comforted.

"If you don't have any more questions, I think you're finished here," Silas tells Taylor.

Taylor tucks his pad and pen away. "Yeah, I'm done. I'll let you know the outcome of your shop." He turns and heads for the door. "And Teagan. I'm sorry about your shop." Silas walks behind him, closing the door and locking it.

I want this day to be over. What else can go wrong?

"Teagan, I need to talk to you."

And there it is.

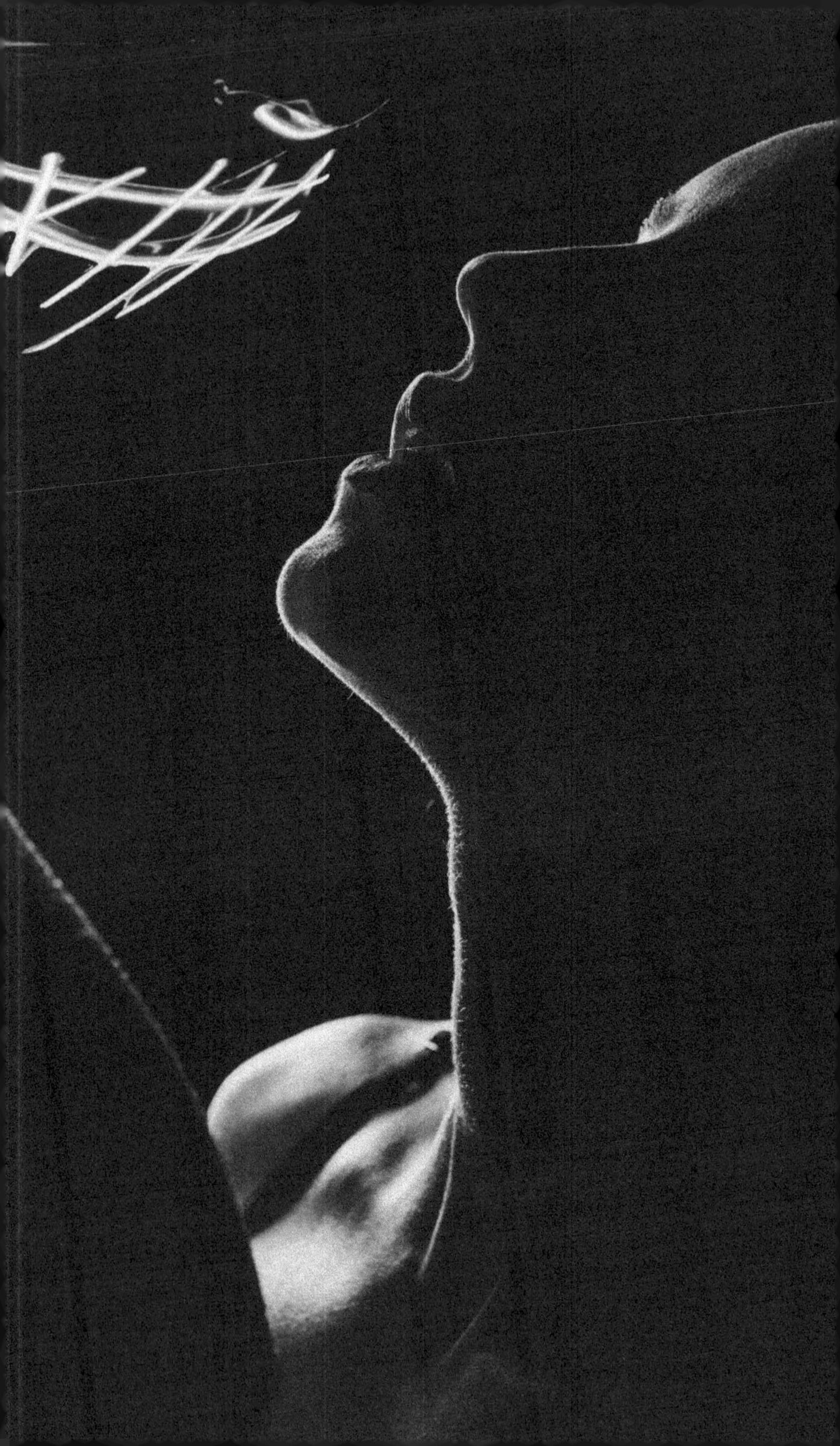

TWENTY-FIVE

SILAS

I won't be afraid to admit it when Teagan sent that text saying she was scared. So many scenarios ran through my mind, and I couldn't ignore her. The one thing I wasn't counting on was Teagan hiding for her life. All her hard work was destroyed in minutes, and no answers. And I should've been there for her, but I was too much of a coward.

At this point, I know I have to be honest with her, though I'm unsure how she will react. I'm prepared for the possibility that she may not want to see me again, and I understand if that's what she decides. I know I deserve it.

I guide Teagan to the couch; when we lock eyes, I see worry. I can't fault her, and I'm worried too. I wait for her to sit, and I shift to sit sideways.

"How bad is this talk, Silas? On a scale of one to ten?"

"A solid nine."

"Jesus Christ. I need a shot of whiskey. Today of all days, you want to break shit down." Leaning back, she rests her head against the couch's backrest. Covering her eyes with the heel of her palms. "Lay it out." She drops her hands, staring straight.

"You've asked about why I moved to Holden. It was to escape some shady people, but that didn't last long. I ended up back there anyway."

"Ended up where?" She tilts her head my way.

"The city," I quietly say.

Her eyebrows furrow, and I can tell she's thinking hard. "But you said you wanted to move to the city but ended up here."

"I left the city. I lived there my whole life and needed a change. I work for a guy named Leroy and have been since I moved out of my parent's house. He caught me one day trying to steal his car; since then, I've been stealing cars for him. I'm not proud of it. I tried to leave, and that's why I moved here, but your past has a way of never letting go."

I let her process everything before telling her the next lie I've been holding in. She slowly nods, closing her eyes and taking a deep breath.

"When you left the first time, is that where you went?"

"Yeah. It was only meant to be a quick job, but Leroy has a way of turning quick jobs into long, torturous ones. I wanted to tell you but didn't have an excuse."

"The truth would've been nice."

"I know, and I'm sorry about that; I just didn't want you to think I was a horrible person for stealing to make a living."

She grabs my hands. "Silas, I'm not a judgmental person. What you do to make a living is none of my business. Unless you kill or rape a person, then we have problems. Otherwise, I won't sit here and tell you what to do with your life. Do I wish you didn't have to do that? Yes, but I'm not going to say how disappointed I am. No one is perfect."

Well, fuck me. Only Teagan could pull the supportive card when I don't deserve it. I should've known she wouldn't judge, but in the back of my mind, that trust card kept flipping over and wouldn't settle.

"My trust issues get in the way, Teagan. I'm try-ing." She moves in for a hug, but I stop her. "I have something else to say, and this one might hurt."

She straightens up and faces me. This is gonna be hard. How do I tell the person that I'm falling for that I've been stalking them and fucked with and without the mask. She's going to hate me. I need to do it quickly, like pulling a band-aid off a hairy leg. I reach behind me and pull the mask that was left on the lawn from behind the pillow. I'm glad I arrived before her, but she never questioned how I got into her house before showing her the mask.

"Aren't you going to ask how I got into your house?"

Her face pales. "I was filled with so many emotions that I never clued in." I notice her hands trembling as I gently try to reach for the necklace hidden beneath her shirt.

I take the mask from behind me and gently place it in her lap, causing her body to tense up a bit. I pull the matching necklace from beneath my hoodie and watch tears fall instantly.

"The first moment I saw you, I wanted you, Tea-gan. But I was a coward; being the new person in town, I didn't know how to be me. So, I hide behind the mask. I didn't think you would like me for me, so I watched you from afar. Then I heard you telling

Elma to mind her business about me, and that was the first time in my life somebody had stood up for me. I've never had that before. But I didn't know if you were just doing it to be nice or because you liked me. So, I still hid behind the mask. And with each passing day, as I got to know you, I didn't know how to lose the mask and be myself around you; I didn't want you to hate me."

She drops her head back. "You didn't want to hurt me. You realize how stupid that sounds. You built this entire relationship on lies." Her gaze meets mine, her eyes cold and void of emotion. "How can I ever trust you? You took advantage of me and our friendship. Does that hold no value to you?"

"That wasn't my intention; I need you to know that. I hid because I didn't want you to know I was a failure."

Her eyes widen, and she touches her chest. "Oh, so this is about you?" And points to me.

I grind my teeth in frustration. "No."

"Then break it down for me because it seems like you're turning it around, so it's my fault now."

This argument isn't getting me anywhere, and how the fuck did we start fighting? I expected her to cry and scream at me to leave her house, not this.

"You're getting my words mixed up. I never once said it was your fault." She raises her hand, stopping me.

"I didn't want you to think I was a failure. That's damn near blaming me for you to be acting like a coward, Silas. It's not my fault that you aren't brave enough to get your shit together and be the person that you are. You could've ended your stalking ways days after we met; you fucked me in the cornfield a fucking week ago," she yells. "How do you think that makes me feel? Do you have any idea how scared I've been knowing there's been someone follow-ing me around? And here it's been you this whole time, and you acted unfazed during the day when we hung out." She moves across the couch, curling her knees into her chest. "Oh my god. You fucking followed me after I left your place to the park," she softly murmurs, resting her head on her knees.

I stand and head to the window, drawing the cur-tain open. "The first time I broke into your house was shortly after I saw you. I laid in your bed, and all I could smell was you, Teagan. It sounds weird, but I think you were meant for me." I take the chance and glance at her. Her face is still resting on her knees, but she's watching me with tears streaming down her face.

"How many times have you broken into my house, Silas?"

"Three."

She closes her eyes and nods. I can't tell her the second time was the first time I slid my fingers inside of her; she can forever think it was a dream. I can't ruin all of her trust in me, and I'm already a piece of shit; I can't sink much lower.

"Say something, Dimples. Please."

She reaches for her necklace, and my heart stutters. "Silas, I truly liked you, but I'm unsure if we can fix this. You destroyed all my trust in you. How do you expect me to ever believe you again? Do I want to know how you filled this necklace?"

"It was the night we slept together here before I left you the second time." I reach for my necklace. "I always wanted you close to my heart, no matter where I went, and I wished to be next to yours, too."

"I'm not sure about this anymore. I think you should go."

And there it is. The words I've been dreading this entire conversation. "Please, Teagan, can we try to work this out?"

"I'm sorry, Silas, but I don't think I can think right now. You've thrown so much at me, and I need time."

I tuck my hand into my pocket, feeling like a beaten puppy. I realize I am to blame and understand the pain it has caused. It was a mistake on my part; I had hoped she would be understanding. Now that I think about it, why would she be? I stalked her, for Christ's sake and for what? It got us nowhere.

I walk toward her, kneeling in front of her. "No, Dimples. I'm sorry. My actions were thoughtless, and I see that now. I hope you can forgive me." I lean up, kissing her forehead. "Take care, Teagan."

I grab the mask and walk away for the third time. I feel like all I do is walk away from her. I head for my car, parked down the block. It doesn't feel right to leave her alone after what happened today. I turn my car around and park outside her house; I don't care if she calls the cops on my ass. No one is getting to her.

I don't care what Leroy says; we need to fix Teagan's problem with Nancy. Grabbing my burner phone, I dial Leroy. And my call goes unanswered. Why am I not surprised. I'm tempted to do this by myself. I need to figure out who was involved with today's act and go from there. They all need to pay for what they did. I want my hands on Nancy's Land Rover, not that it would matter; she'll only go out and buy a new one. I need to hit her where it hurts the most. Her reputation, someone in this town, has to have dirt on her. But the question is, who?

The other question is, who in this town will talk to me to try to knock that cunt off her throne. I've been an outcast since I moved here; no one has spoken to me. Then again, I didn't go out of my way to talk to anyone either.

The only person I can think about is the shit goblin. Do I want to ask him? She's probably already called him and told him what a horrible person I am. Now that I think about it, there is one other person.

And I don't like it either.

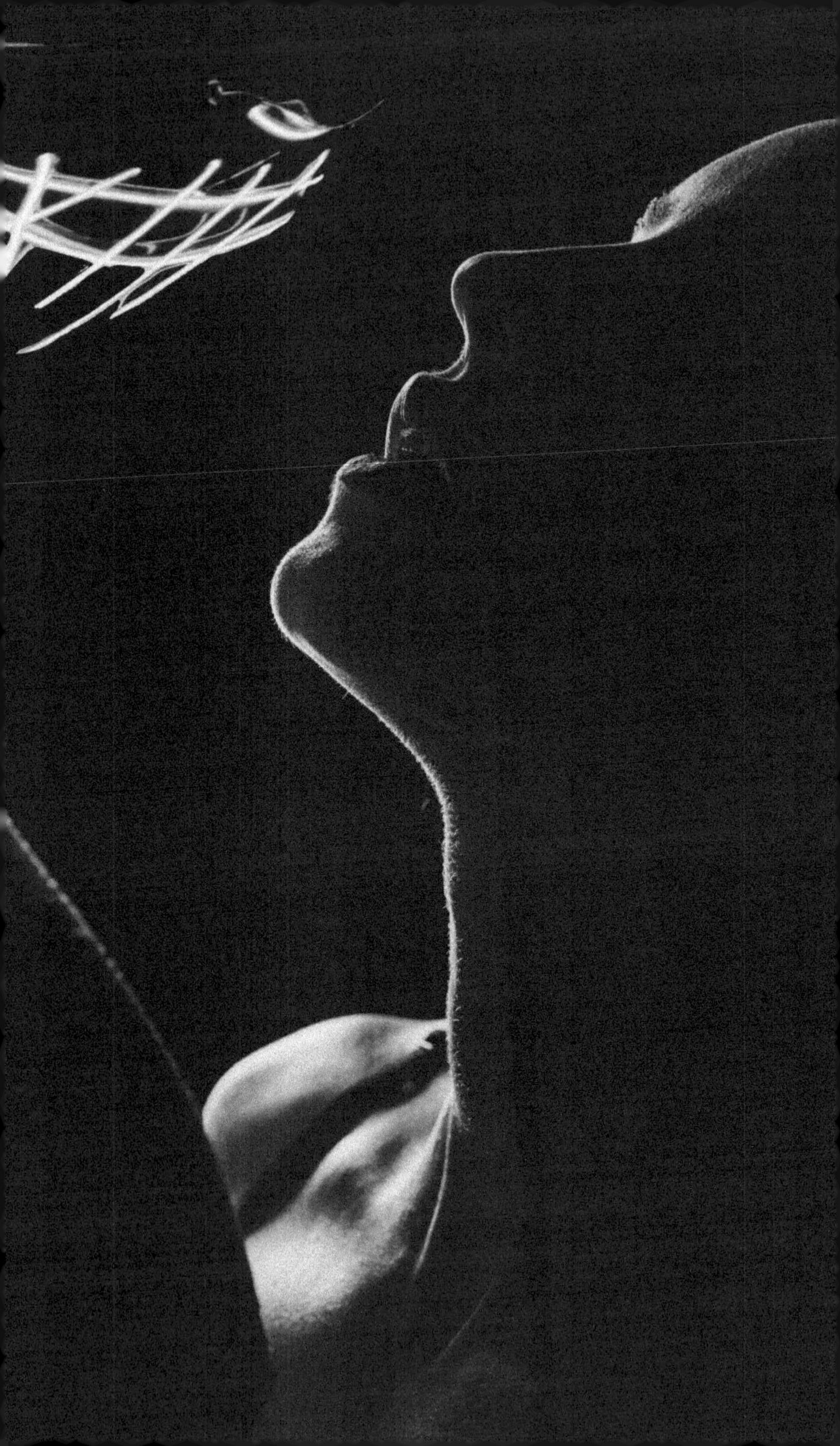

TWENTY-SIX

TEAGAN

I'm at a loss for words.

A double identity wasn't what I expected to hear from Silas. I never kept secrets from him. He, on the other hand, kept a ton from me. I just wanted him to be honest with me, but he couldn't do that until he felt guilty. It makes me wonder if he did it because he felt bad for me or him. That guilty conscience finally caught up to him.

I'm left picking my broken heart up off the floor, wondering if I'll be able to forgive him, maybe, eventually, but it will take me some time. I don't think I'll be able to fully trust him again. I'll always believe in the depths of my soul that whatever he says is a lie. The thing about trust is once it's broken, it'll take time to heal, and even once it's healed, you'll never fully trust in that thing again. Because in the forefront, you'll wonder if it'll betray you again like it did in the past.

I head back into the kitchen, and the ribs that Silas was excited to have are still sitting on the counter. I open the container and toss it in the garbage. I won't be able to eat them without picturing his stupid grin now. I place my food back in the fridge; my appetite is officially gone.

The silence of the house is tormenting me. I'm not feeling like being by myself, but I also don't want any company right now. It's a vicious circle, one that I probably won't break. I never told Jace about Silas; the only one who knew was Ivory. She told me he might be afraid to be judged for his past, but this isn't about his past. This is a whole new ball game. He lied to me about a secret identity.

I walk around the house, checking every lock. I suddenly felt that familiar sense of paranoia creeping back in. I can't tell if it's because of Silas or the events of earlier today. I can only hope nothing else happens for the rest of the day.

I grab a thing of ice cream and a spoon and head to the bathroom. I could use some relaxation right now, and a nice hot bath sounds like the perfect way to unwind without resorting to alcohol. Setting my ice cream on the counter, I turn the water on until it's the right temperature and add the plug. I watch the water start to fill, wondering if I missed the signs when I was with Silas dressed up in the mask. He spoke to me, but I never picked up that it was him.

As I slip out of my clothes, I reach for my ice cream and spoon before settling into the tub. The hot water welcomes me as I sink in, allowing all my worries to melt away or at least try to melt away. The more I lay here, the more my mind wonders about every interaction. Nothing gave away that stalker boy, and Silas were the same person. Silas had a hint of woodsy scent, and the stalker boy wasn't into cologne.

Nothing adds up. He hid it so well.

I wake up in a drenched sweat; having a nightmare is not how I want to wake up for the day. It's bad enough that I was in my shop yesterday during the ordeal, but now it's haunting me. Even though I despise it, I need to inspect the shop and assess the extent of the damage. But the thought of going alone spikes my blood. I can't always rely on my parents, and I can't bear seeing their faces when they see the damage—not knowing how excited they were when I opened it.

It's either Jace or Ivory. I know Jace is my best friend, but he has a life and a job, and I can't keep relying on him. Ivory is too good-hearted to be placed in that situation, which would crush her to see everything. The only thing left is to bite the bullet and go alone; it's my sole responsibility, and I should do it alone. I can't always rely on other people.

When I step outside, I first notice an old, rusted minivan parked outside my place. As I get closer, I see Silas fast asleep in the driver's seat. Of course, he wouldn't leave me alone. I didn't ask for much, just space and he couldn't even listen to that. As much as I want to bang on the window and scare him, I walk away. Who's to say he wouldn't follow me if he were awake?

The walk to the shop feels different from any other time, and nothing brings me joy. I had a ton of ideas lined up for this month at the shop, but now they'll never happen. Nancy stole my dreams yesterday; now I'm unsure what to do. As the shop draws nearer, my anxiety starts to creep up, and I find myself imagining the worst-case scenario so I won't be caught off guard.

I feel my hands trembling as I near the corner, my heart picking up the pace. The thought of any surprises makes me anxious. With a deep breath, I push myself to take that final step and make the turn. My eyes tear up when I see Dad and John standing outside my shop. Every window, including the door, is covered in plywood.

John nods to me when he sees me approaching. When Dad turns to me, it's clear how upset he is.

"Small fry. What are you doing here?" He pulls me in for a hug. "I'm sorry about the shop," he whispers next to my ear.

"Thanks, Dad. I came to check on the place, but I see you two beat me here."

"Jace called and asked if I could help, and in return, I called John. Have you seen inside yet?"

I face the front of the shop, and my heart sinks. It looks like an abandoned shop that no one wants. It doesn't exactly shout, 'I'm a bookshop!' Maybe it should team up with the record store next door and form a support group for run down shops.

"We can head inside if you want. We can't touch anything since it's an ongoing investigation." John holds the door open, Dad heads in first, and I hang back. "It's okay to be nervous, Teagan. But the fears must be met, or they'll never disappear. Do not fear what has passed; as old leaves fall, they create space for new growth. This tree is yours, Teagan. Time to make it flourish once more."

I absorb his words. He's right. We rebuilt it once we could do it again. But what if the same thing happens again?

"I'm scared, John."

"Of what? Going inside?"

My gaze shifts beyond the door, where fragments of bookshelves lie strewn across the floor. "What if this happens again, this last month has been shit, John. I can't handle any more heartbreak."

He grips my shoulder. "I understand that, and I promise it'll get easier."

I want to believe him, but it's hard. I don't have any faith that everyone will be caught, Nancy won't be punished for this, and I'll be blamed still. I take a deep breath and step inside. Now, I wish Jace had given me a little heads-up. The entire place is destroyed. Nothing is left untouched; even the computer is smashed on the floor. The floor is strewn with torn pages from books, while the bookshelves appear to have been brutally attacked with axes.

Dad comes by my side and wraps his arm around my shoulders. "Any word from the cops?"

I scoff. "Taylor came by yesterday, and from his questions, he made it sound like I was the problem. I don't have much faith in him."

"Neither do I. You should call your lawyer and tell him what happened. I don't want any of this coming back on you. This is bullshit; maybe I should talk to Nancy and finally hash it out with her."

I rest my head on his shoulder. "I've always wondered why she had her radar set on me, not that I blame you, Dad, but I swear if you started something and this is the outcome, I'm going to be pissed."

"Yeah, you're gonna be pissed."

I had a feeling it had something to do with Dad. Shit rolls downhill and now I have to deal with it all. If I knew talking to Nancy wouldn't work against me, I would be demanding answers. With my luck, Taylor follows her around like a dog in heat. Maybe I should call Sam and see what he says. Nancy attacked, which goes beyond a threatening note.

"I think I've seen enough. Thanks again for being here."

"Anything for you, Small fry. Want me to drive you home?" He guides me to the door, but John is blocking it. "What's wrong?" Dad shuffles me behind him.

He speaks over his shoulder. "There's an SUV parked out front, and the driver is just watching the shop. They haven't moved in minutes. I'm not sure who they are."

"I'm gonna say someone that's with Nancy, this is bullshit. What would happen if you came down, and we weren't here?"

I don't want to think about that. If I think about it, my mind will wonder where it shouldn't be, and I'll never want to leave my house until all of this is wrapped up. I know whoever is outside is with Nancy; she sent them to scare me. Obviously, she didn't get what she wanted out of yesterday, and I'm the unfinished business.

"Want me to scare them?" John asks.

Dad moves next to John, making his presence known. If having two tall, muscular guys standing there doesn't intimidate you, I'm not sure what will. The sound of the engine revving in reverse and the tires squealing as they drive off is music to my ears.

"I'll drive you home," Dad says, tension laced in his voice.

There's so much I want to say, but I can't think of the words. Because what can you say to one of the people that can be responsible for all the shit that is going wrong, I don't think Dad ever intended for any of this to happen. I don't think he knew it could turn out like this. Whatever issue Nancy and Dad have, they need to figure it out because it's officially getting dangerous. Getting Nancy to listen can be a bit of a challenge; she's on a war path, and I seem to be in her crosshairs.

Rounding the street to my house, I feel my heart leap up my throat when I see a minivan parked out front of my home. I forgot all about Silas parked out front. Doesn't he have to eat or take a piss? He can't seriously stay here all the time.

Dad pulls into my small driveway and glares at Silas. "Who's the soccer mom?"

I laugh. He's not wrong. I mean, name one other male who drives around in a minivan. "That would be Silas."

"Why is he parked out front, and why didn't he go with you this morning?"

"That's a long story, one I don't feel like getting into at this second."

He turns to me. "If he somehow hurt you, you let me know, and I'll tune the fucker in."

"Of that, I am certain. Silas? Please, he's a piece of cake for me to deal with."

Dad laughs, hitting the steering wheel. "I taught you well."

I give him a quick hug and hop out of the truck, and I don't even look toward Silas as I make my way to the front door. He doesn't deserve my time. I have to keep moving forward; there's no space for him in my life anymore. I've got to tackle one mess at a time, and Silas is right at the bottom of that list.

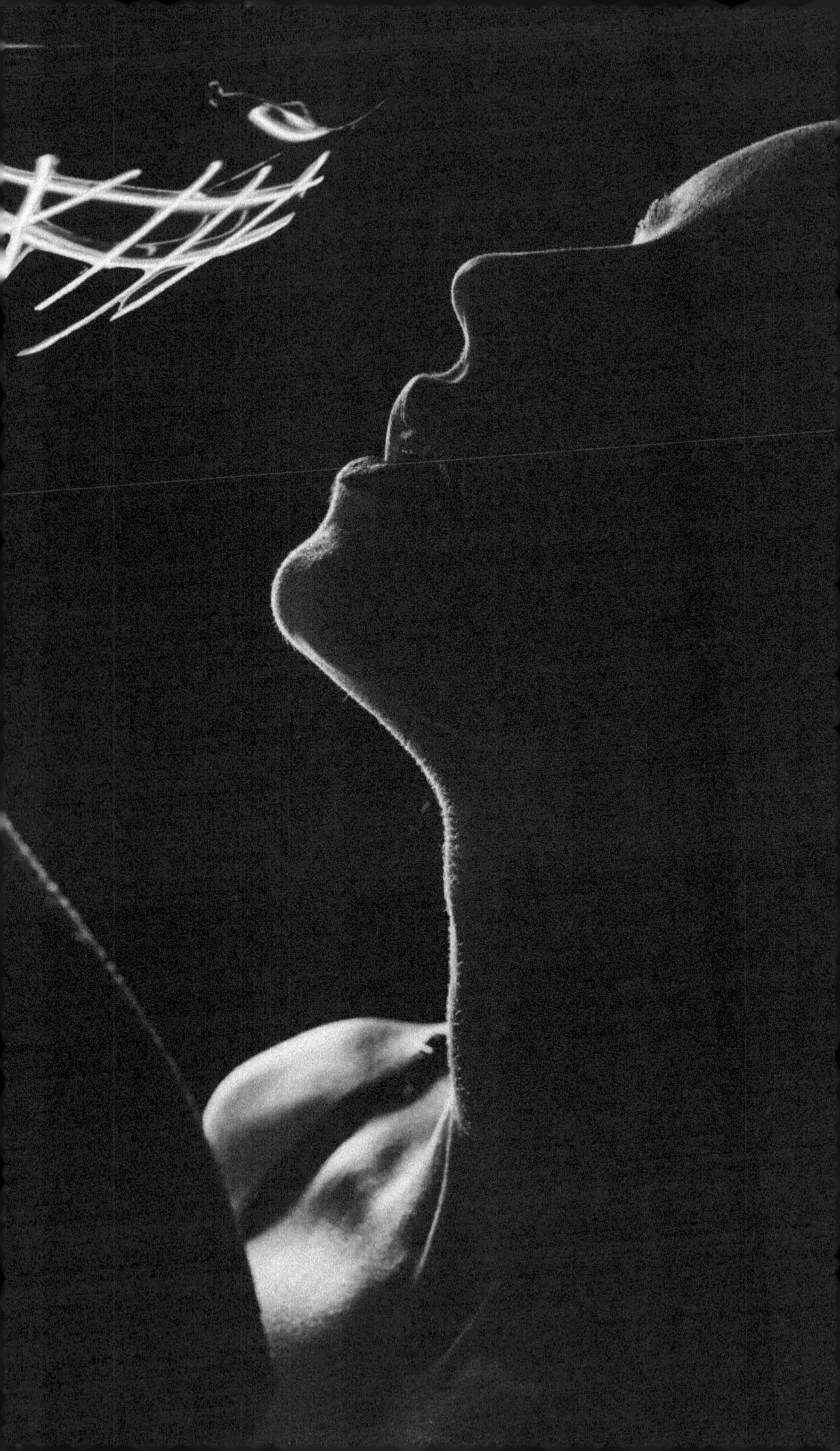

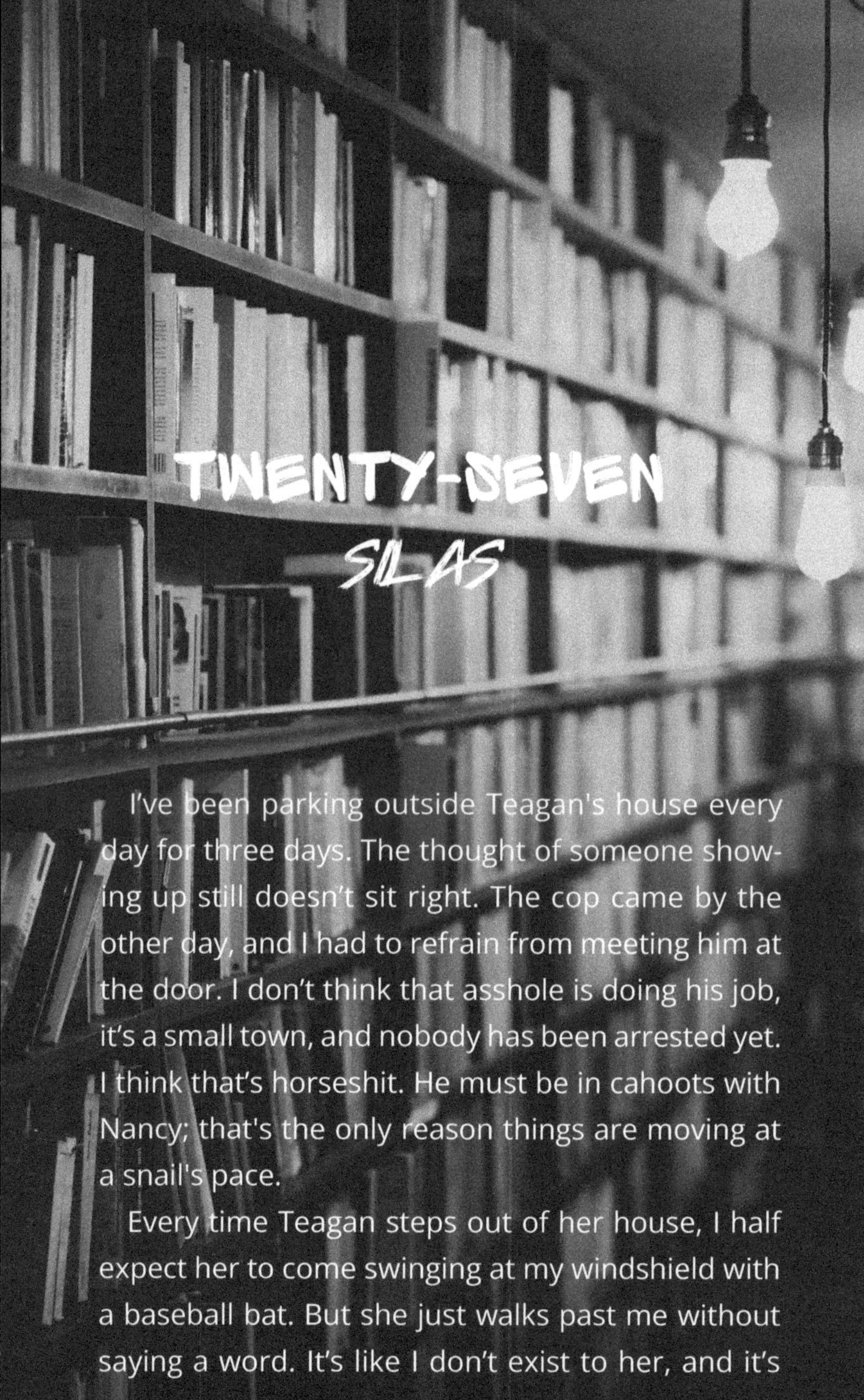

TWENTY-SEVEN

SILAS

I've been parking outside Teagan's house every day for three days. The thought of someone showing up still doesn't sit right. The cop came by the other day, and I had to refrain from meeting him at the door. I don't think that asshole is doing his job, it's a small town, and nobody has been arrested yet. I think that's horseshit. He must be in cahoots with Nancy; that's the only reason things are moving at a snail's pace.

Every time Teagan steps out of her house, I half expect her to come swinging at my windshield with a baseball bat. But she just walks past me without saying a word. It's like I don't exist to her, and it's the worst feeling in the world. But I'll take it; it's my punishment.

I've been trying to find a way to talk to the one person I've been dreading, and I'm not sure I trust them. With the way the rumour mill circles, it won't take long before everyone knows what I've been up to. I need to play my cards right. Leroy and some guys plan to crash at my place when they roll into town tonight. It would be a bit of a stretch to say I'm psyched about it, but it'll be easier to plan, so I shouldn't complain.

When a white Range Rover approaches Teagan's house it causes, the hairs on my neck rise. Only one family in this town drives Range Rovers—the Montgomery's. The SUV parks across from her house, and I blindly reach for the crowbar on the passenger seat, never taking my eyes off the car. When they don't move for five minutes, I text Teagan.

Me: Don't open the door no matter what you hear.

Stepping out of my car, I grab the crowbar and casually walk towards the vehicle. The thought that things could go awry hasn't even crossed my mind. Tapping on the driver's window, they ignore me. I tap again.

"I only wanna talk; roll it down."

The window moves an inch, not enough to see who's behind the wheel, which only irritates me. My grip tightens on the bar.

"That's all your getting, who the fuck are you?" The prick behind the wheel asks.

I laugh because this guy thinks he is a hotshot. "Well, considering you're parked outside my girl's place, I'll do the questioning. Which Montgomery are you?"

"Why does it matter to you?"

I tap the crowbar on his window. "It fuckin' matters. Answer the question before I smash the window in."

"Blaine, the son."

That explains the attitude. I see that the apple doesn't fall far from the tree. Spoiled breeds spoiled.

"Why are you lurking around here? I highly doubt it's for a casual chat over milk and cookies. Did your mommy send you on a spying mission so you can feel like James Bond?"

He rolls the window down, and I get a look at him. His golden locks so slicked back with gel, that not even a hurricane could mess them up. And don't get me started on his tan cable knit sweater and cream tailor pants. They speak volumes.

"Don't fucking talk to me that way. Do you know who I am?"

I shrug. "Nah, and I don't care. When you start lurking like a fucking creep, you don't get to ask questions." I run my crowbar along his door. "Either you leave with this car intact, or" I step back and swing. The bar hits the passenger door with a loud crunching sound.

Blaine swings his door open, jumping out. "What the fuck!" he yells, touching the fresh dent in his precious car. "You'll pay for that."

"I doubt that. Tell me why you're here, or I'll do it again." I move closer to him, stopping inches from his chest. When he doesn't speak, I back up and move to the front of his car. It would be a shame if those headlights broke. I swing back.

"Whoa, wait, I'll tell you."

I drop my arm and stare at him. "Speak."

"My mother sent me over to give Teagan a scare. She doesn't want her reopening a business in town."

"Why?" I'm trying not to lose my temper, but the more this asshole talks, the more I can feel it bubbling over.

"Something about family issues, it's been going on for years. I never asked, and I only do what she tells me."

Family issues, are you kidding me? She's taking shit out on Teagan cause she can't be a grownup and talk about her problems. I slam the crowbar into the headlight, watching plastic pieces wash over the pavement. Blaine jumps at me, throwing a punch towards my face, connecting with my mouth.

"You asshole." He huffs.

The metallic flavour of blood grazes my tongue. I deliver a powerful blow to his stomach, causing him to double over in pain, coughing uncontrollably. I take the chance to destroy his other headlight.

"Don't ever come back here again, or it won't be the car that gets hit with the crowbar next."

"You'll pay for this." He holds his stomach as he walks to his door. "Mark my word."

"I'm not scared of you or your family."

He slams the door, and I step back as he peels away. I touch my lip, feeling the puffiness settling in. I'll admit it was exciting to be in a fight; it was too bad it didn't last long. I head back to my car, still not knowing the reason behind Nancy and her hatred. Besides family issues. With Teagan's family? I need answers. I ignore, looking at her house as I climb back into my car.

I grab my phone to let Leroy know we need to move tonight but my phone is blown up with messages from Teagan.

Teagan: What's going on?

Teagan: Silas answer me, who is outside? Why do you have a weapon?

Teagan: What the fuck is Blaine doing here?

Teagan: If you don't answer I'm coming out, this is bullshit. This isn't your fight you aren't even meant to be around me anymore. I don't need a babysitter. I asked for space and you can't even do that, I feel suffocated still. I think it's time for you to leave.

I knew my time would come to an end here. And Teagan's right. I need to give her space to think; she can't do that with me hanging around all the time. She'll only hate me more. I'm sure with the scare I gave Blaine, Nancy will think twice about sending anyone else over here. I start the car and head off back to my house. I'll admit it'll be nice to stretch out; my ass was getting sore from this horrible seat.

After dinner, three knocks came on the door, a brief pause, and another knock. There's only one person who knocks like that—Leroy. He started knocking like that so no one would shoot him; he might be a little paranoid. I put my vodka on the coffee table and move to the door. I open the door and find Leroy, Buck, Griff and Weldon, each holding a duffle bag.

"It looks like you guys are ready for a fucking sleepover." I tease.

Leroy steps forward. "If any of you pricks cuddle with me, I'll shoot you."

Buck laughs, swinging his bag over his shoulder. "Don't be like that, L. You love my big muscles wrapped around your body." He walks past me, patting me on the shoulder.

Buck is a giant compared to me in both directions. His shirt has probably ripped every stitch in its sleeve, trying to hang onto his biceps. But he's a teddy bear deep down.

Griff rolls his eye and shoves his way into the house; I was never a fan of his. His ego is the size of Russia, and I would love to knock it down a peg or two. Maybe I'll be the reason why he loses his other eye.

"Silas, my man." Weldon pulls me in for a hug and slaps my back. "It's been a while, keeping out of trouble?"

I lick my lip and laugh. "Sure, if you call smashing up a Rover with a crowbar keeping out of trouble."

He throws his head back and barks out a deep laugh. "And this is why I love having you around, you and that impulsiveness. Come, brother, we have so much to catch up on."

My house has never been this full before, and I'm unsure how I feel about it. I'm not used to so many people around all at once, but I need to remind myself that I'm doing all of this for Teagan. She needs the help even if she doesn't know it. I can't let what happened today or to her shop happen again, and if she hates me more after, I'm willing to take that.

"Silas, what's the plan?" Leroy asks as he tosses his bag to the floor and falls on the couch, kicking his feet up on the coffee table.

Buck and Griff follow his lead while Wel stands by the front window.

"That's what we need to discuss. I had a run-in with the bitches brat today."

Griff points to his lip. "That would explain the new look."

"I wasn't expecting a preppy asshole to be swinging at me. Let alone showing up at my girl's house to do his mommy's work. I swear this bitch is like a cockroach. No one in this town will deal with her."

"Don't worry, we'll deal with the cunt." Buck grins. "I'm not afraid to hit a woman if she has it coming."

"I have someone to talk to first, but she loves to spread rumours around town, and with all of you guys here, her lips will be moving a mile a minute now. We need to find her fast."

I'm not looking forward to talking to Elma, but she's the only one who would have all the information on everyone in this town, including Nancy and this so-called family drama.

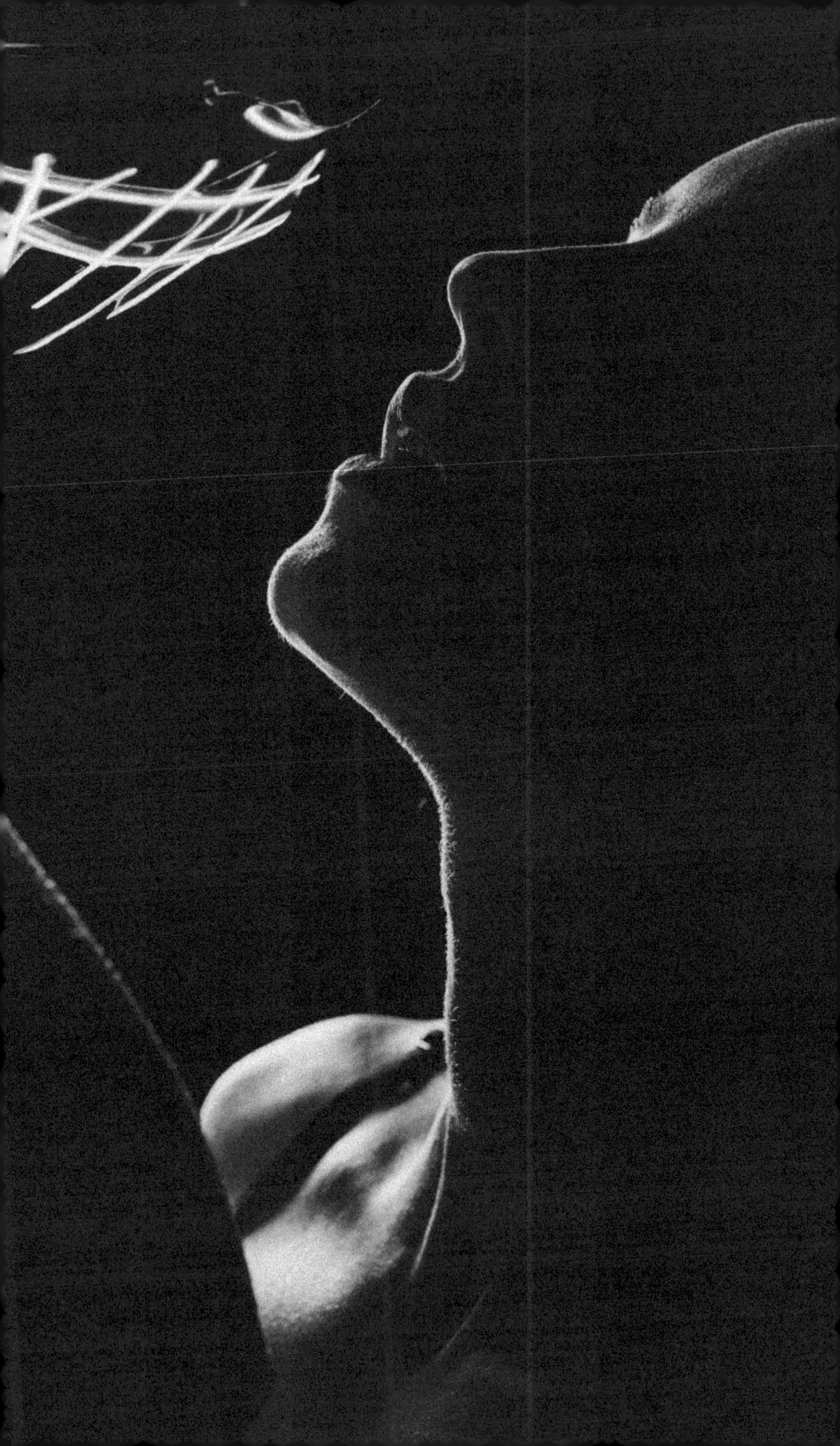

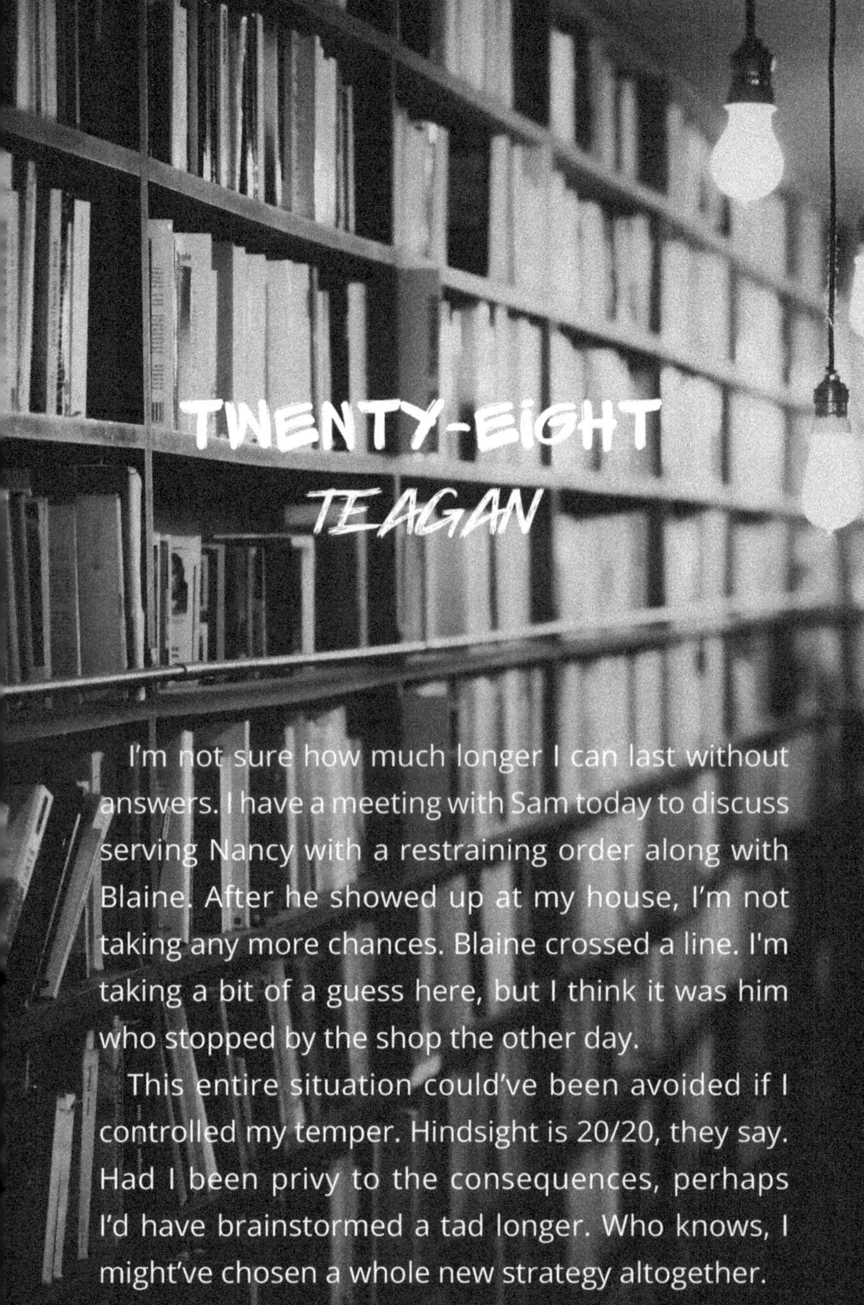

TWENTY-EIGHT
TEAGAN

I'm not sure how much longer I can last without answers. I have a meeting with Sam today to discuss serving Nancy with a restraining order along with Blaine. After he showed up at my house, I'm not taking any more chances. Blaine crossed a line. I'm taking a bit of a guess here, but I think it was him who stopped by the shop the other day.

This entire situation could've been avoided if I controlled my temper. Hindsight is 20/20, they say. Had I been privy to the consequences, perhaps I'd have brainstormed a tad longer. Who knows, I might've chosen a whole new strategy altogether.

Like burning her fucking house down.

I need to keep myself busy, or my mind will wander to Silas. I've been trying hard to forget about him, but it's more complicated than I thought. I grab the necklace that I hid behind my sweater. I didn't have the heart to take it off. I have to stop myself from reaching for my phone to text him; I'm the one who told him to leave me. It's just one of those things, the heart wants what it wants, and I gotta resist the urge.

There's no need for me to feel bad about not speaking to him. He's the one who caused this mess, so why should I be the one carrying the guilt? Does he even feel anything at all? Did he sit outside of my house to torment me? These are the things that irritate me. My brain can't stop overthinking.

Sam emerges from the back office and smiles at me. "Ready?"

"No, but I don't have a choice."

I follow him to a small room with only a table and chair. "This should be quick. I'll go over the paperwork and take it to the police station for you. Since you witnessed Nancy at your business, we can restrain her from going one hundred feet from you and explain what happened with Blaine."

"He showed up at my house, and I'm sure he was at my shop when I was there with Dad and John just watching us."

"But he didn't do anything to inflict harm?"

"No," I slowly say.

He writes a few things down on his legal pad. "That might be an issue; once he does, we can take the next step, but until then, there isn't anything we can do. I've been in contact with Taylor, and he still doesn't have any suspects arrested, and if I'm being frank, I think he's full of shit when he says that. It's a small town, Teagan. He knows who did it."

"I was afraid of that. No one is going to pay for what they did. What am I supposed to do in the meantime?"

Sam drops his pen and folds his hands. "Honestly, Teagan. I'm not sure. If the cops won't do anything, there isn't anything I can do. I'm only a lawyer. Law enforcement is where I draw the line."

"Awesome. Now I have to keep an eye out because this town can't seem to get their act together with the police. How fun."

"I'm sorry. But the bright side, Nancy will be off your back."

I give him the thumbs up. "Go me."

I leave his office the same as last time, hopeless. Why is it so hard to get what I want? A restraining order on Nancy isn't going to do shit when she can send her preppy ass son to do her dirty work. They can both go to hell if they think I'm going down without a fight.

I take a slight detour home, I'm back to being nothing without my shop. I need to find a hobby to pass the time away. But in the meantime, I'll take up this hobby. I park down the street between two cars, trying my hardest to blend in. I lean my seat back, trying to make it less noticeable.

City Hall is busy today, and I never realized how many people need to come here. Did I have to come here today? Yes. Inside? No. I keep thinking about it and I'm starting to feel like a bit of a stalker myself. The thing I bitched Silas out for. But it's not the same thing, Nancy threatened my life, and Silas lied to me.

As I start to doze off, a white Rover squeals into the employee parking area. How convenient that Blaine would choose this time to visit mommy. He sure got his fancy SUV fixed quickly, I guess when you have money, you can do almost anything, even throw a hissy when you didn't get picked to become the new chief of the fire department. I'm still pissed about that.

Jace should be riding that wave.

Instead, they voted for another chief, one that Blaine approved of. I have no idea why Blaine is even in the fire department. He's the worst firefighter, no one wants to work with him. I would feel bad if he wasn't such an asshole. I knew I should've beat him up in school when I had the chance. That would've given the Montgomery family something to fight over.

I honestly don't even know why I'm sitting here, what will I accomplish, that they both are in the same building. This should be when I'm out enjoying myself. But no, my little brain wants to see them together for some strange reason. I want to see Nancy, the evil look on her face. I can feel myself becoming completely fixated on her; honestly, I don't even recognize myself anymore.

I need to get the fuck out of here before I can't escape, this isn't healthy. I need to trust that Sam will do what he needs to do, but it's everyone else that I don't trust. Who am I supposed to call when something happens again? It's not the cops, and they could turn everything around and blame it on me. If either Blaine or Nancy catches me here, I'll be in trouble even though it's a public building.

I readjust my seat and start the car. I have one other detour to make. This one is the stupidest one to make. Silas lives on a quiet street, and I'll never know why I feel the need to check up on him. Perhaps the mere act of sporting his blood like a fashion accessory is magically transforming me into a mini version of him, complete with his creepy stalker tendencies.

His house comes into view, and it looks like a party house. I pull over to stare at vehicles that are parked in front of his house. I don't understand how he could have so many people over; not once did he mention friends when he was around me. He has the nerve to celebrate having hurting me. Unreal.

I observe a beefed-up dude with muscles for days strut out of the door. He stands on the steps and lights a smoke. He scans the neighbourhood and then spots my car. My body lowers in the seat involuntarily when he walks toward me. Being here wasn't the brightest idea, then again, I wasn't expecting Hercules to come storming across the street.

He taps on my window with his knuckles and points down. "Roll down the window, miss." His deep voice vibrates inside the car.

I open the window about an inch. I don't know this guy hells if I'm opening it all the way. He chuckles and shakes his head. "You know, if I wanted to get inside the car, I could always force my way in."

Fuck, he has a point. I roll it down, and he leans in, folding his arms on the door and grins.

"Can I help you?" I ask, leaning away from him.

"I think that's my line. Wanna tell me why you're stalking houses?" He raises a dark brow.

I touch my chest and fake shock. "I'm not stalking. Who would do such a thing?"

"You. Spill it, what did my boy do to you?"

So he is one of Silas' friends. Or is this a work friend? Does he also steal cars? I have so many questions I want to ask.

"I'm not saying anything to you. I don't even know you. Why would I bare my soul to you?"

He shrugs; his muscles tighten when he does. "I've been told I'm a good listener. And if he did anything to hurt you, I won't stand for it."

I bite my lip. The urge to tell him everything that has happened is on the tip of my tongue. Does he even care that his so-called friend duped me into believing that he was a good guy, but in the end, he's nothing but a lying dirtbag?

"Sugar, it's okay. Silas is a hard guy to understand. Believe me, I've known him for years, and he still doesn't open up to me. He didn't have an easy life, and his trust in others doesn't come easy. But if he hurt you, I need to know."

I stare at Silas' house, wondering where he is inside. "He didn't hurt me physically." I turn to look at Hercules. "But he destroyed me. I trusted him, and he threw it all away for what? I don't understand why he would do it."

"What did he do?" his voice drops low.

"He pretended to be someone he wasn't. Silas had so many chances to come clean and never took it. Why hide? He took advantage of me, and I looked like an idiot."

He drops his head. "Fuckin' idiot," he mumbles. He looks back at me. "The mask?"

"Yeah, how'd you know?"

"He's been hiding behind that thing for years; it's almost like his security blanket when he meets someone new. But he doesn't know how to take it off. He's been scared to be his true self, and I'm afraid he no longer knows how. But I promise, Sugar. He's in that house, and all he talks about is you and how he fucked it up. You're the first one who has really seen him for who he is and never once tried to pressure him for more than he was willing to offer."

I'm at a loss for words. If Silas had been upfront, all of this could've been avoided. His friend shouldn't be the one that has to explain it. Why can't I hear this from Silas?

"It's not fair, that's all."

"I know it's not, but I promise it'll get easier."

"How are you such a wise one on relationships?"

He shakes his head. "I've been through my share of heartache and learnt my lessons many times over. But I've never got a second chance."

"If you were to have a second chance, would you take it?"

"In a heartbeat, Sugar."

His words sink in, but I'm not ready to forgive Silas yet. Maybe someday I'll be ready to try again, but not yet.

"I should get going. My stalker days are finished."

"Did you get everything you needed?"

"I guess. You can tell Silas Blaine fixed his Rover, so maybe you should cause the damage next time."

He laughs, backing away. "I'll do that, just for you. Take care."

The drive home isn't long enough to think about, but Hercules gave me a lot to think about. But I still have other things to worry about before I forgive Silas.

Like the asshole that is parked in my driveway.

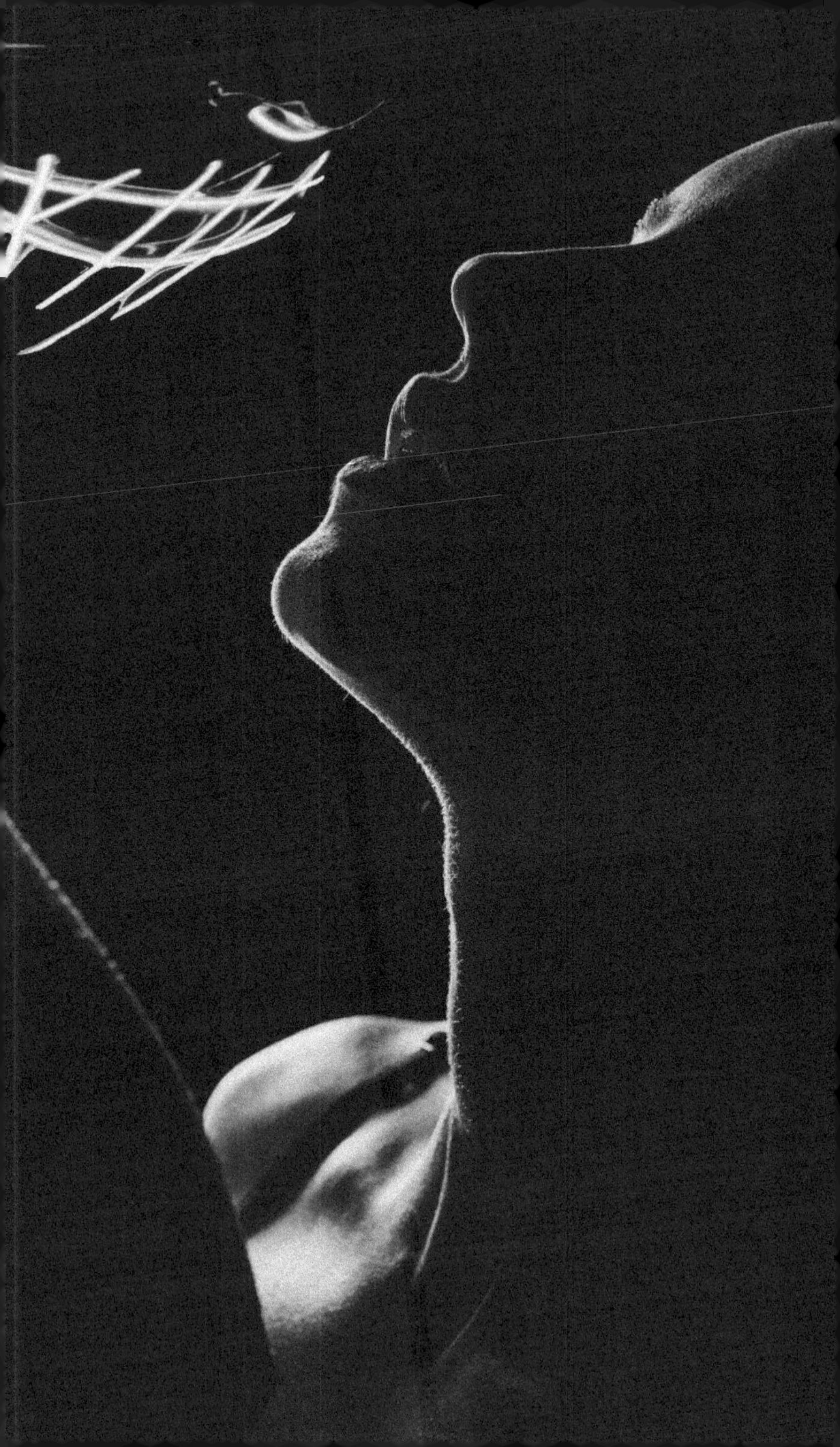

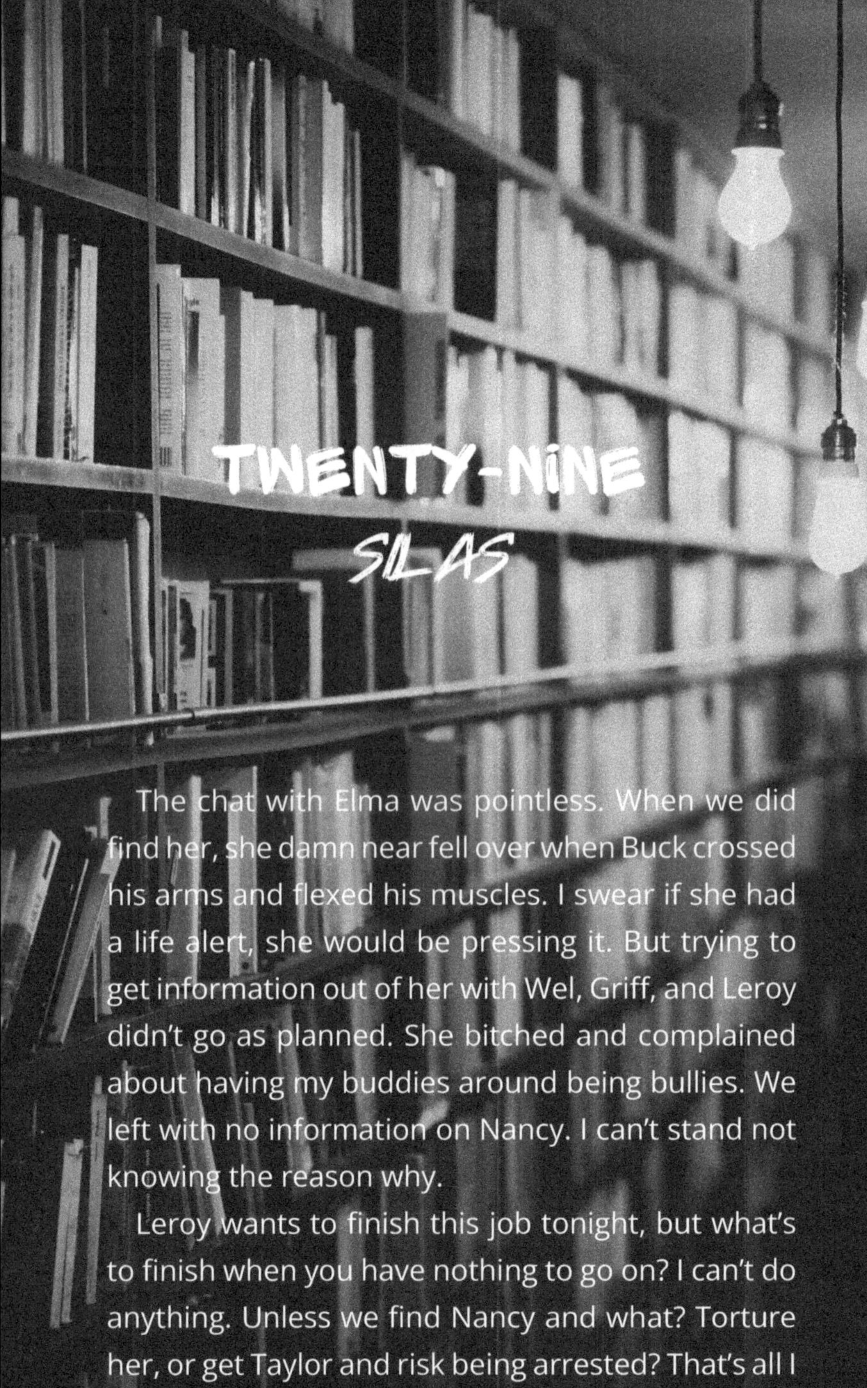

TWENTY-NINE

SILAS

The chat with Elma was pointless. When we did find her, she damn near fell over when Buck crossed his arms and flexed his muscles. I swear if she had a life alert, she would be pressing it. But trying to get information out of her with Wel, Griff, and Leroy didn't go as planned. She bitched and complained about having my buddies around being bullies. We left with no information on Nancy. I can't stand not knowing the reason why.

Leroy wants to finish this job tonight, but what's to finish when you have nothing to go on? I can't do anything. Unless we find Nancy and what? Torture her, or get Taylor and risk being arrested? That's all I can think of for a plan, and I'm leaning toward Taylor because the cunt isn't doing his job.

Buck comes storming back into the house and points at me.

"You fuckin' idiot, you ruined it, didn't you?"

Griff and Wel stare at him, then at me. "I didn't do shit, we're still planning."

"Not this, with her. How could you fuck it up?"

I've never seen Buck so worked up before. How the hell did he talk to Teagan? "Was she here?" I turn to the front window.

"She was, she's gone now. Looks like your stalking ways have rubbed off on her."

I closed my eyes, feeling ashamed. They must've had a decent talk. Buck and his big mouth. "What did you say to her?"

"Nothing that she shouldn't have known from the beginning. I can't believe you, Silas. You're a grown-ass man. Why are you lying? There's no reason for it."

"I was afraid."

"Of what? Why are you so afraid of showing the real you?"

"Because I don't like being vulnerable, and the thought of her not liking me hurts, so I hid."

He walks over to me, placing his hands on my shoulders. "Silas, but you didn't hide from her; you showed her the real you, and she still stayed. You fucked up when you had the mask on and hid that from her. Can't you see, she liked you from the beginning."

"That's enough of the mushy shit. We have work to finish," Leroy says as he enters the living room.

"Aww, L. Don't be like that. Just helping my boy get his girl back." Buck pats my cheek before sitting on the couch.

"Maybe the dipshit should'nt of fucked it up in the first place. Now he's trying to play hero by fixing her mistakes," Griff says, looking annoyed.

I go to move, but Wel smacks the back of his head. "Don't be a prick. Just cause you can't get your dick sucked doesn't mean you have to be a shrivelled up wiener to the rest of us."

Griff touches his head and glares at Weldon. "Touch me again, and you'll lose the hand."

"I'm not scared."

It was a mistake inviting them. I'm still wrapping my head around the idea of Teagan and Buck talking. He's right, though, she never once belittled me. She always stayed true to who she was and never held back with me, yet I struggled to reciprocate that level of honesty.

Is Griff, right? I'm acting like Teagan's hero by fixing what happened to her. Is that how she'll see this?

I hope that isn't the case. I only want what is owed to her, and a part of me owes it to her. It's my way of making up for my wrongdoings. I don't expect her to forgive me, and we go back to how things were, but I need her to know that I'll still do anything for her. I want to be friends.

"I say we kidnap the cunt and see what we can get out of her," Griff says, pulling me from my thoughts.

"We aren't doing that," I snap at him.

"I say we grab her kid. He knows something," Weldon adds.

I completely overlooked Blaine. He's always attached to his mother's hip, of course, he would have the inside scoop of what happened and who was involved. The asshole was probably there destroying her shop.

"We go after him. And I want his car." Only Leroy would want Blaine's car after we beat the shit out of him.

"Where does he live?"

I laugh and look at Buck. "Where do you think?"

"With his parents? What does his dad do?" Weldon asks.

Now that I think about it, I never asked about his dad. I always assumed he worked for the town; maybe I'm wrong. The guys stare at me, but I don't know what to say. The Montgomery's are a mystery to me. No one in this town talks about them.

"If he lets his woman and son cause terror, he's gotta be a pussy." Griff beamed like he discovered a prize.

"I think we get the whole family," Leroy says, shrugging.

I hold up my hands. "Okay, this is getting out of hand. This isn't why I asked you all here. Originally, it was to get Nancy. Now the focus is on identifying who is to blame for the destruction of Teagan's shop, rather than condemning an entire family."

"Yeah, but dragging the whole family makes it more fun, don't you think?" Weldon casually leans back on the couch, folding his arms behind his head.

Oh, this is going to go wrong in so many ways.

"Gather the gear. We leave at sundown." Leroy claps his hand, always in charge.

Even outside of the city, Leroy acts in charge. I'm not going to argue this might have been my idea, but I can't lead for shit. We all break into our areas, getting our gear ready, but I can't help but think of Teagan. Why did she stop in today? It's the one thing I can't get out of my head. Did something happen? I need to push it out of my mind and focus on this task, or I'll blow it.

Leroy is determined to drive, so I hop in the front seat, and the guys pile into the back of the SUV. I direct Leroy to where Nancy's house is, and it turns out it's the place where I threw my bottle of vodka. Who knew? I hope I made the right decision with this.

We pull into Holden's wealthy neighbourhood as the sky is darkening. Silence fills the SUV as everyone mentally readies themselves for tonight. Failure is not an option. Griff and Weldon check their guns, and Buck has his eyes closed. I'm unsure if he's sleeping or imagining what he's about to accomplish. Either way, I'm not going to touch him. I like my life.

"We should park here and watch the house until we know who's all coming and going. Since we don't know much about the husband, we can't go barging in yet." Leroy pulls the vehicle over so we can keep an eye on the house.

"And what do we do if no one comes or goes?" Buck drawls out.

"Then we force our way in." Griff cocks his gun.

This isn't gonna end well, and Griff will go in guns a blazin' because that's what he always does. And he's always left scratching his head, wondering why Leroy is so against the idea of him participating in carjacking. It's like he's oblivious to the fact that he never considers the consequences or takes the time to listen to Leroy's concerns.

Do I feel bad that I never told Teagan the entire truth about what I do? Maybe a little, but she doesn't need to know this side of the business. I don't need her wrapped up in kidnapping and everything else we do. This life isn't for her; she's too good for it.

"Heads up, we have movement." Leroy straightens in his seat.

Weldon moves his way in between Leroy and me and watches as a black Mercedes pulls into the driveway. "Who's that?"

"I'm gonna go out on a limb here and say the husband."

"You're an ass, Silas."

"Ask a dumb question, get a dumb answer."

"Will you two be quiet, I swear you're worse than children," Leroy says from the corner of his mouth, too busy to look at us.

I didn't believe my eyes when I saw a tall, slim guy with salt and pepper hair emerge from the car. He wasn't at all who I expected to be Nancy's spouse. I had imagined someone young and fit, able to handle her antics. He grabs his briefcase, stops, opens it and answers his phone. He throws his hand in the air and points to the house.

"Dudes pissed with whoever called him," Buck points out.

I watch as he opens the car door and climbs back in. "Should we follow him?"

"I'm thinkin' so, whoever called has to be either Nancy or Blaine because no one pisses off the man of the house more than a loved one." Leroy starts the car and pops it into gear. He waits until Mr. Montgomery passes us before making a U-turn.

"I was kinda hoping to see inside that house," Griff mumbles, fixing his eye patch.

"No, you wanted to see what you could steal. Why lie about it," Weldon laughed as he spoke, moving back into his seat.

"Same thing, dickhole."

Leroy drives a good distance from the Mercedes in a part of Holden that I've never been to. Now, I'm curious where we're going. What can possibly be out in the industrial part of this town? Is Mr. Montgomery in some shady business that no one knows about? He rolls into a parking lot with one big cinder block building. It's got four massive garage doors stretching across its length.

He pulls up to the third one, and the door opens. A guy wearing a utility vest walks out and greets him. I lean forward, trying to get a better look at the dude. But he doesn't look familiar.

"This seems like a drug deal," Buck states the obvious.

"What should we do?" Weldon enquires.

"I say we go in there and shoot it up." Griff taps his gun on the window.

Leroy quickly turns in his seat. "Yeah, and then what? Risk the cops showing up, and then this is all for naught. Start thinking with your brain and not with your trigger finger, for fuck's sake. We wait until they both go in, then move in—two in the back and three in the front. Weldon and Silas go in the rear; you have two minutes to gain entry. Buck, Griff and I will take the front. You two head out now." He points to Wel and me.

I exit the car and enter the chilly night, watching the wind play with trash in the parking lot. Wel comes up behind me, patting my back.

"We've got this, I'm hoping there are answers in there, and we didn't just fuck this all up."

"That's what I hope. Going in blind, not a fan."

We quickly make our way around the building, stopping at the shop door. Weldon looks at me, and I dig into my bag for the lock-picking kit. With a quick twist, I get the door unlocked.

"Time?"

"We have less than a minute."

As Weldon stands ready by the door, I grasp the doorknob tightly in anticipation. After one last glance at the time, he gives a confident nod, and I boldly swing the door open.

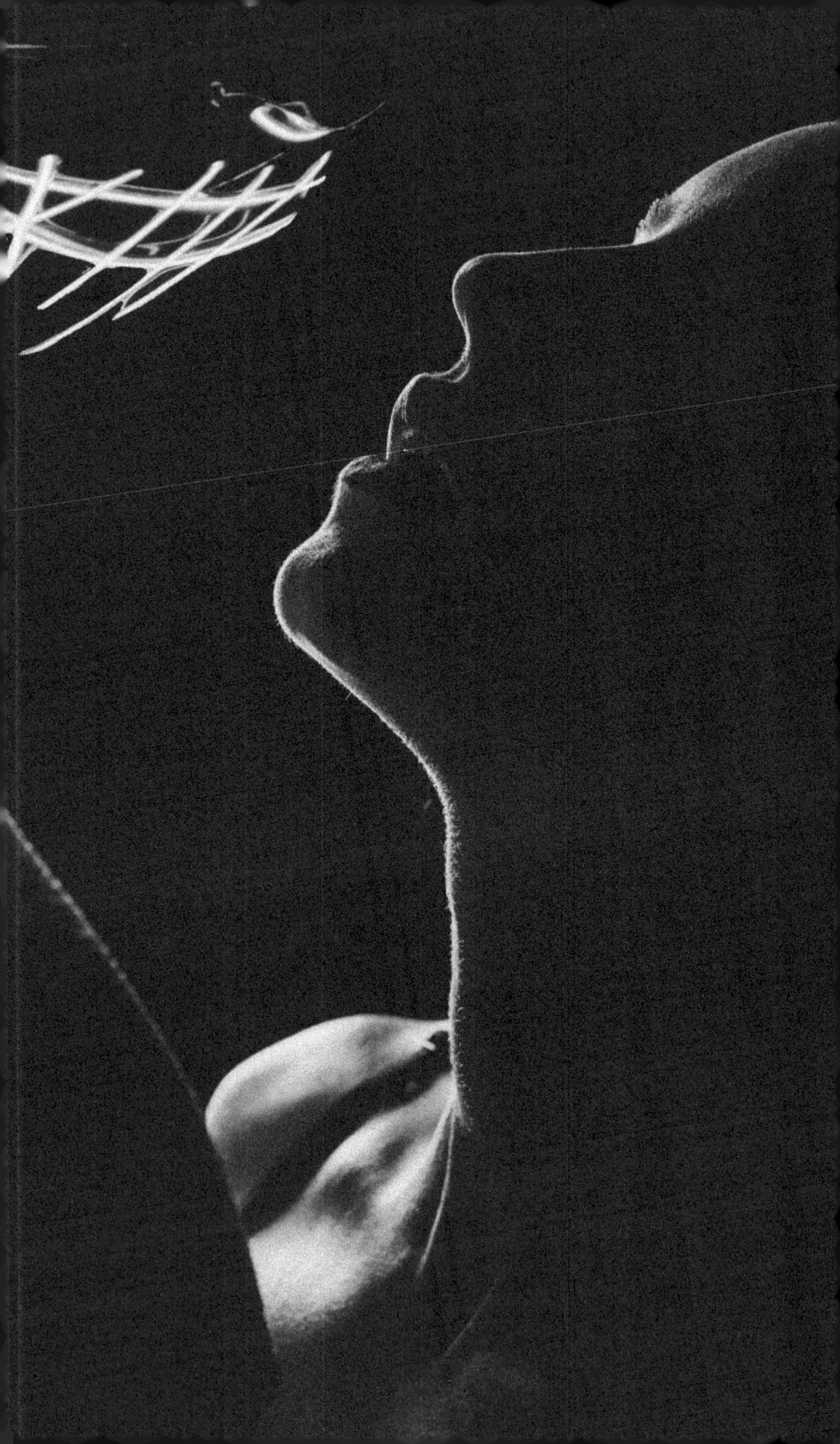

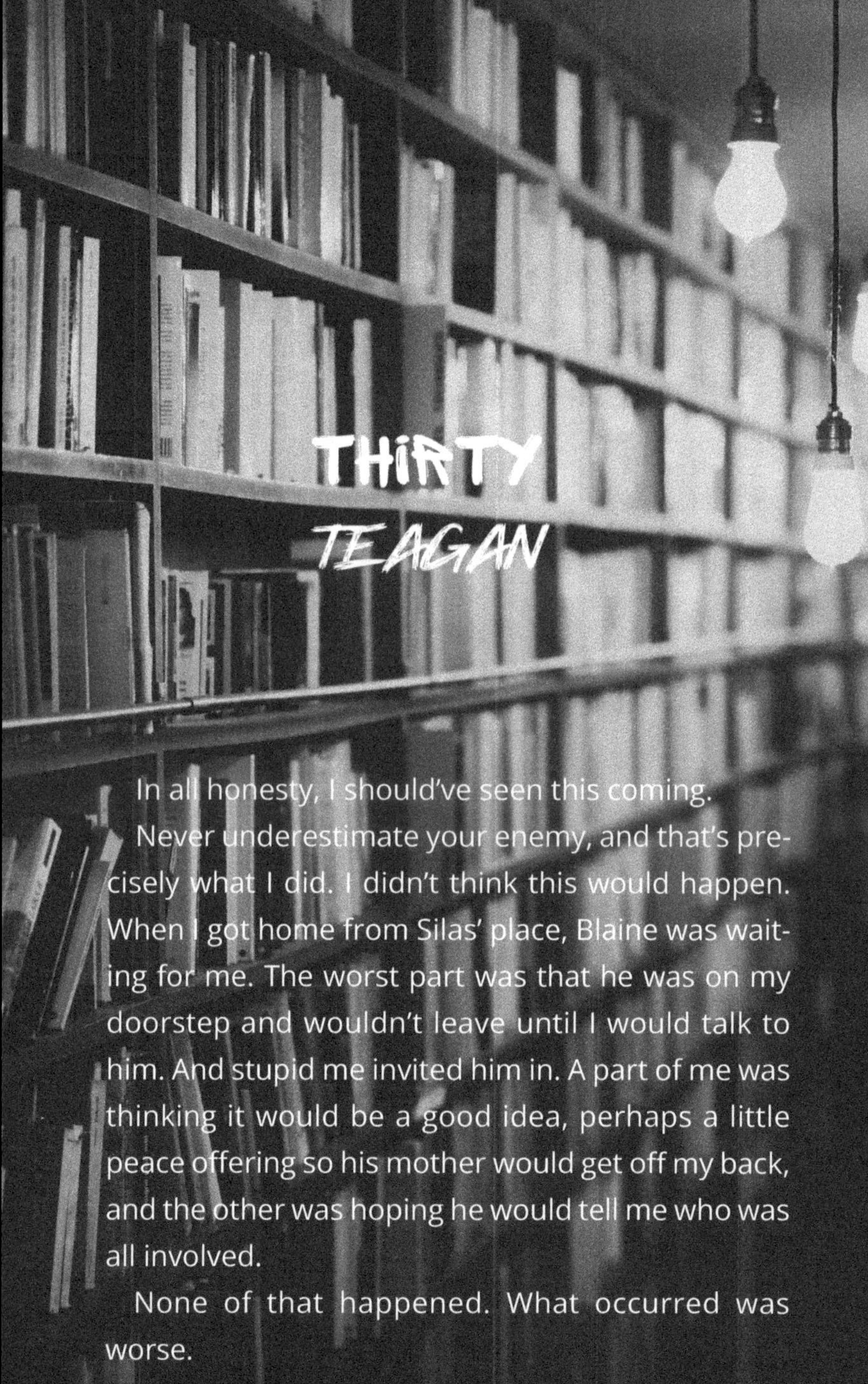

THIRTY

TEAGAN

In all honesty, I should've seen this coming.

Never underestimate your enemy, and that's pre-cisely what I did. I didn't think this would happen. When I got home from Silas' place, Blaine was wait-ing for me. The worst part was that he was on my doorstep and wouldn't leave until I would talk to him. And stupid me invited him in. A part of me was thinking it would be a good idea, perhaps a little peace offering so his mother would get off my back, and the other was hoping he would tell me who was all involved.

None of that happened. What occurred was worse.

"Blaine, I don't have time for this. You can't be here."

"Oh, don't be like that. I only came for a small chat. Invite me in." He gives me that disgusting grin.

"Fine, but I want something from you in return." This is stupid of me; I know better. Blaine can't be trusted.

I unlock my door and enter before him; when I hear the door close, the lock engages my heart races. I swing around to take Blaine in. He leans against the door and crosses his arms, never taking his eyes off me.

"Do you know why our families hate each other?" He asks.

I back away until I hit the wall. "No, it's been a mystery."

"It all started when your father and my mother went to school together. Such a long time to hold a grudge, don't you think?" He glances at the ceiling.

I nod silently.

"If your father only stayed out of my mother's business, this would've been easier for you. She was never meant to work at a desk writing permits for this shitty town. She was meant to run it. But Caleb ruined it."

"How?" A shiver ran down my spine when Blaine snapped his head toward me.

"He stumbled upon her father's drug business and went to the cops, tarnished her name in this town until she met my father. You don't get where you are in this town without status, and thanks to your father, he took that from her."

"How is that my fault? I didn't do anything wrong."

He shrugs. "If Mother didn't get her life, why should the daughter of the one that took it from her have one."

Are you kidding me, she's doing all this because Dad went to the cops on her dad and took her status away. You can't tell that anything happened to her. She's still living the high life. I think this is still all a ploy. I can't trust anything Blaine says.

"Who destroyed my shop?"

"Oh, I can't tell you that."

"Then you can leave. I have nothing else to discuss."

He steps forward. "That's not going to work for me, you see. I can't have you walking around town yapping that trap of yours. It's bad enough that you have a restraining order on Mother, and that looks bad to her. I need you to disappear."

Panic unfurls in my chest; disappear how? A noise from the kitchen draws my attention. When I turn, I find two other men standing by my island. "What the hell are you doing in my house?" That sounds like a reasonable thing to ask. Deep down, I know why they are here, the exact reason why Blaine won't move away from the door. I take a long, deep breath and brace myself. Blaine, I can handle, but these two are huge compared to me. I'm not sure I can take them on.

I turn to Blaine and act fast. I knee him in the stomach, making him fall forward; I shove him to the side and reach for the deadbolt. I'm able to unlock it, but a hand grabs my hair before I can open the door. I scream in pain as I'm tossed to the floor. A large boot presses on my stomach until I can't breathe. I claw at his calf, trying to loosen his pressure, but I fail. A hand with a cloth comes into view, and I wiggle my head out of the way.

"Fuck...you," I manage to say.

"We were told not to touch you that way, or we would be tag teaming right now," The big ass stepping on my chest says.

The one holding the cloth drops to his knees and presses it to my nose. I take a deep breath, and the world starts to get cloudy.

"We need to hurry and get her out of the house before anyone sees. Grab her; we can put her in my car," I faintly hear Blaine speak.

My body is lifted as if it's floating; my limbs hang. No matter how much I try to move them, nothing works. The asshat with the cloth places it back on my face, and my eyes close, leaving me in a world of darkness.

And so I sit tied to a chair in a dirty, disgusting place while men all around me chat like it's a boy club. I take the time to look around and plan an escape route. I glare at the two dickheads that placed me in this situation, even though it's my fault. Wherever Blaine is, he's on my shit list. Why should I disappear just because your mommy didn't get her way?

I'm beyond irritated, not even scared that I got kidnapped because it's Holden, for fuck's sake. Nothing ever happens here, and I'm not going to be a statistic. Call me jaded, but I'm not going down without a fight. I attempt to wiggle the ropes binding my wrists, but they only dig deeper into my skin, sending sharp fibres that make my toes curl.

I can't give up; there isn't anyone coming to my rescue. I rock back and forth, trying to tip the chair. It won't be the smartest move, but I should at least be able to get my feet free. I'm getting the chair close to being on two legs when it's jerked forward.

"Not the smartest move, princess. Either you stop, or we can finish the job for good."

I glare at the one that placed the cloth on my face and mumble in the fabric that's tied around my face. I yell at him, telling him I hate him and wish he would die.

He leans forward, gets in my face and laughs. "You can say whatever you want, but it won't work. The boss will be here shortly so I suggest you be on your best behaviour."

And I suggest you get out of my face. I jerk my head forward fast and hard, cracking my forehead into his nose. He hollers, holding his bloody nose.

"You cunt." He slaps me across the face; the pain was so sharp blackness gnawed at the edges of my vision.

He's at the top of my shit list, then Blaine. The massive shop door rolls open, and I try to get a clear look at who is outside, but from where I'm sitting, the wall blocks my view. The boy club eagerly greets whoever steps out of the car. When the mystery man does step into view, I damn near shit my pants.

Mr. Montgomery himself.

He glances at me, and one of the men whispers something to him. Mr. Montgomery's eyebrow raises. He heads toward me; I swallow hard when he stops before me. His finger dips under the cloth, gliding along my cheek, pulling it free.

"Miss Moore, what a pleasant surprise."

"Mayor, can't say the same."

He opens his mouth to answer, but chaos erupts. The Mayor whips around and stands behind me as the back door flings open, and Silas and a red-headed guy with a beard. The front has more going on as three guys storm in, including Hercules, an older guy and a bald guy covered in tattoos and an eye patch.

I turn back to Silas and watch him, trying to figure out how he got here. He stares at me in shock.

"Hey, Sunshine." I smile at Silas because I have no idea what to do in this situation.

Ginger laughs and nudges Silas. "I like her already."

"Can you not." He punches Ginger in the arm. "Teagan, I'll deal with you later."

"What the fuck is going on here?" Mr. Montgomery calls out, gripping my hair tight until I hiss in pain.

My gaze bounces from guy to guy holding guns. I'm feeling super lost right now. I don't think anybody has a clue about what's happening anymore. With increasing force, Mr. Montgomery yanks on my hair, tilting my chin upwards, causing tears to well up at the corners of my eyes.

"Someone tell me why you assholes decided to barge into my place without introductions?"

"If you want introductions so bad, how about you tell us who you are and why you have a girl tied to a chair?"

I can't tell who is speaking anymore, but it's not Silas, Hercules or that Ginger guy. Mr. Montgomery forcefully pulls my head to the side, causing a sharp pain to shoot up my neck. I grit my teeth and breathe sharply through my nose.

"This isn't your concern; it's a family issue," he spat the words out like poison.

"Fuck your family, you stupid prick," I bit the words out. I watch his jaw tick.

"Oh, I'm tired of this." He holds a gun and shoots.

The echo of the gunshot blazes through my ears, sending my senses reeling. As I'm thrown to the floor, the weight of my body landing on my shoulder causes a searing burn. Chaos is erupting all around; I watch from the floor as guys hide behind shelving units, boxes and a car as everyone fires shots. I keep trying to wiggle free from my ropes, but it's still no use. I kick my feet, trying to loosen the ropes around my ankles.

I'm defeated. I can only hope I don't get shot in the crossfire. I close my eyes and try to ignore what's going on, and if something happens, at least I won't see it coming. And as much as I'm angry at Silas, I can't see if something happens to him.

A hand lands on my shoulder, and my eyes shoot open. I stare into familiar green eyes. I choke back a sob when Silas cups my cheek.

"Shh, Dimples. I'm here."

My tough girl act crumbles, and the tears flow freely. Silas backs away and pulls a knife out; he keeps one hand on me and guides it down my side to my ankle. His touch alone soothes me. He tugs on the rope as he slices through. My top leg drops to the floor, and I groan.

"I'm gonna cut your wrist free; it might hurt, so bear with me."

Silas slides the knife through the rope, and I take a deep breath as the pain hits my stomach, and my fingers tighten in response.

"Fuck."

"I know. I'm trying to be gentle."

A gunshot goes off near my head, and I flinch.

"Teagan, you have to stay still."

"Oh, I'm sorry, Your Royal Highness. I'm not used to having assholes shooting their peashooters around my fucking head." I side-eye him.

"I missed your sarcasm."

And who's fault is that? It wasn't mine; I didn't do anything to ruin what we had going on. He may be acting like my white knight, but that's not enough for me to forget what he did. Pressure on my shoulder is relieved when he frees my wrists, and it drops forward. I roll onto my stomach and stay there, trying to find comfort from the cold cement flooring.

Silas places his hand on my back. "Teagan, we need to get you out of here."

"Si, we need to leave before the cops show up; we lost the husband somewhere."

I roll onto my back with a groan and see it's Hercules. "Hey, big guy."

"Hey, Sugar. We need to go. Can you walk?"

I move my ankles, and sharp pain radiates up my legs. Nothing compared to my bleeding wrists. "Yeah, I can walk." I prop myself up on my elbows and attempt to turn my head, but Silas blocks my view.

"You don't need to see anything, Dimples."

"Don't Dimples me when a dead guy is laying over there." I'm beyond pissed. And so much is running through my mind. How the fuck did he figure out about this place? Is he in on this? Is this a part of his carjacking life?

Hercules grabs me by the armpits, lifting me. Silas tries to reach for me, but I quickly dodge out of his way. "Don't fucking touch me. You may have saved me, but our relationship ends there. I haven't forgiven you, and we are not friends."

Hercules looks at Silas, pressing his lips together. "I'll take her back; you probably should keep your distance for now."

He wraps his arm around my waist, and I grip his shoulder. He slowly walks as I hobble alongside him; the cold air hits me like a freight train, sending shivers down my body. Hercules pulls me in closer as we near an SUV with a group of guys standing around.

"Buck, what are you doing?" The old man shakes his head.

"We need to get her home; we can't leave her here, Leroy," Hercules tells him.

"You ditched the sack of shit, did you?" The baldie asks.

Hercules growls. "Griff shut the fuck up."

Ginger smacks Griff on the back of the head. "You wonder why you can't get a woman. That fucking mouth of yours. You can stay behind with Silas and find a car."

"Weldon, fuck off. I'm not staying with him. He's on his own."

Maybe I should find my ride home. These guys act like a group of teenage girls. "Don't you guys still have to find the mayor?" I remind them.

"Who's the mayor?" Silas says from behind me.

I look over my shoulder. "Mr. Montgomery. You didn't know?"

"Are you kidding me? We had a shootout with the goddamn mayor?" I look at Leroy, who is now pacing.

Sirens scream in the distance and Hercules' hand tightens on my waist. "We need to leave now. In the car, Sugar."

Leroy climbs into the driver's seat, and Griff and Weldon climb into the back. Leaving Silas, Hercules, and I standing outside.

"Get the fuck in, we don't have time for this," Leroy yells from his window.

Silas runs to the front, and Hercules helps me climb into the back. "What about you?"

"Easy, L, pop the back open." The back hatch opens, and Hercules grins at me before closing the door. This can't be happening. I'm a simple book-store owner, and now I'm caught up in a mess. Take me back to a few days ago when I didn't know this didn't exist.

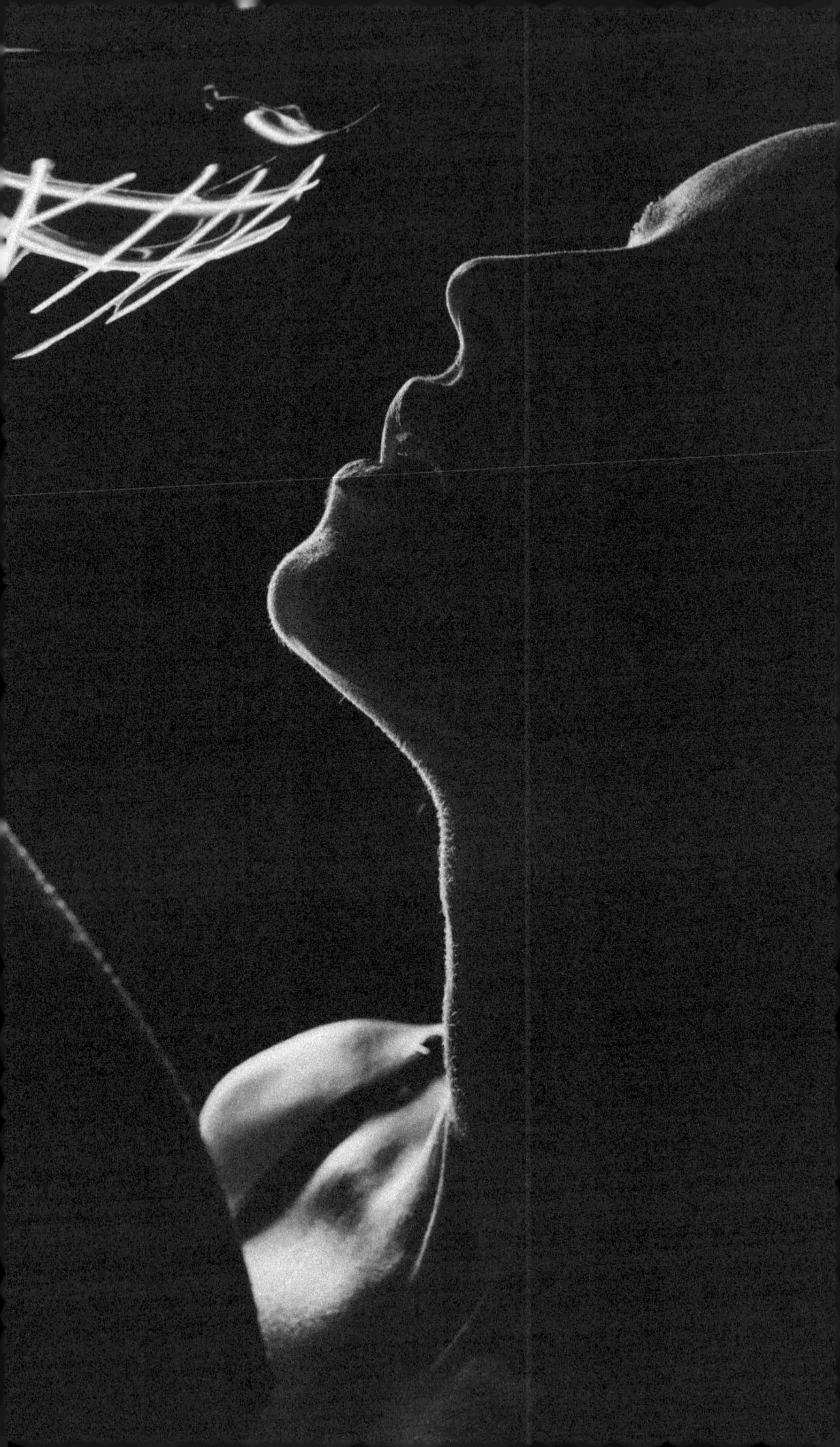

THIRTY-ONE

SILAS

The tension in the car is suffocating. I knew she wouldn't forgive me, but her words cut me deep. I royally fucked it up with her, and I'll never be able to get it back. When I stepped into that shop and saw that asshole standing next to Teagan, I damn near lost my shit. How did she end up there in the first place? Buck had just seen her at my house a few hours beforehand.

I turn in my seat and stare at her. She looks so at ease, with her head comfortably resting on Weldon's shoulder. Her wrists have stopped bleeding, and I pray they don't leave scars. I resist the urge to ask the questions that are bouncing in my head. Who knows if she'll even answer me.

"So, the mayor is a crooked sonofabitch. Who would've known." Leroy chuckles. "Didn't see that one coming."

I face the front. "I should've. Explains why his wife is a cunt."

"You don't even know the half of it," Teagan mumbles.

"Well, fill us in," Griff ordered forcefully.

"No need to be a dick about it, baldie. Didn't mommy teach you fucking manners?"

The car fills with laughter. I watch her from over my shoulder, and she combs her fingers through her tangled hair; her mouth pulls into a slight grimace when she moves her wrist wrong. I look into her eyes and notice a tear forming as our gazes lock. My own eyes narrow in concern.

"No need to be a bitch, didn't your mommy teach you that."

The car goes quiet, and I watch Teagan. Her eyes are still on me, and her face has gone hard. I've seen that look once before.

"My mom is the reason why I am a bitch. Your dad must be a pussy because you act like one to be picking on a woman. Grow a pair asshole."

Griff goes to reach for her when Buck and I move. Weldon blocks her, and Leroy slams on the brakes.

"That is enough. If you can't handle backtalk from a fucking woman, get the hell out of the car. She's right you are a pussy, Griff. Jesus Christ, can't we just get back to the house in one piece," Leroy barks.

Buck pushes Griff back into his seat, and I swear if he touches her just once, he's fuckin' dead.

"Sorry," Teagan spoke softly.

"Not meant at you, Firecracker." Leroy continues the drive as we sit quietly.

My place appears on the horizon, and I couldn't be more relieved to see it. After everything that's happened, we could all use a little breathing room. I need to have a heart-to-heart with Teagan, just the two of us. Leroy pulls into the driveway, and a light turns on in the house.

"Expecting company?" he asks, looking out the windshield.

"No." The sounds of guns being cocked has my heart racing. I turn to Teagan, who's gone pale. "Stay in the car, lay on the floor and don't move. Can you do that for me?"

A tremor shook her lips. "Yeah."

"Good girl, I'll knock on the window when it's time to open the door." I squeeze her knee before getting out. This isn't what I want for her; she somehow still got sucked into my life without knowing it. I know what I need to do, but selfishly, I don't want to do it.

Leroy points at Griff and Buck to take the back while Weldon, Leroy, and I take the front. Whoever is in my house better pray because they aren't leaving. Leroy stands to the left and Weldon to the right of the door. I kneel in front of Weldon, hold my fingers, and count down from three. Leroy turns the doorknob and flings the door open.

When no guns go off, we slowly enter. Buck and Griff meet us in the living room, looking confused.

"Upstairs?" Weldon suggests.

Where else would they be? It's not that big of a house; we gradually take each step, listening as we go. We break into our groups at the landing. My bedroom is dark when we enter, which doesn't surprise me. I never open the curtains. I mindlessly walk around the bed for the nightstand and flick the lamp on. The room is empty, and my heart settles down.

"I'm getting tired of this shit," I tell the guys.

"It has to be a joke. Are you sure Teagan isn't just playing you 'cause you pissed her off?" Leroy looks at me seriously.

"She would never do that; I was there from the start of this when Nancy did all this shit to Teagan. Before she suspected that I lied to her."

Weldon raises his eyebrow. "Are you sure she never suspected you?"

"Look, Teagan wouldn't do any of this. If you don't believe me, you can leave." My jaw tightened as I tried to reel in my frustration. I can't believe they would say things like that. Why would Teagan go out of her way and get kidnapped?

A shot goes off from down the hall, and I jump over the bed and take off to the spare room. I grab the doorjamb, coming to a stop. I try to understand what is happening in the room, but my brain won't catch up.

"You piece of shit," Blaine yells at Griff. "You shot me." He grabs his thigh, trying to stop the bleeding, but the blood runs through his fingers and drips onto the hardwood floor.

"What in the world?" Weldon asks in shock.

I step into the room, rounding Blaine taking in the piece of shit. "Why are you in my house?"

He spits at my feet. "Fuck you, I don't have to tell you anything."

I swing my foot and kick him in the kidney; he falls onto his side, moaning in pain. "Wanna bet?

Start talking, or we shoot again, this time someplace where you can't dig the bullet out."

Griff steps forward, placing his gun on Blaine's stomach.

"Okay, fine. I came for Teagan. I know you have her. Hand her over."

"That's never gonna happen. Now try again." I step on his fingers, and he screams in pain, shaking his hand to get it loose.

A creak in the hallway has us turning our attention and pointing our guns. Teagan stands there. She takes a tentative step back, reaching for the wall, and she falls to her knees. I quickly dash out of the room and drop to my knees next to her, scooping her in my arms.

"I'm sorry." I brush her hair to the side and kiss her forehead. "What are you doing out of the car?"

She buries her head into my chest. "I got worried. It was quiet, then I heard gunfire."

Blaine cries from the guest room, and she looks up at me. I shake my head. "You don't need to know."

"No, but you should know what Blaine said to me."

I take a deep inhale and stare down the hall. Blaine is still on the floor with the guys standing over him. Leroy looks over at me and raises a brow. I nod him over so he can hear what Teagan has to say because if Blaine needs to die, he has to hold Teagan for me.

"What's going on? Sorry about all the guns, Firecracker. Can never be too cautious."

"My fault." She nods. "I'll yell next time to put the boy toys away."

Leroy shakes his head. "A pistol even under stress. Okay, why am I out here and not in there messing his face up?"

"Go ahead, tell me what Blaine said to you."

She softly hisses as she lays her hands gently on my shoulders for support as she stands up. Slowly, she makes her way to the other side of the hall, bowing her head. As she begins to talk, my vision starts to build blinders. I can feel the rage building; he's the reason why she was kidnapped over some family bullshit that happened between Nancy and Teagan's dad. Are you kidding me? Her dad knew about this the entire time and never said or did anything. He put his daughter in danger.

"Clear something up for me, Firecracker. How is this all centred around you?"

"Nancy wanted revenge because she never got to live her dream in this town. Her name was tarnished. Yet she married into a well-known name, her husband is the mayor, but she's pushing papers in an office."

"And that is your problem, how? I'm not sure how kidnapping you and wanting you to disappear will solve all her problems," Leroy says, looking confused.

Teagan shrugs. "I'm struggling to get it, too. There's definitely something else we're not getting, and the only solution I can think of is just to go ask Dad."

"Griff, tie that asshole up. It's a wrap for the night, and we'll finish this tomorrow. Silas, take care of her; she needs to sleep."

Teagan meets my eyes, and I can tell what she's thinking. "It's alright; you can trust me on this one." I guide her to my room, and she sinks onto my bed.

"Did you want a shower?"

"Silas? I need you to tell me the truth."

I sit next to her, resting my elbows on my knees. "The truth about what?"

"All of this, Silas. No one that jacks cars shoots people. What are you hiding? I thought we talked about this."

"This business isn't always easy, and people get shot. Do you see why I wanted to leave this life? Who wants to live like this all the time? I wanted to keep it away from you, yet you somehow still got into it."

"That wasn't your fault. I had beef with Nancy for years. I'm sure this all happened because I got a restraining order on her, and that set her over the edge. There has to be a reason why she wants my side of Main Street empty."

"You think that's why she's down there?" I toss my hat onto the bed and run my fingers through my hair.

"The record store next to me was always busy. One day, the owner came down with a cold and never recovered. I have a feeling Nancy was behind it."

"What about the boutique?"

She shakes her head and lays down. "The boutique got an eviction notice; they have to move out at the end of the month."

How is this happening in this town? Does no one care? "And only you have been fighting her?"

"Yeah, and it doesn't help that there is family history. I didn't think they would go this far." She holds up her wrists. The angry, bloody line stares back at me. A reminder that if I didn't lie, I would've been with her.

"We should get your wrists cleaned before infection sets in."

I drag her up and into the bathroom. She sits on the toilet, and I dig the first aid kit out from under the sink. "How bad do they hurt?"

"Not so bad now, just when I move them."

I grab the antiseptic and spray it along the rope burn; she inhales sharply when it hits her skin. "Sorry."

"It's cold, that's all."

I gently clean the wound, trying not to make it bleed. "Have a shower, then I'll wrap them; I'll find you a shirt and boxers."

"Thanks, Silas. For everything. Even earlier, I came off as a bitch when you cut me loose; maybe my emotions were a little high. Mr. Montgomery isn't someone you want to be mixed up in. You know who he is, right?"

"No, who is he."

"Nancy's dad used to run drugs in this town, remember? Now, Mr. Montgomery does it. Where do you think all the drugs go?"

"The city?"

"I would watch your back next time you go carjacking in the city."

I step out of the bathroom and close the door. I find her a change of clothes and leave it on the bed; I step out of the room, closing the door behind me. I go and see the guys downstairs.

"How is she?" Buck asks, closing the fridge and cracking open a beer.

"Ah, she's fine. She also informed me who the mayor is." I grab a beer, drinking half of it.

"Do tell before I get older." Leroy folds his arms, leaning back in the kitchen chair.

"Where's Blaine?" I look around but don't see him.

"I shoved him in the upstairs closet; he won't be getting out anytime soon," Griff chuckles.

"His dad is the drug dealer, not Wolf. This entire time, we were wrong."

"The mayor gig is a cover up?" Weldon confirmed. "What a douchebag. Why not give it to his wife? She damn near acts like it."

"I think that's why she acts like it; he's never here. It has nothing to do with family issues; she doesn't want Teagan's dad to get suspicious again. That's all what this is. So, run the daughter out of town, and no one will be wiser." Buck states the obvious.

"Can't have her shop be targeted and no one else on that street," I add.

Leroy snaps his finger. "Bingo. Teagan never did anything wrong; Nancy has been trying to cover up for her husband and found a way to do that."

"The only thing left is to expose them all." Griff raises his beer.

We all raise our beers and drink. Now I understand why Elma wouldn't talk about that family. Too much was at risk. I leave the guys and check on Teagan. I quietly open the door and find her sleeping in bed. No matter how much I don't want to leave her,

I need to. After tomorrow, she'll have to move on without me.

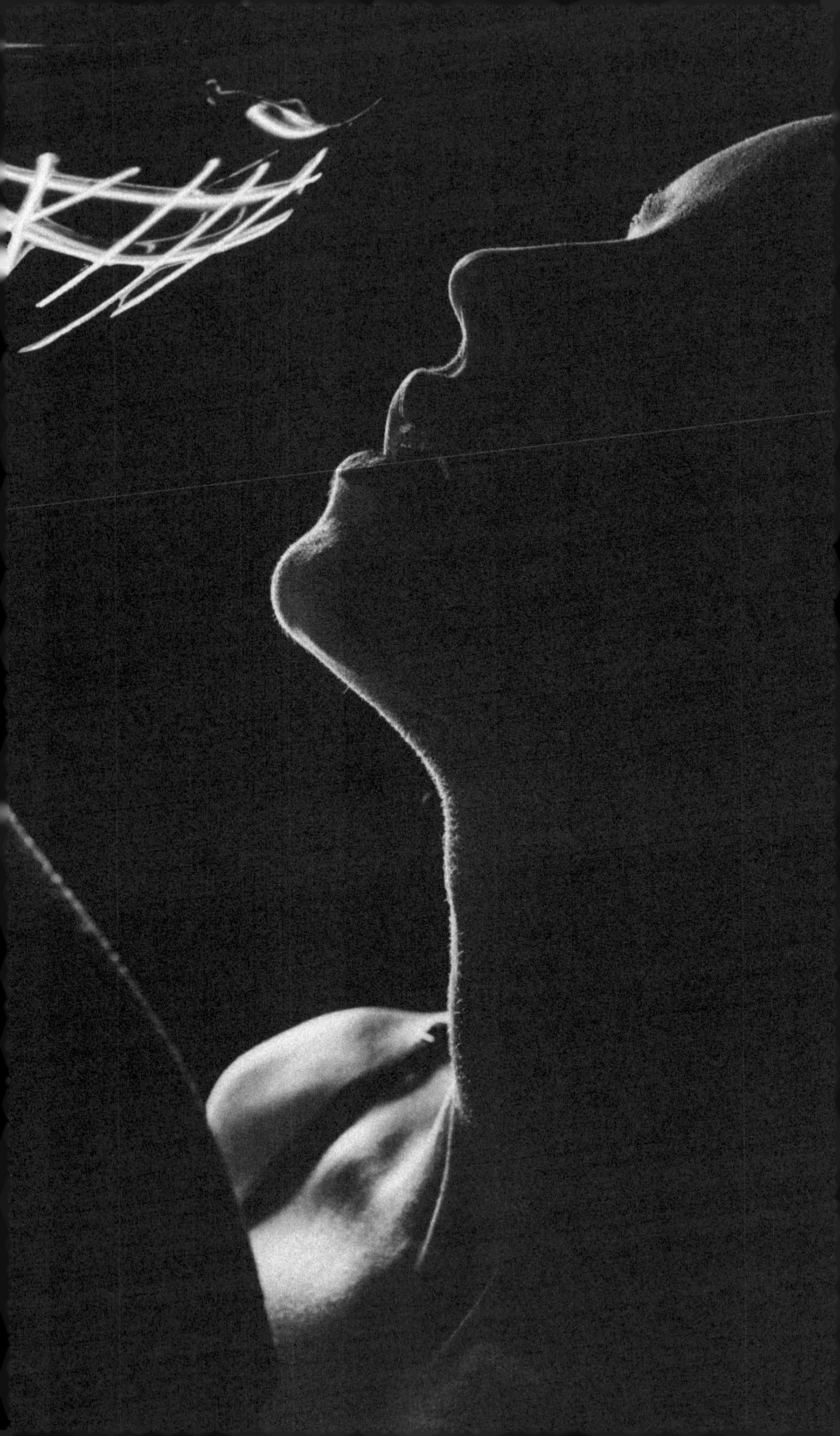

THIRTY-TWO

TEAGAN

I lie awake in Silas' bed when the sun peeks through the curtains, wondering how all this unfolded. I wish Dad would've filled me in on the entire Nancy bullshit when it started; it would've saved me a lifetime of problems. Now I'm in over my head. I haven't gotten a single answer, and I don't think I ever will. Maybe being in Holden isn't for me anymore.

I grab my clothes and quickly get dressed; I need to see Dad and get some answers. My wrists are stiff; I hope they don't leave a scar. I dig through Silas' closet for a hoodie to cover them. I'm not ready to answer those questions if Mom or Dad see them.

I open the door and poke my head out, the house is quiet, and I have no idea where any of the guys are or where Blaine is.

I tip-toe down the stairs, and on the last step, I place my shoes on. I get close to the door when a throat clears behind me.

"Where you off to, Firecracker?"

"Out." I reach for the doorknob.

"You aren't gonna say goodbye to him?"

I look over my shoulder and watch Leroy drink his coffee. "Why would I? He's nothing to me; he had his chance and ruined it. I'm not getting into this with you, and I don't even know you."

"No, you don't. But I know Silas. He's a good kid, a little stupid, but he has a good heart. It was his idea to find out who was responsible for destroying your shop. That's why we all came down here; Silas wanted to get your shop back so you could feel safe."

"It doesn't matter because, in the end, I have nothing now." I open the door and step outside.

"Firecracker, he does deserve a second chance."

I close the door; why does everyone love to tell me what to do? Do they not see how lying to me about a secret identity is wrong? It's like they are brushing that off like it's nothing. When I'm ready, I'll think about it. Until then, he doesn't get an answer.

I'm not even sure what time it is when I walk up the pathway to Mom and Dad's without my phone I'm clueless. I take the backway and go through the yard; if they are up, they'll be outside having morning coffee on the deck. I round the corner and hear them chatting away.

"Teagan? What are you doing here so early?" Mom stands, coming to the steps.

"I need to talk to Dad, it's important." Mom pulls me up the stairs, rubbing my arm as she pulls me in for a side hug.

"Of course, did you want a tea?"

"No, that's okay."

"Morning, Small fry. What brings you to the old folks home?" Dad smiles, setting his tablet on the patio table.

"Nancy, tell me everything now." I stand there watching Dad. He looks at Mom and then back at me.

"I should've told you from the start. That's my fault. I used to work for Nancy's dad, and if you're asking, you already know what he did. I'm not proud of my past, but I also wanted out of that life, so I went to the cops. Nancy found out and has been trying to bring me down ever since. Her dad went to jail for years, and after he was released, he fell ill mysteriously. I believe Nancy tried to kill him, but it's hard to say. Now that Jordan runs that world, Nancy controls the town. That's why she's always going after you; she wants revenge on me but can't."

I'm shocked. I stand there speechless. "Why didn't you tell me all of this before I started my beef with the bitch? She ruined my business."

"I didn't think she would go this far."

I throw my hands in the air, getting frustrated. "Serious. The record store owner dies randomly. The boutique is getting evicted, and mysteriously, the fire hydrant goes rampant, and that's not good enough; my shop gets destroyed on opening day. Why does she want that side of the street?"

"What's behind your shop?"

"The bar?"

Dad shrugs like he expects me to figure out what the answer is.

"She wants to run the drugs through that street," Mom cuts in.

Well, shit. No wonder why Taylor is so far up her asshole. He's in on all of this. I'm too deep in this; how the fuck do I get out of it. Dad touches my wrist, and I jerk away. He grasps my arm, and I try to pull away, but he pulls me closer and slides up the hoodie sleeve. Mom gasps, tugging my other arm and sliding the sleeve back.

"Who did this?" Dad barks.

I look between them. Mom has tears streaming down her face, and the muscles in Dad's jaw clenched and his nostrils flared.

"Mr. Montgomery and Blaine."

"Fucking Jordan, I'll kill that prick. Leave him to me; I know the cops in the city. Where's Blaine?"

I'm not sure how to answer that one. Then they'll ask more questions, and I won't be able to answer them. "He's tied up at the moment."

"Good, keep him that way. Let me make a phone call and I'll get the Jordan situation under control. Where's Nancy?"

I shrug. "No clue, I'm guessing wherever her husband is."

Leave it to Dad to finish this whole shitshow that he started. But in the end, I know what I need to do. Holden isn't the place for me anymore. I can't remain here, knowing everything I try to do will forever be tainted. The people in this town will start to hear the rumour soon about what happened and won't support me again; I'll never be able to reopen my shop. It's permanently closed after what happened. If Nancy doesn't get busted, I'm done no matter what.

The reality of what happened is slowly creeping in. I need to escape; I slowly back away without a word and leave the yard. I can't stay here anymore, and it might be rash to think of it so soon after last night's ordeal, but I don't care.

My house comes into view, and my heart races, only sealing the deal more for me. If I don't feel safe coming home, it's not going to work. I'll forever be watching my back when I enter this house. The dominos are falling, and I can't stand them back up fast enough.

I step slowly through the front door, and my body stiffens. The rag that was used on me lays on the floor in the living room, and all I can picture is the two guys standing over me. I make my way to my bedroom and pack a bag.

THE END

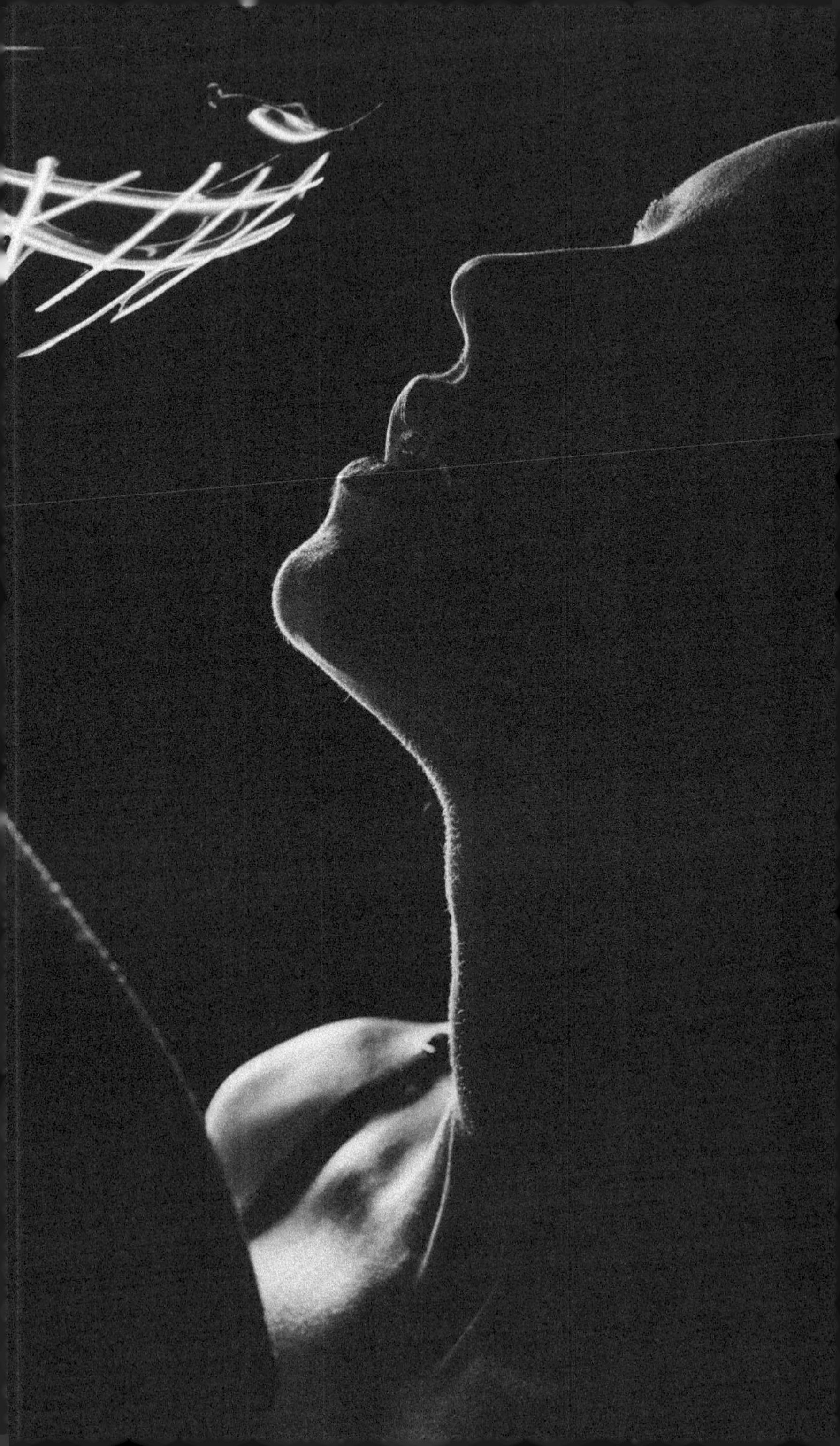

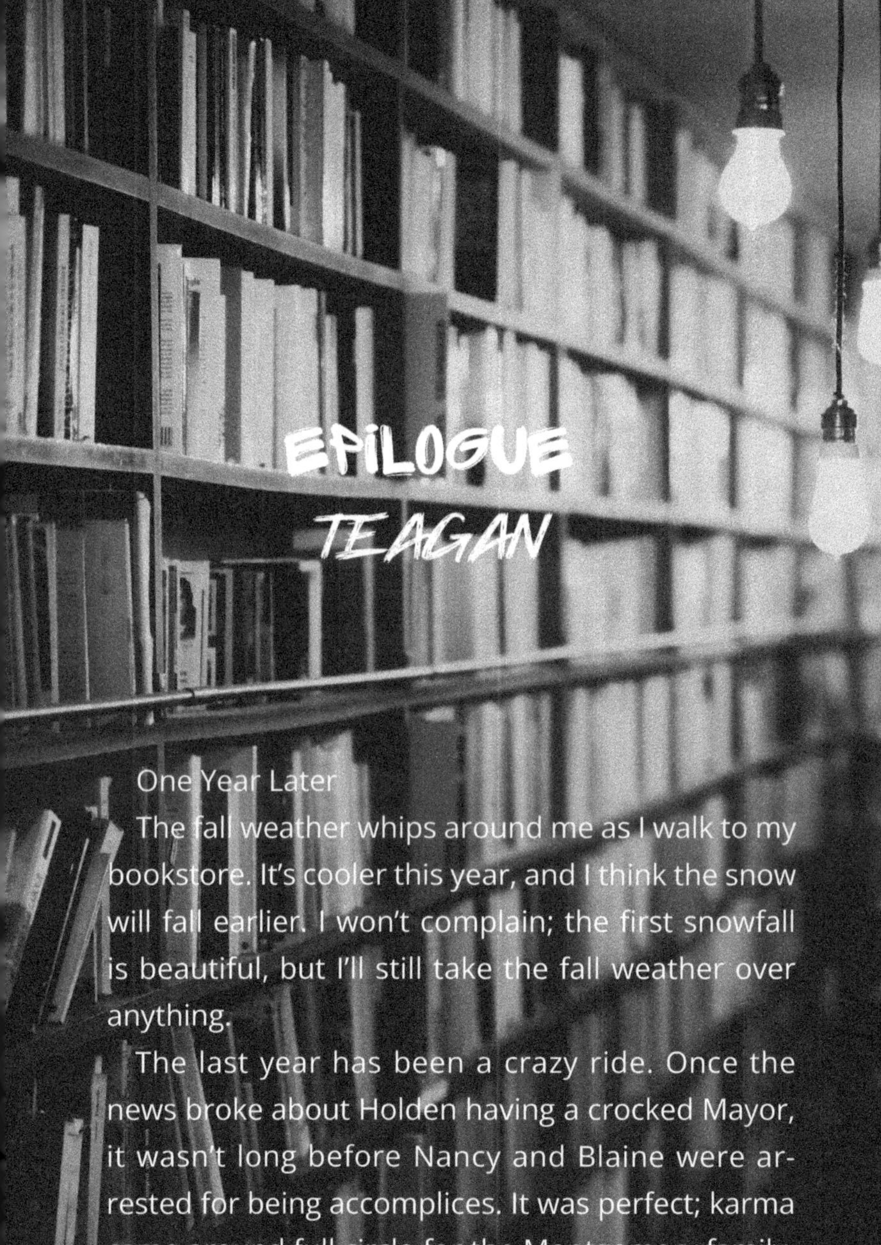

EPILOGUE

TEAGAN

One Year Later

The fall weather whips around me as I walk to my bookstore. It's cooler this year, and I think the snow will fall earlier. I won't complain; the first snowfall is beautiful, but I'll still take the fall weather over anything.

The last year has been a crazy ride. Once the news broke about Holden having a crocked Mayor, it wasn't long before Nancy and Blaine were arrested for being accomplices. It was perfect; karma came around full circle for the Montgomery family, after all, but it wasn't enough to bring me back.

During those initial months, Jace and Ivory were my rocks, always there to support and guide me. I leaned on them more than I ever thought I would. I didn't want to return to my house, and once I told them what had happened, they moved me without question. Jace wanted to go out and kill Blaine, but I told him what Silas and his boys had done, and he cooled down. Then he dived into the questions about who this Silas was. That opened up a wound I wasn't ready for.

I never talked to Silas after that night. I couldn't bring myself to do it. I hope deep down that he moved on and found someone that he can trust being his authentic self with; I won't lie. I miss him. I have no idea if he stayed in Holden or moved away; I hung up my stalker ways that one and only day.

I unlock the front door to The Dancing Goats Bookshop, listening to the bell go off when I push the door open. I flick the lights on, and my shop comes alive. This is my love, and it's drama free. The fact that Elma isn't here talking about random gossip is the best.

The shop is busy a few hours after I open, and it's non-stop moving. I have two employees, and I'm so thankful for them. I'm busy scanning stock into the computer when a book drops on the counter. When I look up, I freeze.

Green, intense eyes lock onto mine. I'll never forget those eyes; I've missed them every day for a year.

"Hey, Dimples."

Stinging fills my eyes as I try to hold the tears back. Silas hasn't changed at all; still wearing the same baseball cap. "Hi, Sunshine."

"How's life treating you?"

I shrug. "Better, I guess, you?"

"Mmm, not so bad. I like the shop." He looks around and smiles.

"Thanks. I figured a fresh start was what I needed. Did you move back to the city?"

"Yeah, my girl moved here, so I figured it would be easier if I were here too."

My heart sinks. Of course, he would move on. It's been a year; why wouldn't he? I would be foolish to think he wouldn't.

"That's great. I'm glad."

"Thanks, I'm proud of her. She also opened a shop here."

"Oh, that's amazing." I take his book and scan it. "Is her shop close by? Is that how you found the bookshop?"

"Sorta."

I see he still doesn't like to open up; not much has changed. When I look at the book, it's the third book in the series he's reading. I can't help but grin. "Good choice. I hope you enjoy this one."

"Thanks, I'll get to it one day. My nights are usually busy."

"I hear ya. Mine are, too."

He chuckles. "I know. I've been watching you still."

ALSO BY

A HITMAN'S DUET
MYLES
CARTER

RUSSO MAFIA SERIES
UNBROKEN
UNBEARABLE
UNDENIABLE

STRANGERS OF EASTWOOD
STRANGERS OF THE NIGHT
STRANGERS OF THE TOWN
STRANGERS OF THE CROWD

RAVENWOOD ACADEMY
ATTICUS
ASHTON
MADDOX

STANDALONE
CHRISTMAS UNWRAPPED

PAINFULLY OURS
PAINFULLY MERRY

ABOUT THE AUTHOR

HELLO, LOVES! IM A CANADIAN ROMANCE WRITER WHOS ALL ABOUT THE STEAMY AND DARK STUFF. HORROR BOOKS, MOVIES, AND MUSIC? YES, PLEASE! I HAVE A LITTLE TRUE CRIME OBSESSION, BUT ILL JUST CALL IT RESEARCH AND PRETEND IT'S NORMAL. IF YOU CRAVE LOVE STORIES THAT PUSH THE LIMITS OF LUST, TRUST, AND DESIRE, YOU'VE COME TO THE RIGHT PLACE.

FOLLOW ME FOR EXCLUSIVE SNEAK PEEKS, GIVEAWAYS, AND BEHIND-THE-SCENES GLIMPSES INTO MY WRITING PROCESS. AND IF YOU WANT TO KEEP UP WITH MY LATEST RELEASES OR CONNECT ON SOCIAL MEDIA.

LET'S DIVE INTO THE SHADOWS TOGETHER, DARLINGS.

www.ingramcontent.com/pod-product-compliance
Lightning Source LLC
Chambersburg PA
CBHW070408310726
48977CB00003B/602